Praise for the Cutthroat Business mysteries

"Move over Stephanie Plum, there is a sassy, sexy sleuth in town! If you enjoy your cozy mysteries with a good shot of romance, and a love triangle with a sexy bad boy and a Southern gentleman in the mix, then you will love this. Very reminiscent of the Stephanie Plum books, but the laughs are louder, the romance is sexier and there is a great murder mystery to top it off."

—Bella McGuire, *Cozy Mystery Book Reviews*

"A frothy girl drink of houses, hunks and whodunit narrated in a breezy first person."

—Lyda Phillips, *The Nashville Scene*

"VERDICT: The hilarious dialog and the tension between Savannah and Rafe will delight fans of chick-lit mysteries and romantic suspense."

—Jo Ann Vicarel, *Library Journal*

"Equal parts charming and sexy, with a side of suspense. Hero and heroine, Savannah Martin and Rafe Collier, are a pairing of perfection."

—Paige Crutcher, *examiner.com*

"Hooks you in the first page and doesn't let go until the last!"

—Lynda Coker, *Between the Pages*

"Enough wit and sexual chemistry to rival Janet Evanovich."

—Tasha Alexander,
New York Times bestselling author of *Murder in the Floating City*

Also in this series:

A CUTTHROAT BUSINESS

HOT PROPERTY

CONTRACT PENDING

CLOSE TO HOME

A DONE DEAL

CONTINGENT ON APPROVAL

CHANGE OF HEART

Savannah Martin has always been a good girl, doing what was expected and fully expecting life to fall into place in its turn. But when her perfect husband turns out to be a lying, cheating slimeball—and bad in bed to boot—Savannah kicks the jerk to the curb and embarks on life on her own terms. With a new apartment, a new career, and a brand new outlook on life, she's all set to take the world by storm. If only the world would stop throwing her curveballs...

When Savannah Martin's fellow Realtor and friend Lila Vaughn is robbed during an open house, Savannah rushes to the rescue with tea and sympathy, or at least a really good lunch and a shoulder to cry on. However, Lila seems more peeved than distraught, and her main gripe is that the sexy robber who tied her to a kitchen chair—for her own good—didn't follow her suggestion to tie her to the bed instead.

Lila's description of the man fits Savannah's old school-mate Rafael Collier to a T. Rafe has recently turned up in Savannah's life again, and he isn't above doing a little breaking and entering. Metro Nashville Homicide Detective Tamara Grimaldi is of the same opinion, and when Lila turns up dead, tied to her bed and strangled, Rafe becomes a suspect.

Now Savannah must get busy finding the real murderer before Detective Grimaldi can arrest the wrong man.

HOT
PROPERTY

Jenna Bennett

HOT PROPERTY
SAVANNAH MARTIN MYSTERY #2

This is a work of fiction. Names, characters, places and incidents either are the product of the author's imagination or are used fictitiously, and any resemblance to actual persons, living or dead, business establishments, events or locales is entirely coincidental.

Interior design: April Martinez, Graphicfantastic.com

ISBN: 978-0615868530

MAGPIE INK

One

The first open house robbery took place on the second Sunday in August, just at the time I was busy apprehending a murderer.

Before I go any further, I guess I should make it clear that I'm not actually in the business of law enforcement. Walker Lamont was the first, and I sincerely hope the last, murderer I'll encounter.

My name is Savannah Martin, and what I am, is a Realtor. Walker was my boss. Up until the moment I happened to be standing next to him when he came face to face with someone who could put him in the wrong place at the wrong time, we'd had a very good relationship, and I'm sure he meant it sincerely when he apologized for having to kill me.

But I digress. As I was pushing the business end of a lipstick into Walker's back, trying to make him believe it was a gun, another Realtor—Kieran Greene with RE/MAX—was being gagged and tied to a chair on the other side of town. After he was safely trussed, four masked men proceeded to strip the house of anything of value and cart it off in a rented moving van, leaving Kieran sitting in the kitchen waiting to be rescued.

The incident made the news, but was treated as sort of a sidebar to Walker's arrest. Violence against Realtors, Part II. Poor Kieran's ordeal was buried on page 4 of the *Nashville Banner* and received scant attention from anyone. It wasn't until the next Sunday, when the same thing happened again, that the real estate community sat up and took notice.

The first I heard of this second robbery was at the weekly staff meeting on Monday morning. With Walker in jail, Timothy Briggs had taken over as managing broker of Walker Lamont Realty, and he was the one who brought it up. "Before we talk about holding open houses next weekend," he said, leaning back in Walker's leather chair and folding his manicured hands across his flat stomach, "I guess we should discuss what happened yesterday. I assume you've all heard the news?"

He looked around the table, his baby-blue eyes bright.

I raised my hand. "I haven't. What happened yesterday?"

"Oh, Savannah, it was just awful!" Heidi Hoppenfeldt was busy chomping her way through the three dozen donuts Tim had brought in for us to share, and when she spoke, a fine spray of crumbs arched out of her mouth and landed on her ample bosom. She was on the other side of the table from me, so I wasn't hit, but the people on either side of her leaned away.

"What's awful?" I said. And added, mentally, "*apart from Heidi's table manners.*"

Tim smirked. "Didn't you catch the news last night, darling? My goodness, you must have had a busy day. It was on the five o'clock, six o'clock, nine o'clock *and* ten o'clock news!"

"I was in Sweetwater this weekend," I said. Sweetwater is my hometown, a small place an hour or so south of Nashville. My mother and my two siblings live there, along with their spouses and children, my aunt Regina, and various old friends and acquaintances. "I had dinner with a friend before I drove back, so I didn't get home until after eleven. And I didn't listen to the radio in the car."

Tim smacked his lips appreciatively. "And how is the scrumptious Mr. Collier?"

A few of the girls and the other (gay) guys tittered. Tim has an outspoken and unrequited crush on Rafael Collier, who's an old acquaintance of mine, also from Sweetwater. Rafe isn't gay—not by any stretch of the imagination—but Tim likes to dream.

"He's fine," I said repressively.

"He certainly is," Tim agreed, with a saucy grin.

I rolled my eyes. "You know what I mean. I haven't seen him for a few days, but he seemed all right on Thursday. And we're not dating."

"You were dating last weekend at Fidelio's," Tim pointed out. A whisper, like a breath of wind through stiff grass, spread around the table. Fidelio's is one of the nicest (and most expensive) restaurants in Nashville; the sort of place where country music stars dine and normal people can only afford to go on special occasions. It's not the kind of place one takes a casual acquaintance, unless one has serious designs on her. Which Rafe does. (He wants to sleep with me. And he hasn't made any secret of it, so I don't see why I should.) But if he had thought that wining and dining me at Fidelio's would make me give in to his predatory charms, he must have been disappointed. He didn't get so much as a goodnight kiss when he brought me home, although I'd wager that my near-faint when he suggested it may have been almost as gratifying to his undeniable ego.

"It was a business dinner," I said firmly. "And it's none of your concern. Yesterday I had dinner with someone else. Someone you haven't met."

"You get around, don't you, darling?" Tim smirked.

I narrowed my eyes. Tim added, "Well, since you missed the news... There was another open house robbery yesterday."

I blinked. "Like the one last week? When the owners came home and found their Realtor bound and gagged in the kitchen?"

Tim nodded. "Poor Kieran. He'll never be the same." He clicked his tongue sympathetically and then brightened. "This time the Realtor was Lila Vaughn, with Worthington Properties."

I must have made a noise, for he added, "Do you know her?"

I nodded. "I took real estate classes with Lila Vaughn. We got together for lunch less than two weeks ago." Just after the ordeal with Walker, in fact. She'd wanted to hear the scoop.

"I saw her on the news yesterday," Heidi mumbled, spraying another shower of crumbs across the table. The donut box was slowly emptying out.

"They interviewed her?" That sounded like Lila. She was an aggressive go-getter, willing to do pretty much whatever it took to get ahead, and she probably considered the news coverage free advertising. I could easily see her pushing through any fear or discomfort she was feeling to get her face on TV. She'd exhorted me to do the same thing last time we spoke, and to take advantage of the media circus surrounding Walker's arrest.

Heidi nodded. "Black girl, pretty, with long, curly hair."

"That's her. What happened?" I looked around the table.

"The same thing as last time," Tim said. "Just before the open house was over, a group of men showed up. They tied Lila to a chair and spent twenty or thirty minutes carrying everything of value out of the house. Electronics, jewelry, rugs, paintings. The house was full and they got it all."

"Was Lila hurt?"

Tim shrugged. "The news didn't say. The owners found her when they came home later."

"Gosh," I said, "she must have been terrified."

We all thought about Lila's ordeal and—I'm sure—thanked God it had happened to her and not to us.

"In light of all this," Tim broke the silence, "those of you with open houses scheduled for this weekend may want to take some extra precautions. Get a friend to come with you so you don't have to be alone. Keep the doors locked between visitors, or stay on the porch or outside in the yard where people can see you. Arrange to call a friend every fifteen minutes. You know, all the usual things."

"The same things my daddy told me when I was sixteen and started dating," one of the women said with a grin.

Tim nodded. "And that reminds me... Savannah, I can usually count on you to host an open house for me, but if you'd rather not, under the circumstances..." He let the sentence trail off suggestively. I grimaced. At the last open house I hosted, someone had tried to kill me, which didn't make me particularly eager to try again. Until the open house robbers were caught, I'd just as soon not tempt fate.

However, I couldn't in good conscience say no. Tim was, for all intents and purposes, my boss, now that Walker was languishing in jail, and although he couldn't really order me to do anything—like all Realtors, I'm an independent contractor and responsible only to myself—I didn't think it would go over very well to refuse. In my roughly eight weeks on the job, I hadn't brought in so much as a dime in commissions.

"Sure. I'm happy to help." I don't think I sounded happy, but I got the words out.

"Excellent." Tim showed all his capped teeth in a blinding smile. The conversation went on to the houses he and the others wanted to hold open next weekend, and I tuned out while I let my mind wander.

Poor Lila, what a horrible thing to have happen. She wasn't the most delicate of women, bless her heart – not by a long shot – but still, surely something like this would be enough to put the wind up anyone. I'd had to deal with some scary stuff myself in the past few weeks, and I was becoming quite an expert on heart-stopping terror. I should definitely give her a call to commiserate, once the meeting was over. IfI scraped the bottom of my purse, I could come up with enough change to pay for lunch.

"Does that sound OK, Savannah?" Tim's voice said. I nodded vaguely. "I'll put you down for that, then. Thank you."

"No problem." I had no idea what I'd just agreed to do, but I wasn't willing to admit I hadn't been paying attention by asking him to repeat it. I'd figure it out later.

Tim giggled. "If you're worried, maybe you should ask Mr. Collier to keep you company. He looks like he'd be able to handle any number of robbers."

Rafe would be more likely to be aiding and abetting them, but I didn't say so. "I'll keep the suggestion in mind," I said instead, cooly.

"Do that, darling. And if you don't, maybe I'll ask him to guard *my* body instead." Tim tittered.

I rolled my eyes. "Don't be surprised if you find yourself tied to a chair, in that case."

"Darling!" Tim bleated, seemingly overcome with emotion. He fanned himself with a limp hand as the rest of the room laughed. I blushed.

AFTER THE MEETING BROKE UP, I headed for my office, otherwise known as the converted coat closet off the reception area. It's hardly big enough to turn around in, but I've managed to squeeze in a miniature desk with a laptop, and a chair. While the computer booted up, I put a call in to Lila. She didn't pick up—she was probably inundated with phone calls, the way I had been after the incident with Walker and the lipstick—so I left a message on her voice mail, inviting her to lunch just as soon as she could dig herself out from under all the reporters and colleagues and just plain nosy-parkers who wanted to talk to her about what had happened.

That done, I turned my attention to the computer, which had finished booting up while I was telephoning.

Everything is computerized these days, so it wasn't hard to find more information about what had happened. The *Nashville Banner's* website and the *Tennessean's* website both had articles about the robberies, as did all four of the local TV-station websites. Several of them had dug up pictures of Lila to accompany the articles, but they were posed and didn't give me any idea of how my friend was holding up under the pressure. There were pictures of Kieran Greene, too, and he looked like a dark-haired Tim, with lots of white teeth, perfect hair, and skin as smooth as a baby's bottom.

After reading the various accounts, I pieced together a basic story of what had happened. At some point between 3:30 and 4 pm on Sunday afternoon, when the open houses were beginning to wind down and the Realtors were alone inside, a moving van had pulled into the driveway of each house. Possibly the same moving van in both cases, possibly not. The jury was still out on that. Four masked men had walked into the house, which—of course—was unlocked. That's the whole point of an open house, to get as many prospective buyers as possible to come in and browse. Lila and Kieran were tied to chairs in their respective kitchens, while the men stripped the houses of anything of value and carried it out to the moving van. When each house was empty of valuables, or they had gotten what they came for, they walked out, leaving Lila and Kieran bound and gagged in the kitchen. The whole thing hadn't taken any more than ten minutes from beginning to end. Luckily for both Realtors, the owners had come home within an hour or two, although it was anybody's guess what would have happened if they hadn't. Poor Kieran or Lila could have been sitting there until midnight or longer.

None of the websites had managed a good description of the criminals, not even as to race or gender. Both Realtors were fairly certain they had been men, but it was difficult to be sure even of that, as they were all dressed in padded coveralls and boots, with ski masks covering their faces and heads, and with gloves on their hands. It seemed almost miraculous that none of them had passed out from heat exhaustion in the 90°F weather, but we keep our air conditioners cranked up high in Nashville in the summer, and if they'd only been dressed like that for thirty minutes or so, maybe it hadn't been such a big deal. And the loot had certainly been worth a little discomfort. The estimated loss was more than forty grand in one house, and closer to sixty in the other. Not bad for a half hour's work. There were no fingerprints or obvious DNA found in either house—both open houses had had at least a dozen visitors who had to be eliminated first—and although some of the neighbors had seen the moving vans, no one had thought anything of it, since the houses, after all, were for sale. And because all of the hauling had been done through the garage or back doors, none of the neighbors had gotten more than a brief glimpse of the robbers.

On impulse, I picked up the phone again. It was a number I had called a fair few times during the preceding couple of weeks, and I had more or less memorized it. It was answered on the second ring. "Metro PD. Homicide. Tamara Grimaldi."

"Hi, Detective," I said politely. "Savannah Martin."

A beat passed, while the detective adjusted to my voice. It was a week or so since we'd spoken, and with Walker safely behind bars and his crimes solved, she must be wondering why I was calling. "Yes, Ms. Martin. What can I do for you?"

"I just wanted to say hello," I said. A disbelieving silence greeted this announcement, and I grimaced. "All right, I wanted to ask you something."

Another beat passed. "Does this have to do with your boyfriend?"

"What boyfriend? Todd?"

"Who's Todd? I'm talking about Mr. Collier."

Of course. Tim isn't the only one who thinks Rafe and I have something going on.

"He's not my boyfriend." Although I couldn't stop myself from adding, "What has he done now?"

"Nothing I know of," Tamara Grimaldi said.

"So why would you think I'm calling about him? No, never mind. Don't answer that. I wanted to ask you about these open house robberies. You know, when a bunch of guys tie up a Realtor and steal everything in the house?"

"Can't help you there, I'm afraid," Detective Grimaldi said. "Until someone gets killed, it's not my problem."

"Let's hope it doesn't come to that. So you don't know anything about it?"

"No more than you do, I expect. Just what's in the news. From what little I've gathered, it doesn't seem as if the robbers are trying to hurt anyone. Neither Realtor was harmed, and Ms. Vaughn said the man who tied her up, told her it was for her own protection."

"That's good to know, anyway," I said. "Tim has asked me to host an open house for him this weekend."

Tamara Grimaldi's voice turned serious. "Be careful. Bring a friend with you if you can. And if you encounter these people, the best thing you can do is exactly what they tell you. Don't give them a reason to harm you, or—God forbid—take you with them when they leave. Once you're on their turf, your chances of survival fall to almost nil."

I promised I wouldn't, with a shudder. "But you don't think they're dangerous?"

"Everyone's dangerous," Detective Grimaldi said, "under the right circumstances. Even you. But so far, this particular group hasn't exhibited any particularly violent tendencies. Unless you gave them a reason, I don't think they'd treat you any differently than they treated Mr. Greene or Ms. Vaughn."

I nodded. "Do the police have any... um... leads?"

"None I'm at liberty to discuss," Detective Grimaldi said. And relented. "As I said, it isn't my case. But between you and me, I don't think there's much. They're good. The vans have been from different companies, and so far, no one has seen their faces well enough to identify them. The neighbors assumed they were hired by the homeowners to move the furniture out, so no one paid attention, and the robbers wore masks inside the house. We're not even sure how many of them there are. Mr. Greene was too shook up to notice details, and because they were all wearing the same thing, and for all intents and purposes looked exactly the same, Ms. Vaughn couldn't be certain. We're going on the assumption that there are four."

"And you have no idea where or when they're going to strike again, or how to catch them?"

"Not a one," Detective Grimaldi said cheerfully.

I bit my lip. "Can't you set up a sting, or something? Stake out the open houses to see if they show up?"

"If we had some idea of where they'd be, we could. But it's too early to predict trends. Chances are the next open house will also be in the seven hundred thousand to million dollar range, and have something in it worth taking. In one case it was paintings, in the other electronic equipment. But there are a lot of houses that fit that bill, and unfortunately, the Metropolitan Nashville Police Department doesn't have unlimited resources at its disposal. We can't put an undercover cop in every single open house in South Nashville on Sunday afternoon. Or even in the two or three dozen that fit the criteria."

I nodded. "Let me know if there's anything I can do to help. Lila Vaughn is a friend of mine, and until they're caught, we're all jumpy."

Detective Grimaldi said she'd keep me in mind, and we said our goodbyes and hung up.

No sooner had I put the desk phone down, than my cell phone rang. I glanced at the display before I answered, and had to work on making my voice sound chipper when I answered. "Hi, Mother."

"Good morning, Savannah," my mother's soft Southern voice said. "How are you, darling?"

"I'm fine, thank you. And you?"

"Just wonderful, dear. Thank you for asking. I'm just making a quick call before meeting your aunt for lunch. I wanted to make sure you got home all right last night. After your dinner, I mean."

"If I'd had an accident between Sweetwater and Nashville," I said, "you would have been the first to hear about it. You're the emergency contact in my cell phone. My ICE number. And I didn't have much to drink with dinner. Just a single glass of Sauvignon Blanc. It wouldn't have registered on a Breathalyzer test, let alone have made me run off the road."

"That's good, darling." I could hear her draw breath, and I held my own.

All of this had been small-talk, testing the water before taking the plunge, and now we came to the real conversation. What would it be this time? That I wasn't getting any younger and should marry Todd Satterfield before it was too late? That I shouldn't have divorced Bradley to begin with? That—God forbid!—my brother Dix had told her I'd had dinner with Rafe Collier once, and she was calling to tell me I was disowned?

She said, "I hear another Realtor was robbed this weekend."

"Oh." I breathed out. That wasn't as bad as it could have been. "Yes, her name was Lila Vaughn. We're friends."

"That young woman they interviewed on the news? She seemed very…" Mother hesitated delicately, "forward."

"She's not shy and retiring," I admitted, "but she's nice." If a lot more aggressive than I was brought up to be.

"You're being careful, aren't you, darling?"

We'd had this exact same conversation just a few weeks ago, after Brenda Puckett was murdered. And then again after Walker had tried to shoot me. "Yes, Mother," I said. "Of course I am. Tim has already talked to us about taking special precautions when we're showing houses, and I'm thinking about getting a weapon of some sort. A can of Mace or pepper spray to keep in my handbag."

"That sounds like a good idea," Mother agreed. "Maybe I can ask Sheriff Satterfield if he has some advice he can give you."

"That would be nice," I said politely, although I didn't really need the help. Many Realtors carry some sort of weapon for protection, so there were people right here in the office I could ask, and if I wanted a truly professional opinion, I could call Tamara Grimaldi for help. Or Rafe, who would, at least, be able to tell me which weapon he himself would most prefer not to be faced with. While Sheriff Satterfield would tell his son what I was doing, and then Todd would worry about me shooting myself in the foot or accidentally frying my brain with nerve gas.

I knew from experience that nothing would derail my mother once she'd gotten an idea in her head, however, so I didn't bother to try to talk her out of it. "Thank you." If I went along quietly, maybe she'd decide it wasn't such a big deal, and would forget to talk to Bob Satterfield.

"It's no problem. I'm happy to help. I hope you and Todd had a nice time last night?" She sounded optimistic.

"Very nice," I answered demurely. "Thank you. Todd is good company."

When he isn't lecturing me, or going on and on about Rafe, at any rate. Somehow he has gotten this *idee fixe* that Rafe is a danger to my virtue—correct as far as it goes—and he feels that it's up to him to protect me. So he's harping rather obsessively on Rafe's baser qualities and my need to be careful. The real problem, from my point of view, is that Todd doesn't think I'm capable of handling my own affairs, although telling him so would only make him believe something is going on when it isn't, so I hadn't.

"That's good. Well, darling, I guess I should go. Regina and I are discussing the plans for this year's Christmas Tour of Homes." Aunt Regina is my late father's sister, and also the society columnist for my hometown newspaper.

"That's it?" I blurted.

Mother's didn't answer, and I added, "I mean, was that all you wanted? You just called to make sure I had a good time with Todd?"

"And to tell you to be careful. You do seem to be quite a magnet for trouble, darling, with discovering Mrs. Puckett's body and being held at gunpoint by that nice Mr. Lamont. A mother just worries, that's all." The tail end of the statement hung in the air, unspoken: Especially when her daughter is all alone in the world and '*are you sure you shouldn't remarry, Savannah; you're not getting any younger, you know.*'

"Right," I said. "Thank you, Mother. I'll be careful. No more dead bodies for me, I promise. And no more murderers, either."

And I believed it. I honestly did. I just didn't realize how quickly another dead body and another murderer were going to be littering my path.

But the thing is, had I known, I doubt I would have acted any differently anyway. I did what I had to do, and that's really all there is to it.

Two

Fidelio's Restaurant is located off Murphy Road, on the snobby west side of town.

I don't have fond feelings for the place. My ex-husband took me there to celebrate our first (and last) wedding anniversary, and invited his paralegal assistant (and future wife) to join us. I spent my anniversary dinner twiddling my thumbs while my husband and his mistress talked shop. Our marriage didn't last long after that, and Bradley married Shelby a week after our divorce was final. Todd knew the story, but still insisted on taking me to Fidelio's whenever he was in town. And as Tim had pointed out, it was also where Rafe had taken me last Saturday, on our date-that-wasn't-a-date. Although, to be fair to Rafe, he didn't know my history with the place; he was just determined not to be outdone by Todd. At least I assume that had been his motivation, as it was hardly the kind of place he himself frequented.

Today, I was there to meet Lila Vaughn, who had chosen it because it was close to her office. She had called me back later in the day on Monday, and had agreed to go to lunch. But because her phone had been ringing off the hook since the robbery, and because she had more to do than she could handle, she couldn't get away until Thursday.

She swept in ten minutes late, air-kissed the gray-haired maitre d' and sailed through the restaurant while men of all ages stopped with their forks halfway to their mouths to stare at her. She air-kissed me, too, before she sank onto the chair opposite and grinned.

"Hi, girlfriend. Sorry I'm late."

I smiled back. Lila is outgoing, effusive, and even a little brash. I was brought up to be ladylike and polite. In spite of our differences, we get along amazingly well. "No problem. I know you're busy. And you look great. As always."

Lila dresses to attract attention. Today, she was wearing a bright red sundress with practically no back and her long hair was tumbling over her shoulders in calculated disarray. Men all over the restaurant were ignoring their companions to look at her.

"I work at it, babe." She leaned back on the chair and crossed one impossibly long leg over the other. Her already short skirt rode up another few inches, exposing a perfectly toned thigh. I'd kill for Lila's figure. "So how are you?"

"I'm doing better, thank you. What about you?"

"I can't complain. It's amazing what a little publicity can do for a person's career. I'm working with several buyer-prospects, and just after I got off the phone with you on Monday, someone called and wanted me to do a listing presentation today. I had to put them off, just so I could be here."

"That was nice of you," I said, not sure if I would have been able to be as magnanimous. I really, really needed to make some money, and sooner rather than later. The divorce settlement from Bradley was dwindling almost daily, and if I didn't make a sale soon, I'd have to go back to the make-up counter at the mall.

Lila shrugged. "They'll keep till tomorrow. So how about you? Are you working with anyone?"

"A few people." One young couple, to be exact. And our association was in the very early stages; we hadn't gone out to look at any properties yet. "Nobody special."

"Maybe you should arrange to get tied to a chair and robbed," Lila said. She drew breath to go on. But just then the waiter appeared, and saved me from what would probably be a bracing lecture on ditching my ladylike upbringing and going after what I wanted more aggressively.

She ordered a Diet Coke, while I asked for water with lemon. Water is free, and a penny saved is a penny earned. The waiter disappeared, and we scanned the menus until he came back a minute later with our drinks. Lila asked for a Cobb salad with low-fat dressing on the side while I ordered a Chicken Caesar. The waiter departed and we got back to business, but by then Lila had either forgotten what she was going to say, or thought better of it. "So how's everything at the office?" she asked instead.

I gave a shrug. "I guess it's all right. Different, with Tim at the helm. Although he's doing an OK job, I suppose. Everything's getting done that needs to get done, and we're still making money, although I don't know how long that'll last. Brenda Puckett was our biggest income producer, and she's dead. Tim was our second biggest, but he doesn't have much time to go out and make sales now that he's in charge. He'll probably miss it. I'm not sure he has quite the right personality for leadership, either, bless his heart."

Proper, sophisticated Walker would never, ever have made the comments about my personal life that Tim had made at the meeting on Monday morning. And although I hadn't said anything to him about it, I thought he had spoken rather inappropriately, especially in front of everyone else. It would have been bad enough to talk that way to me privately, but at a sales meeting with the whole staff present...!

"What's he done now?" Lila asked.

I made a face. "Oh, he just told the whole office that I'm dating Rafael Collier. At the staff meeting on Monday morning. Just because he saw us having dinner together last week."

"Is this the guy you were telling me about, the one who was with you when you found Brenda Puckett's body? So you *are* dating him!"

I shook my head firmly. "It wasn't a date. It was just dinner."

"You sure?"

"Yes, of course I'm sure. I'm not interested in him that way."

"Right." Lila didn't even try to hide her amusement. "I don't know, girlfriend. Have you even had a man since you got divorced? He asked you out, so he's obviously interested, and if I remember the way you described him, he's not repulsive. Are you sure you shouldn't go for it?"

"It's not that easy," I answered.

Lila didn't speak, just arched her brows questioningly. I added, "You don't know my family."

"Aren't you allowed to date anyone? Or is it just him?"

"Mostly just him. Or anybody like him. Or maybe just anybody but Todd."

"Who's Todd? Oh, wait. He's that guy you dated in high school, right? The one your mother keeps throwing at you?"

I nodded. "Rafe went to school with us too, but I never had anything to do with him. He was the boy my mother always warned me about. The boy all the mothers warned their daughters about."

"So what's wrong with him?" Lila asked.

I hesitated, before settling for the general, "He's just very different from me."

"Different, how?" Lila said. She was relentless; it was one of her biggest strengths as a Realtor. Unlike me, who was brought up to be polite and courteous, Lila took every 'no' as a challenge, and wouldn't back down from anything. Tenacious to a fault.

"Different in every way. I grew up in a mansion. One of the antebellum ones south of Columbia, on the Antebellum Trail. He grew up in a mobile home, in a trailer park on the other side of town. I can trace my family tree back to the Civil War; he only learned who his father was two weeks ago. I went to finishing school after graduation; he went to jail. I drive a Volvo, for God's sake, and he rides a Harley-Davidson!"

Lila thought for a moment. "So he's what people down here call white trash?"

Lila's from Detroit, where I guess they call it something else.

"His mother's family was." I'd certainly heard the Colliers described that way often enough. Not by anyone in *my* family, of course. We don't use words like those. Think them, perhaps, but don't utter them out loud. "His father was black, so mostly what people called him was *that colored boy.*"

Or more often, *LaDonna Collier's good-for-nothing colored boy*, but I didn't think I should say that to Lila.

"Oh-ho!" Lila said.

"I grew up in a very small, very segregated town. There were black neighborhoods and white neighborhoods, but very few that were mixed. Black people go to black churches and white people to white churches on Sunday morning, and there were no black children in my elementary school. They all went to the other elementary school, on the other side of town. It wasn't until high school that we all ended up together."

"I don't imagine your daddy would be best pleased if you brought home a black boyfriend, then."

Lila took a sip of her Diet Coke. Each long fingernail was painted as red as her dress and decorated with a tiny flower.

"It's not my daddy who's the problem," I said, inspecting my own ladylike French manicure. "He's in heaven, where I'm pretty sure they're beyond petty concerns like skin color. My mother, however, is still here."

"Is she a racist?"

I bit my lip while I tried to form the words. I didn't want to make Lila angry, or worse, hurt her feelings, and we hadn't known each other long enough yet to get to the point where we could say just about anything to each other without giving offense. At the same time, I wanted her to understand what it was like being a Martin. "She has nothing against black people. She deals with them – you – every day, and she does it politely and courteously. It's not like she puts on a white hood and rides out at night to burn crosses on people's lawns. Or chases people off her land with a shotgun, the way Rafe's grandfather did. It's more a case of..."

I hesitated, searching for the right way to explain things, "...them and us. Heck, my brother-in-law Jonathan was given a terrible time when he first started dating my sister Catherine, and he isn't even black, just a Yankee. My mother is just very aware that not everyone is up to her standard."

"Hunh," Lila said.

I shrugged. "She can't help the way she was brought up, any more than the rest of us can. She's not a bad person, really."

Lila didn't answer, though I don't think she was convinced.

"All right," she said, "so I don't suppose you can really get too involved with this guy, then. Not if you want to avoid trouble. But didn't you tell me that your family lives an hour or more away? What's to keep you from jumping in the sack with him? They'd never know."

"They'd find out. Somehow, my family always finds out. Besides, I don't really want to jump in the sack with him. I wasn't brought up to sleep around."

Lila arched her brows. "You've been divorced for how long, again? Almost two years, isn't it? Girlfriend, I don't think indulging yourself for once would count as sleeping around."

"Maybe not," I admitted. "But I don't really want to."

"You sure?"

"Yes, of course I'm sure. Why?"

"Oh, no reason. I was just thinking…"

Her voice was too innocent, and I narrowed my eyes. "Thinking about what?"

"Well… you know what they say about black men, don't you?" She smirked.

"I'm not sure I do," I said.

She told me.

I blushed.

It wasn't until the waiter had arrived with our salads and we were both busy shoveling lettuce into our mouths that she glanced over at me. "Aren't you going to ask me about what happened this weekend?"

"I don't want to pry…" I began.

Lila snorted. "My phone's been ringing off the hook all week, and I've talked myself hoarse. So don't be shy. You want to hear about it?"

"If you don't mind telling me," I said.

She grinned. "Not at all. It was… interesting."

"Don't you mean scary?"

"Not as much as you'd think. You've probably read the stories, right?"

I nodded.

"There were four of them, I think, and they tied me to a chair in the kitchen, before they stripped the house and left."

"That's what I heard," I said. "What was the interesting part?"

Lila smiled. "The interesting part was the guy who did the tying-up."

"What about him?"

"Oh, girlfriend!" She rolled her eyes expressively. "This guy was hot!"

I wrinkled my forehead. "How do you know? I thought they wore masks. That's what the newspapers said."

"They did. But I could see the way he moved. And his eyes. They were this really deep, dark brown—almost black—and with the most amazing eyelashes. And he had this really sexy voice.

Listen to this: before they left, he came into the kitchen and sat on the table in front of me, and then he brushed the hair out of my face and told me to be good…".

I dropped my fork. It clattered on the edge of the plate, but for once I wasn't aware of the horrible breach of manners. "Oh, my God! He touched you? Weren't you scared?"

"It wasn't like that," Lila said. "Though *you* might have been scared. I suggested that maybe he'd like to tie me to the bed instead."

She smiled. I stared at her, and I'm sorry to have to report that my mouth was hanging open. At least it wasn't full. "Are you insane?"

"Why?"

"You don't know this guy from Adam! He might hurt you!"

"He didn't seem like the type," Lila said.

I rolled my eyes. "That's probably what they said about Ted Bundy."

"I doubt it." She kept forking up lettuce, unrepentantly.

I closed my mouth and made an attempt to sound more worldly when I opened it again. "What did he say? When you asked him to tie you to the bed?"

"He declined. Very nicely. *Some other time, darlin'.*" She lowered her voice to a husky baritone, then grinned at my stupefied expression. I smiled back, automatically, and lowered my eyes to the Caesar. Silence reigned, broken only by the clinking of silverware and muted chewing. Not from me; any appetite I'd had was gone and I was pushing the croutons around on my plate, too busy thinking to be able to process chewing and swallowing right now.

After a minute or two I ventured, "You'd probably recognize his voice, right?"

"If I heard it again? Sure. He picked up one of my business cards and put it in his pocket, and then he winked. I keep hoping he'll call!" She sighed.

"Oh, surely not!" I said, and then caught myself. "I mean, really, Lila. Don't be stupid. I appreciate the fact that you thought he was attractive, but if he calls, put him off and then call the police. Please. Don't take any chances with someone you don't know."

"Don't worry about me, girlfriend. I can take care of myself."

After a second, she added, "Although he'll probably never call."

"Probably not," I admitted. At least I hoped he wouldn't.

Lila grinned. "And meanwhile, if you don't want this Collier-guy for yourself, you can always send him my way."

"I'll think about it," I said, although I knew that it would be a cold day in hell before I put Lila Vaughn and Rafe Collier together.

We parted company after another fifteen minutes or so, with more air kisses and promises to get together again soon. I let my forced and cheerful smile slide off my lips as I walked to my car.

Exactly one week prior to my lunch with Lila, almost to the minute, I had made myself a vow. That was when I had visited 101 Potsdam Street to give Rafe the last of the paperwork pertaining to his grandmother's house—the house where Walker Lamont had killed Brenda Puckett—and it had also been when, to show his gratitude, he had kissed me. Rafe, I mean, not Walker. Walker bats for the other team.

Because of a distressing tendency to pass out every time Rafe comes into my personal space, I can't give you any of the details, but I know I promised myself that if I survived with my virtue and sanity intact, I would stay away from him in the future. It was with the utmost trepidation that I dialed the only telephone number I had for him, and waited for someone to pick up on the other end of the line.

"Storage," a gruff voice grunted. I hesitated. The first time I'd called the number, it had belonged to a car lot; the second time, a pawn shop.

"This is... um... Savannah Martin?" I phrased the statement as a question, expecting some sort of acknowledgement. None came. But at least the phone wasn't hung up, so I decided to push on as if everything was normal. "I'm trying to get in touch with Rafe Collier."

"Nobody here by that name," the voice said. It was familiar. (No, it didn't belong to Rafe. This guy's name was Wendell. I'd met him once. Briefly.)

"I'm sorry to hear that. I need to reach him rather urgently. Maybe you'd be so kind as to pass on the message if you happen to see him?"

Wendell didn't say a word, although he didn't hang up, either.

"Thanks," I said, and severed the connection myself, wondering— not for the first time—about the people Rafe was involved with.

SEVEN O'CLOCK SAW ME BACK at Fidelio's again, greeting the same gray-haired maitre d' as had been here for the lunch shift. "Welcome back, signorina," he said politely, bowing, "good evening, signor."

Todd nodded, frowning. I could tell he was curious, but he contained himself until we were seated at a table in the romantic, dusky section of the restaurant, where big, ferny plants provided plenty of cover and tinkling fountains drowned out private conversations. "What did he mean, *welcome back*? Have you been here recently?"

"Lunch," I said succinctly.

Todd looked at me, suspiciously. "It wasn't with Collier, was it? I thought you said you wouldn't be seeing him again, now that he's got his grandmother's house back."

"I haven't seen Rafe for more than a week," I said calmly. It was a week and approximately six and a half hours, but who was counting? "If it'll make you feel better, you can ask the maitre d'. I had lunch with a girlfriend. Her name is Lila Vaughn."

And may I state for the record that under normal circumstances, I wouldn't be eating at Fidelio's twice in one day. I live on crackers and canned tuna the rest of the time; it's only when someone else is footing the bill that I get to go to places like this. I had scraped the bottom of my checking account to pay for my half of the lunch today, and I wouldn't have been able to afford to pay for dinner.

One thing about Todd, he's easily distracted. "Wasn't she the one who was assaulted this weekend? At that open house?"

I nodded. "Although assaulted wasn't really..."

"I read about it in the paper," Todd interrupted. "You're being careful, aren't you, Savannah?"

I told him I was. "But apparently it wasn't as big a deal as the news made it sound. The robbers didn't touch her, and she wasn't shaken up much at all. She was more disappointed that the man who tied her to the chair didn't choose to take advantage of her."

"Oh." Todd wrinkled his aristocratic noise. "One of those."

I shrugged. There's something about a remark like that, that makes it almost irresistible to say something even worse, just for shock value. And Lila was my friend; I didn't want him to think poorly of her. However, anything I said to Todd had a way of getting back to my mother and brother in Sweetwater, so I resisted the temptation.

"I have to host an open house this weekend," I said instead, "so I wanted to find out as much as I could about what had happened, just to be prepared. Plus, Lila and I are friends. I thought she might need a shoulder to cry on."

"Not everyone is as sensitive as you, Savannah," Todd said. I simpered. Until he changed the subject. He was like a dog worrying a bone. "So you haven't seen Collier at all?"

"Not since last Thursday. I already told you that." And between you and me, I wasn't looking forward to seeing him again. Not after that kiss. I mean, what would I say the next time we met? Should I make reference to it, or pretend it never happened? And what if he tried to kiss me again?!

"Are you all right, Savannah?" Todd inquired solicitously. I looked at him, blankly, and he added, "You're flushed. Here's the waiter. Would you like some ice water?"

"I think I'm OK, thanks. I was just... um... thinking." I smiled graciously at the hovering waiter. "White wine, please."

"And signor?"

Todd ordered a glass of Merlot, and the waiter withdrew. Todd added, "I'm sorry if my talking about it is upsetting you, Savannah. It's just that I know Collier, and he's not someone a nice girl like you should get involved with. I'm concerned about you."

"And I appreciate your concern," I said, just like I had done all the other times he had told me the same thing, "but you don't have to be. I'm not involved with Rafe, and I don't see any way that I ever will be. You seem to be forgetting that I went to school with him too, and heard all the same stories you did."

Todd didn't look mollified. "You're a lady, Savannah. There are stories nobody would have told you."

Before I could ask, the waiter showed up with our drinks and hovered, obsequiously. Todd ordered veal piccata, I asked for chicken marsala. The waiter withdrew.

"So tell me what's going on in Sweetwater this week," I said brightly, before Todd could return to the previous subject. It wasn't that I minded his concern, exactly; it was more that his harping seemed a little misplaced. We hadn't been dating exclusively since high school, and although I still liked and cared for Todd, and hoped he felt the same way about me, I didn't think that our current relationship was such that he had any right to question how I spent my time. I certainly wouldn't presume to question how he spent his. Obviously Todd disagreed.

We talked about home and people we both knew until the food arrived, and then Todd began regaling me with stories from his work. Like everyone else in my family, and like my unlamented ex-husband Bradley, Todd is a lawyer. But where my brother Dix and my brother-in-law Jonathan specialize in family and inheritance law, and where Bradley is a divorce attorney, Todd has gone into criminal law. He worked in the district attorney's office in Columbia, while he lived with his daddy in a big four-square in the heart of Sweetwater.

The waiter brought our food in the middle of one of his amusing anecdotes about life at the courthouse, and Todd kept talking between bites. I smiled, nodded, and nibbled while I listened. It wasn't necessary for me to say anything; he kept the conversation going all by himself, with just the occasional encouraging murmur from me.

We were just getting to the end of dinner when my cell phone rang. My heart sank, along with my stomach. Of all the times for Rafe to return my call...!

"Aren't you going to answer that?" Todd asked, looking at me. I avoided his eyes by flipping the phone open to look at the display. I didn't recognize the number, but that didn't mean anything. "It could be important."

"I doubt it," I answered, putting the phone down next to my plate, where it kept sounding the Alleluia-chorus. "I think I know who it is, and I don't really want to talk to him right now."

Todd's bluish-gray eyes narrowed. "Is Collier bothering you?" He reached out and snagged the phone before I could stop him. I leaned back on my chair, biting my lip, while he lifted it to his ear. His terse greeting was a masterpiece of manly competence. "Satterfield."

The phone squawked. As I watched, the heightened color left his cheeks and his pleasant features took on a slightly sheepish cast. "Of course. My apologies. Here she is." He handed me the phone across the table. "Someone named Gary Lee."

"Oh!" I snatched the phone out of his hand and put it to my ear. "Gary Lee? Hi!"

"Hi, Savannah," Gary Lee Hodges said politely. "How are you?"

"I'm fine. And you?" I was practically panting with excitement, and Todd didn't look happy. I smiled apologetically at him, but I don't think he quite caught my drift, because his expression became even stonier than before.

"We're fine," Gary Lee said. "Hey, me and Charlene have been looking at these houses you've been e-mailing us..."

"Yes?"

"And we've found one we wanna take a look at. Real pretty—Tudor-like, you know—and with a real nice master bedroom with a skylight and stuff."

"Sure," I said, nodding rapidly. "I'd love to show it to you. What's a good time for you?"

"How 'bout tomorrow? I ain't got nothing going on in the afternoon, and Charlene gets off work early."

"I'm not busy tomorrow afternoon. How about 3 o'clock? Or 3:30? That should give us plenty of time."

Gary Lee allowed as how 3:30 would suit him and his wife just fine, and we agreed to meet then. I shut the cell phone off, beaming.

"Plenty of time for what?" Todd wanted to know. I turned my attention to him.

"I beg your pardon...? Oh, that was Gary Lee Hodges."

"I gathered that. Who's Gary Lee?"

"Haven't I told you about him? He's half of that young couple who came to see Rafe's grandmother's house two weeks ago. We've been staying in touch, and now they want me to show them something else." I beamed.

"That's great," Todd said, hiding his enthusiasm well. "So Mrs. Hodges will be there, as well?"

"Charlene? Sure. Why would Gary Lee look at houses without her?"

Todd didn't answer. "Why didn't you want to take the call in front of me?"

"Oh, that wasn't... I mean..." I hesitated, flushing; my mind casting about for something plausible. Something other than the truth, which was that I had expected it to be Rafe, and *that* was the call I didn't want to take in front of Todd. "It wasn't that I didn't want to take the call in front of you, exactly. Or that I didn't want to talk to Gary Lee. I just thought it was impolite to conduct business on the phone when we were having dinner together. *You* don't talk business on the phone when we're on a date."

I smiled. Todd smiled back, and although I thought I could still detect a shadow of suspicion in the depths of his blue-gray eyes, he didn't question me further.

He had cheesecake and I had coffee for dessert, and then he drove me home in his cushy SUV. I snuggled into the buttersoft seat and enjoyed the smell of new leather upholstery. There's nothing wrong with my Volvo, but it's almost five years old, and doesn't smell brand, spanking new anymore.

"You're quiet tonight," Todd said. I shook myself awake.

"Sorry. I was just thinking."

"About...?"

"Oh, this and that. My car. My income. The house I'm showing Gary Lee and Charlene tomorrow. Whether I can find another client at the open house I'm doing for Tim this weekend."

Or if I'd find myself gagged and tied to a chair instead. Maybe I ought to ask Todd to join me so I wouldn't be alone, just in case something happened. But he lived an hour away, and it wasn't fair to impose upon him, plus—honestly—I had my doubts about just how effective he'd be. Todd's just so... civilized, and I couldn't picture him standing up to four masked men—or even women—in coveralls and ski masks. He's more the type who'd nail them to the wall in a courtroom later, after someone else had arrested them.

"You need a husband, Savannah," Todd said, and shocked me into full alertness. I gaped at him, too stunned to speak. He wasn't going to propose, was he? Surely that was a little precipitous? We'd only met again a few weeks ago; before that we hadn't seen each other for four years. I wasn't even sure his divorce from Jolynn was final.

But he didn't say anything else, and I began to breathe again. I could even speak. "I'm not so sure about that. The first time wasn't such a success that I'm in a hurry to try again."

"Maybe you married the wrong man," Todd said. I glanced over at him, but he wasn't looking at me, just keeping his attention on the road.

I guess I couldn't very well deny that. However... "Sometimes it's difficult to know who the right man is. I mean, Bradley seemed like the right man when I married him. Just like you thought Jolynn was the right wife for you when you married her."

Todd didn't answer, and pretty soon we were rolling to a stop outside the gate to my apartment building on East Main Street. Todd started to open his door, and I said quickly, "You don't have to walk me up. It's late, and..."

"Don't be silly." Todd got out of the car and came around to my side. "Of course I'll walk you up. A single woman can never be too careful, especially in a neighborhood like this." He looked around, at the skyline a mile or so to the west, and the cars whizzing by on their way to Ellington Parkway, just to our north. The urban grit was a far cry from sleepy Sweetwater, but not that bad, all things considered.

"East Nashville is actually a very desirable neighborhood these days," I said. "Home prices have doubled and sometimes tripled in the past ten years. We hardly ever have violent crimes anymore. The police have been cracking down on the drug dealers, and even the prostitutes have moved on to grimier pastures. I have a gate, and a private parking space, and a deadbolt and chain on my door. I'm as safe here as anywhere else."

Except maybe tiny, sleepy Sweetwater, where Todd probably wanted to see me.

He didn't answer, but I don't think he was convinced. As we walked upstairs, he kept looking around suspiciously. He didn't complain, however, probably because there wasn't anything for him to complain about. The hallways were freshly painted and carpeted, and well lit by florescent bulbs every few feet. No dark corners where anyone could hide.

"Well..." I said awkwardly when we stood outside the door to my apartment, "thanks for dinner."

Todd turned away from contemplating the hallway and focused on me. "It was my pleasure. I would be happy to provide you with dinner every night, if you'd let me."

"Don't you think going to Fidelio's every night would tax even your wallet?"

I smiled to make it sound like a joke, when in fact it sounded like he was once more gearing up for a proposal.

Todd smiled too, but he didn't answer. "The Broadway production of 'The Phantom of the Opera' is coming to the performing arts center this weekend," he said instead. "I've got two tickets for Saturday night's performance. Would you like to go?"

"I'd love to!"

My mother always told me and my older sister Catherine that we should never seem too available when a gentleman asked us out, but after having looked down the business end of a gun recently, I had resolved to play a little less hard to get. All sorts of opportunities were passing me by, and there were no guarantees that they'd come my way again, or that I'd be alive to take advantage of them if they did.

"I'll pick you up at five, then, and we'll have an early dinner."

"That sounds great," I said. Todd leaned in to kiss me.

"I'll call you tomorrow," he said when he had withdrawn. I nodded. "Contact me if you need anything."

I promised I would. He gave me another quick peck, this one on the cheek, and left. I watched him walk down the hall and around the corner before I pushed the apartment door open and walked inside.

Three

No sooner had I kicked my shoes off and padded into the kitchen in my stocking-feet, than there was a knock on the door. I reversed direction and unlocked the door again, wondering what Todd had forgotten. Had he decided to come out and propose, after all?

"What did you...? Oh!"

"Evening, darlin'."

The man outside lacked Todd's all-American, clean-cut good looks, as well as his $500 suit and impeccable manners. Instead of waiting for me to invite him in, he sauntered across the threshold, brushing against me on the way. Not by accident. I glanced out into the hallway—no sign of Todd—before I followed. "Come in. Make yourself at home."

To my dismay, my heart was thumping a little faster than usual. I was nervous, and not looking forward to teasing answers to my questions out of him. Even so, I can't say I was terribly surprised to see him. I had called him, after all, and it wasn't the first time he'd shown up unannounced on my doormat.

He stopped in the door to the living room and turned to face me. "Thought I already did. Hot date?"

"Dinner with Todd."

Out of my customary high heels, he seemed even taller than usual. I folded my arms across my chest. It was a reflex, although in my more lucid moments I wasn't entirely certain whether I was trying to prevent him from seeing into my cleavage or if it was more of a defense mechanism against the man in general, emotionally as well as physically.

He nodded. "Saw you drive up. Thought maybe he'd be staying the night."

"I didn't see you," I said, diverted. He shrugged. "No, he won't spend the night. I let him walk me to the door and I kissed him goodnight, but that's it. My mother always told me a man won't pay for the cow if he can get the milk for free."

Rafe grinned, white teeth flashing. "So you'll kiss Satterfield, but you won't kiss me?"

So much for pretending last week's kiss had never happened...

"I kissed you. Or let you kiss me, which comes to the same thing."

He shook his head. "No, it don't. I'll show you the difference, if you like."

I stepped back, out of reach. "Some other time."

He grinned, but let it go. "So what can I do for you, darlin'?"

"Oh. Um… Right. I called you, didn't I? I'm never quite sure whether my messages are going to get to you or not. Sometimes you call back, sometimes you don't, and whoever answers the phone—Wendell, isn't it?—never answers it the same way twice. First it was a car lot, then a pawn shop, and today he said it was a storage place. The only consistent thing he says is that you're not there." I realized I was babbling, postponing the inevitable, and I reined myself in. "I wanted to ask you something. Do you want to sit down?"

He quirked a brow—usually I was trying to get him out, not in—but he didn't comment. "Sure."

"The living room is through there." I pointed. "Can I get you anything? Milk, water, sweet tea?"

"Beer?"

"Sorry. Although I think I may have half a bottle of Chardonnay somewhere..." I looked around.

"I ain't that big on wine. But I'll take a glass of tea, if it ain't too much trouble."

"Coming right up." I walked into the kitchen while he headed for the living room. A minute later, when I entered with two glasses of sweet—iced—tea on a tray, I found him not on the sofa, where I'd expected to see him, nor by the balcony doors, looking out at the view—my second guess—but lounging in the doorway to the bedroom, assessing my queen sized bed with an experienced eye. And why I had expected anything different, I don't know. Nevertheless, I stopped as if I'd hit an invisible wall, and blushed. One corner of his mouth curled up, but he didn't speak.

I prodded myself into moving, and put the tray down on the coffee table. "Here you go. It's just instant; I didn't have time to brew fresh."

"You're slipping, darlin'. What'd your mama say?" He removed himself from the door and sauntered around the sofa to retrieve his glass. I did my best to avoid touching him when I handed it over, but without success. His fingertips brushed my knuckles, and I'm not willing to swear it wasn't intentional. Rafe's got the kind of in-your-face sex appeal that a lot of women—and Tim—seem to like, and although I've been brought up to value old-fashioned manners and decorum, I'm not entirely dead below the neck, either. Especially as he doesn't scruple to turn the setting up to scorching hot every time he sees me.

"Cheers." He lifted his glass. I did the same, without thinking. "To us."

He drank. I hesitated, and then took a small sip from my own glass. It was just a toast, and joining in it didn't mean that I acknowledged that there was or ever would be an 'us.'

"So what do you need?" He put the glass down on the table and himself on the sofa, where he leaned back comfortably. He was wearing jeans tonight, and a black T-shirt that molded to his chest and upper arms. I turned away to sit down in a chair, before he could catch me looking. He added, with a grin, "You got someplace you need me to break into for you? Or somebody I can beat some answers out of?"

Recently, we had broken into a storage unit together, in the process of trying to discover who had murdered my two coworkers Brenda Puckett and Clarice Webb, and we had also persuaded a young man to come clean about finding Brenda's dead body and not calling the authorities. Rafe hadn't had to do any actual beating, but the way he had loomed over the youth, cowing him with his six feet three inches and 195 pounds of solid muscle, not to mention the demeanor he had developed in two years behind bars, hadn't hurt. Nineteen-year-old Maurice Washington had sung like the proverbial nightingale.

I shook my head. "I know how much you enjoy doing that sort of thing, but this time, you can give me the answers I need yourself."

"Shoot." He lifted the glass and took another long draught of iced tea, throat moving smoothly as he swallowed. I wasn't sure whether the word was an invitation to ask what I wanted, or a reaction to hearing that there was nothing macho and illegal for him to do.

"Do you know anything about these open house robberies that have been going on for the past two weekends?"

He put the glass down, and I thought there was a watchful look in the depths of his eyes, but it was hard to be sure. They're so dark as to be almost black, and he's learned to hide his feelings and reactions almost too well. "Why?"

"Tim has asked me to host an open house for him this Sunday."

"Yeah? Where?"

I shrugged. I hadn't been paying attention when Tim went over the details on Monday. "Some million-dollar McMansion in Brentwood somewhere."

"Better be careful then, darlin'." Rafe picked the glass up and took another swig. The ice jingled when he put it down on the table again, empty. "So you want me to get you some protection? Gun? Knife? Something untraceable, in case you have to use it?"

"Lord, no!" I moderated my voice. "I'm not going to walk around with a gun in my handbag, thanks all the same. I thought about it after Walker tried to kill me, yes, but I've decided I'm just not comfortable carrying a weapon. More tea?"

"Not right now. You'd be more comfortable once you got used to using it."

"What makes you think I'd want to be comfortable using it? Deliberately shooting someone, or sticking a knife into them? No, thanks. I don't think I have it in me."

"If you had to, you could," Rafe said, in a weird echo of Detective Grimaldi's statement from earlier in the week.

I shrugged. "I appreciate the offer, but no. I don't suppose you'd be willing to give me some... um... personal protection? Stay with me during the open house, just to make sure nothing happens?"

"Guard your body?" He grinned, letting his eyes wander over it. I compressed my lips and willed the incipient blush to stay where it was. "You sure your body'd be safe with me, darlin'?"

I hesitated. "I'd trust you to protect it from someone else coming at it with a knife or a gun." Although not necessarily from himself. But if we were in someone else's house, surely I'd be safe. "And I'd be happy to pay you for your time, if you'd like."

"With your body?"

"No! Don't you ever think about anything else?"

"I'm a man," Rafe said, as if that was an explanation. Maybe it was. "It's a tempting offer, darlin', but I've got plans for Sunday afternoon."

I'd been afraid he'd say that.

He added, blandly, "Maybe you should stay home. Find someone to take your place, or just call Tim and say you're sick."

"I can't do that," I said. "Maybe you could call in sick from whatever it is you're doing, to stay with me."

"If I do that, you're gonna have to make it worth my while."

"Forget it." I said. "I'm not going to sleep with you just so you'll give me two hours of your time."

"Who said anything about sleeping?"

I rolled my eyes. "I'll ask Todd instead."

He smirked. "You think Satterfield can protect you? I could take him with one hand."

"But you're not going to be there, are you?"

I smiled. Neither of us spoke for a moment, until I changed the subject. "I had lunch with Lila Vaughn earlier today; did I tell you?"

"Who?" The question sounded innocent, but I thought I could detect that same watchful quality, this time as an undertone in his voice.

"The Realtor who was hosting the open house that got robbed last weekend."

He nodded. "Friend of yours?"

I explained how I knew Lila. "And she was telling me about what happened, and about this man who tied her to the kitchen chair."

"So?"

"She said she suggested that maybe he'd like to tie her to the bed instead."

Rafe's lips quirked. "I wouldn't recommend doing that if they come to your open house on Sunday, darlin'."

"Because you'd take me up on it?"

"Because..." He stopped, and his eyes narrowed. "You accusing me of something?"

He had asked me this question once before, when I had told him that Sheriff Satterfield in Sweetwater—Todd's daddy—wasn't entirely sure that LaDonna Collier's death was an accident. Rafe's mother had died over the summer, of a drug overdose. There was no evidence to suggest that she hadn't been alone when it happened, and Bob Satterfield had never been able to prove that anyone, let alone Rafe, had had anything to do with it, but at one point he had told me that Rafe was high on his suspect list. I had passed the news on, in a fit of temper over something Rafe said. And I had recoiled when his eyes turned the flat black of a cobra about to strike. The suggestion that he'd be capable of killing his mother had cut deep, into some reserve of icy menace he kept locked inside. This accusation didn't bother him the same way; his response was calculated rather than emotional. As a result, he didn't frighten me. Much.

"I'm not sure," I said, lifting my chin. "All I know is that Lila's description of this guy fit you to a T."

He arched a brow. "No kidding? What did he look like?"

"Tall and dark, with brown eyes and especially long, thick eyelashes." He batted them playfully. "She also said he had a really sexy voice and called her darlin'. And..."

"Yeah?"

"She said he was really hot."

He chuckled. "You think I'm hot?"

"I didn't say *I* did. Lila does."

"Don't you mean Lila would?"

I shrugged. He obviously wasn't going to admit to anything, and I shouldn't really have expected him to. Rafe is a master at keeping things private. I didn't know where he lived when he wasn't at his grandmother's house, didn't know what he did for a living, didn't know how he had spent the past ten years, after he was released from prison... I didn't know anything about him at all, other than what I could see with the naked eye, and the few details he'd volunteered from time to time. If they were even true.

"Sorry I can't help you, darlin'." He got up from the sofa in one smooth movement, like a panther uncoiling. I got to my feet as well, and padded after him toward the door.

"Maybe I'll call Tamara Grimaldi and see if she has the weekend off and wants to hang out with me."

If the suggestion that I was thinking of calling in the cops bothered him, he didn't show it. When he stopped in front of the door and turned to me, he was smiling again. "Tell Tammy I said hi."

Tammy?

"I didn't realize you and the detective were on such intimate terms," I said. She had certainly never asked *me* to call her Tammy.

Rafe didn't answer, just grinned. "Sleep tight, darlin'. Sweet dreams." He reached out and tweaked a strand of hair that had fallen out of my upswept do, twining it around his finger and tucking it behind my ear. The very same thing he—or someone—had done to Lila last Sunday. I stepped back, out of reach.

"You, too."

"Always." The grin widened before he blew me a kiss. "See you around."

"Right," I said to his back.

Of course I couldn't resist the temptation to mention Rafe's pet-name to Detective Grimaldi when I called her the next morning. "By the way," I said sweetly, after the introductions were dispensed with, "Rafe says hi."

"Mr. Collier?" Her voice had a weird undertone, and I wondered if she was blushing. The mental image of a blushing Tamara Grimaldi was bizarre; she was always so put together and seemed so capable. The idea that a man's name could make her blush, was... intriguing.

"I spoke to him last night, and when I told him I'd be calling you today, he said to tell Tammy hi. I didn't realize you two were so chummy."

"He's a chummy sort of guy," the detective said, her voice flat. I didn't bother to hide my grin, since she couldn't see me.

"That's true. He'd flirt with a lamppost if it was wearing a skirt."

She didn't react, and I added, "I asked him if he had time to babysit me on Sunday afternoon, but he said he doesn't. I thought maybe, if you're not working, you'd like to hang out with me. If we're lucky, maybe the open house robbers will show up and you can arrest them."

"Very kind of you to think of me," Tamara Grimaldi said, "but I'm on call this weekend. I'll try to stop by, but if something comes up," I took that to mean '*if somebody gets killed*', "I'll be too busy."

I nodded. "Understandable." And then I hesitated for a second, and two and three, before I added, "I had lunch with Lila Vaughn yesterday."

I could envision the detective's eyebrows arching. "You don't say? And what did Ms. Vaughn have to say about her ordeal? Anything interesting?"

She had better believe it. "Apparently she suggested to the man who was tying her to the chair that maybe he'd like to tie her to the bed instead. I guess she was hoping he'd join her."

It wasn't often I managed to surprise Tamara Grimaldi, but today I succeeded. Twice. "Funny," she said levelly, after a beat, "there isn't anything about that in her statement."

"When did you read her statement? I thought you said it wasn't your case. Not until someone dies, you said."

"After I spoke with you the other day," Detective Grimaldi answered cordially. "I looked it up as a favor, in case there was something there that might be of use to you."

"Oh." I bit my lip. "Sorry."

"No problem. As it turned out, the statement didn't contain much. Certainly less than Ms. Vaughn told you. Did she share with you why she suggested that the robber tie her to the bed?"

"She said he was hot. And before you ask, no, he didn't take his mask off. All she saw were his eyes. She said his voice was sexy, and maybe that was enough for her. I guess her mother never told her not to proposition strange men."

"I guess not," Tamara Grimaldi said. "Did she happen to mention his response?"

"Isn't it obvious? He said no. Or actually, what he said was, *some other time.* Maybe you should mount a guard over Lila, in case he takes her up on it." That would serve the added purpose of keeping her safe, in case I was wrong and it wasn't Rafe she had encountered.

"Hmm..." Detective Grimaldi debated with herself for a moment. "No," she said finally, "I don't think so. Not worth the trouble. I doubt he'd take the chance. Although if he does, and she mentions it to you, maybe you'll be good enough to let me know?"

I hesitated. Off-hand I couldn't think of any reason not to. We'd all be better off once the robbers were safely behind bars; even Lila would agree with that. Probably. And if it was Rafe, and he was stupid enough to take her up on the offer, he deserved to get arrested. "Sure. Next time I talk to her. If she mentions anything that's pertinent to the case, I'll pass it on."

"Thank you, Ms. Martin."

"No problem, Tammy."

"Ms. Martin?"

"Yes, Tammy?"

"Nobody calls me Tammy. Not even my mother."

I smiled. "Would you like me to relay that information to Rafe?"

"No," Tamara Grimaldi said, her voice grim, "that won't be necessary. I'll do that myself."

I suppressed a giggle. "I don't doubt you will. Thanks, Detective. I'll talk to you later."

Tamara Grimaldi grunted something noncommittal, and I hung up, feeling well satisfied with my morning's work. (And if I felt just a little bit guilty, too, I managed to suppress it.) The police had needed to hear what Lila had told me, but—I told myself—naming names would have served no purpose. The man Lila had described sounded like Rafe, yes, but a lot of men have dark eyes with long eyelashes. She hadn't seen any other physical characteristics, so it was hardly conclusive identification. Men who call women darlin' are a dime a dozen, especially here in Nashville, and Rafe wasn't the only male in town with sex appeal. If Detective Grimaldi and her colleagues dug up some actual evidence, I'd come clean about my suspicions, but until then, I'd keep mum.

Four

The house that Gary Lee and Charlene wanted to see was an attractive 1940s pseudo-Tudor cottage in Inglewood. Gary Lee and Charlene were charmed. They charged into the house and started poking around in closets and under the stairs while I followed, smiling maternally, like a nanny with two boisterous charges.

"Look at this, babe. A what-d'ya-call-it... butler's pantry!"

"Oh, isn't that cute!" Charlene was hanging on Gary Lee's arm as well as on his every word. They were only a few years younger than me, but in their newlywed bliss they seemed impossibly young to my jaundiced, divorced eyes.

"Where are the bedrooms at?" Charlene asked after a few minutes. I pointed them up the stairs, just as my cell phone started ringing.

"Knock yourselves out. I'll just stay down here and take this call. Let me know if you have any questions."

Giggling, they promised they would, and then skipped upstairs hand in hand. I wandered out onto the deck and pulled the phone out of my purse. "This is Savannah."

"Hi, girlfriend!"

"Lila? How are you? Is everything all right?"

"Everything's great," Lila said. "I just wanted to let you know that I just took my first listing. For a cute little ranch in West Meade. 1800 square feet, $350,000. If you know anyone who's interested."

"Good for you." I suppressed an unbecoming twinge of envy. "Congratulations."

"Thanks." She hesitated for a second. "Hey, listen, Savannah…"

"Yes?"

"I've been thinking about what you said yesterday. You know, about me being careful and not taking any chances…?"

"Yes?"

"I appreciate you worrying about me. And I won't do anything stupid, I promise. If he calls, I'll sic the cops on him."

"Oh." I said. "OK. Yes, that's probably a good idea."

"That's what you wanted me to do, right?"

"It was. Yes."

"OK, then."

"OK." I didn't know what else to say. Lila didn't say anything, either. I added, awkwardly, "You know…"

"Yes?"

"I may have been a little… um… pushy when I said that. I mean, I don't want anything to happen to you, and it's always good to be careful, but I may have come on a little too strong. I'm sure you're able to decide for yourself who you should trust and who you shouldn't."

Lila sounded surprised. "Really?"

I nodded firmly. "Really." After all, if it was Rafe she had met—and I was pretty sure it was; if it hadn't been, surely he would have said so—it wasn't as if she was in any danger. Even if he did call her, and she agreed to get together with him, he wouldn't harm her. That was one thing I was sure of.

We hung up after another few words, and I headed back into the house. Gary Lee was on his way down the stairs as I came into the foyer. "Charlene's using the little girl's room," he said, tossing his half-long, dark locks in the direction of the upstairs. I smiled.

"No problem. Make yourselves at home." The more comfortable they felt, the more likely they were to want to buy the house, right? That's why we Realtors recommend to our sellers to remove any personal photographs from the house before offering it for sale, and also adding lots and lots of mirrors. Buyers should be able to see themselves in the house. Literally as well as figuratively. Or so goes the conventional wisdom. "What do you think?"

"It's nice," Gary Lee said, looking around, "but I think we'd like to see one or two more before we decide. The bedroom wasn't quite as mind-blowing as we'd hoped."

"All right," I said.

"I don't suppose you've got any time tomorrow to show us a house? There's one over on Avalon Drive we'd like to see. One of the ones you sent us. Nice brick cottage, new kitchen, full basement, master suite upstairs with a double shower..."

"Sure. I'd be happy to. When would you like to meet?"

Gary Lee said that 3:30 would work well again, and we agreed to meet outside the house on Avalon, just as Charlene came skipping down the stairs. Her cheeks were flushed and her eyes shiny, and it looked as if she had liked the present house just fine. But when Gary Lee explained that I had said myself willing to show them the house on Avalon tomorrow, she hooked herself onto his arm and nodded eagerly.

"It's just darling, Savannah. The maple kitchen, and the fireplace, and the master bedroom..." She looked dreamy for a second, and then glanced over at me, apologetically. "I mean, this one was OK, too. It was fine. Great. It's just..." She squeezed Gary Lee's arm and giggled, "that we think we can do better."

Gary Lee nodded.

"It's no problem at all," I said politely. "It's what I'm here for. I'll see you tomorrow at 3:30, outside the house on Avalon. Then we'll see if that one works better for you."

Gary Lee and Charlene exchanged a look and a giggle before Gary Lee tucked his long legs into the couple's tiny hybrid, and Charlene folded herself into the seat next to him, and they drove off with a squeal of tires. I got into the Volvo and sat there for a moment, contemplating my life.

So Gary Lee and Charlene wanted to see another couple of houses before they made up their minds about which they wanted to buy.

Oh, well... nothing wrong with that. I had plenty of time to spare; it wasn't as if I had any other clients fighting for my attention. And if I stuck with them, sooner or later they'd buy something, and I'd finally get that first coveted commission check. Hopefully it would come soon enough to keep me from ending up on the street. And meanwhile, I had plenty of other things to worry about. Not the least of which was Lila and the man who may or may not have been Rafe.

Pretty sure is not the same as absolutely certain, and after having just essentially told Lila that I didn't think she had anything to worry about, it'd be really nice to be absolutely certain, or at least almost positive. I picked up the phone again and called Kieran Greene.

Kieran worked for one of the big national real estate chains, and he must have been pretty good at what he did, because he arrived for our appointment in a brand new Lexus.

He had tried to tell me that he didn't want to talk about what had happened to him, but I had been adamant. Nice, of course, but adamant. And then he had tried to tell me that we could talk on the phone, but I had been firm on that score, as well. I'd have to go further into debt, but Kieran had agreed to meet me for an early dinner at Rotier's, where, over the best cheeseburgers in Nashville, I intended to wring any and every usable scrap of information from him and then hang it out to dry. If he could give me just one piece of information that could either prove or disprove that Rafe had been among the burglars, I could set my mind at ease. About several things.

Rotier's is a tiny hole-in-the-wall near Centennial Park. Once a carriage house for a fashionable West End Avenue home, the building has been occupied by the family-owned restaurant since 1945. The interior is straight out of the 1950s, with naugahyde-upholstered booths and lighted Budweiser-signs on the knotty-pine paneled walls, and the menu—thankfully—leans in the same direction. I may have been spending money I didn't have, but at least I was spending less than I would be elsewhere. Kieran Greene, bless him, was a cheap date.

Up close and in person, his resemblance to Timothy Briggs was less obvious. He was at least ten years older, for one thing, and not as dashing as in the picture I had seen. Possibly the media had dusted off an old photograph, or maybe Kieran himself preferred to use it, because he liked the way he had looked back then. Now he was a middle-aged fuss-pot with thinning hair and the beginnings of a paunch. He was dressed in chinos and a tasteful pale pink shirt under a navy blazer, and his shoes were so highly polished they reflected the ceiling lights. He even wore an ascot, which he tweaked fussily as he took his place on the opposite side of the table with a polite smile. "You must be Savannah."

"And you're Kieran. I recognize you from your picture." A well-placed compliment never hurts.

We shook hands across the table. His was cool and soft.

"Thank you for agreeing to meet me," I added. "I appreciate it."

"A body has to eat," Kieran said demurely, "and you sounded so fierce on the phone, I didn't dare say no."

Oops. My mother would have been mortified to hear me described as fierce. A properly brought up Southern Belle should be docile and pleasant in all circumstances, and always defer to any man in the vicinity. Mom might have made an exception in Kieran's case, but then again, she might not. He did have x-chromosomes, after all, even if he acted prissier than the most properly brought up maiden aunt.

"I'm sorry I upset you," I apologized. "I didn't realize I came on so strong."

"That's OK," Kieran said forgivingly. "I know you didn't mean it. It's just that I've been so emotional lately. After my ordeal weekend before last, you know."

I nodded. "Something like that would be enough to make anyone emotional, I would think. I don't blame you in the least."

"Thank you, sweetie. That's so darling of you." He leaned over and patted my hand.

"Are you sure you don't mind talking about it? I hate asking you to relive a frightening episode."

Kieran sighed bravely. "No, I don't mind. If my horrible experience can help someone else, I'll be happy to tell you about it."

"Thank you." I glanced around. "Let's find a waiter and order, that way we won't be interrupted. And you can tell me all about it while we wait."

Kieran agreed that this made sense, and we ordered our drinks and cheeseburgers and got down to business.

"Like I told you on the phone, I've already spoken to Lila Vaughn," I said, as kind of an introductory statement. Kieran made a moue. I hesitated. "Do you know Lila?"

He shook his head. "Oh, dear me, no. No, no. Not personally. Although I have certainly seen enough of her lately. On the news, in the papers, online..."

I nodded. "She's a lot more resilient than I would be in her situation."

Kieran murmured a musical, "Mmm-hmmm..." as the waiter arrived, and we sat in silence for a moment or two, while he set down our drinks. I was having water again, while Kieran had ordered something with cherries and pearlized onions on a stick upright in clear liquid.

"Well, dear," Kieran said, after a taste, "what exactly is it you want to know about my ordeal? I can tell you about it, or you can ask whatever questions you have. The latter may be more productive. Although maybe I should give you a *precis* first."

"Please," I said. Kieran drew breath and threw himself into a spirited recounting of what was probably the most terrifying—and exciting—thing that had ever happened to him.

I won't bore you with the details. They matched what I had read online in every particular. Kieran had had a relatively successful open house, with more than two dozen visitors, but by the time 3:45 rolled around, the house was empty. He was just beginning to think about closing up shop when he'd heard the rumbling of a big engine in the driveway. Looking out, he saw a moving van backing up to the side door. It confused him, because the owners hadn't told him that anyone was coming to pick anything up, but it didn't worry him.

"I just assumed that they'd forgotten to mention it," he explained. "The stager I brought in recommended that they put some furniture and bric-a-brac in storage, to open the rooms up a little bit, and we'd talked about taking the valuable paintings down and putting them away while the house was on the market. So I didn't think anything of it."

I nodded. "When did you realize that something wasn't right?"

Kieran had realized what was up as soon as the movers walked in. Four men—four *big* men—wearing ski-masks and gloves.

"Yes," I murmured, "that would probably tip me off, too."

Kieran puffed a shaky laugh. As he had been talking, some of the affectations had dropped away, revealing what I recognized was a severely shaken man. "Three of them pushed past me into the house. The fourth grabbed my arm and led me into the kitchen. He was *very* big." Kieran shuddered.

"How big?" I wanted to know. Kieran shook his head despairingly.

"Height, maybe six-two or -three. He towered over me, anyway. And he probably weighed over 200. He was just solid, you know. All muscle. I could feel it through the padded coveralls. And he had dark brown eyes and dark brows, and his skin color was medium. He might have been a light-skinned black, or Hispanic or Mulatto, or even Middle Eastern."

I nodded. "And what did he say to you?"

"He said..." Kieran swallowed, "that if I just did what I was told, he wouldn't hurt me."

"He, or they?"

Kieran shrugged. "He, they... does it matter?"

"Probably not. Was there anything distinctive about his voice? Accent? Dialect? Any words he used?"

I crossed my fingers. I should have known better; whoever it was—Rafe or someone else—wasn't likely to have called Kieran darlin'.

Kieran informed me that no, there hadn't been anything distinctive at all about his voice, other than that he was clearly from the South. Or had been here long enough to be able to manage a reasonable approximation of the dialect.

"So what did he tell you to do?" I asked.

Kieran closed his eyes. "To be quiet and sit on the chair. I did, and he tied my hands and my legs. And then he told me to sit tight until he came back. So I did. They went past with paintings and other things that they put in the truck, but none of the others talked to me."

"And did he come back?" He had for Lila, so I was interested to know if he had for Kieran too, or if it had been just because Lila was Lila.

Kieran nodded. "The others went out with the last load, and I could hear the truck starting. He stopped in the kitchen to make sure I was OK."

"That was nice of him," I said, inanely. Kieran rolled his eyes.

"No, it wasn't. It was horrible and cruel and mean."

"You're right," I said. "Although it sounds as if, everything considered, he could have treated you worse."

Kieran admitted, grudgingly, that he could have. "He explained that they were leaving, and that I had to stay tied up, because if I didn't, I'd be on the phone to the police before the truck had left the yard. He said he was sure that someone would be home to find me before long, but just in case, he'd check later to make sure."

"And you told the police that, of course."

Kieran nodded. "They put a policeman outside and took down the license plate numbers of all the vehicles that drove down the street for the rest of the night. But no one came." He shuddered.

"Maybe someone did, and you just didn't realize it," I said comfortingly. Kieran shook his head. I insisted, "No, really. Maybe your clients got a phone call or something, which they didn't think had anything to do with what had happened. A wrong number, or someone pretending to be from the newspaper or collecting for the police benevolence fund or something." That last lie would appeal to Rafe, I felt sure. To make a phone call pretending to be from the police benevolence fund to see if anyone was home to answer the phone was just the sort of thing he'd do. "I'm sure he wouldn't have let you sit there all night."

"He might!" Kieran said petulantly. I opened my mouth to argue, but thought better of it. We may not be talking about Rafe Collier here, and even if we were—especially if we were—I didn't want to give Kieran the idea that I knew anything.

Luckily, this was at the exact moment when the waiter arrived bearing our food, and Kieran didn't notice my lapse. I watched him cut his burger into neat quarters before he began to eat, daintily, with both pinkies sticking out. His face looked drawn. I decided that I had tormented the poor man enough, and that I needed to leave him alone to eat his dinner in peace. I attempted to put him at ease with an innocuous question about how long he had worked in the real estate business, and we spent a pleasant half hour eating and talking shop. Kieran had twenty years of experience, and was a fount of knowledge. I'd been in the business for roughly two months, and needed all the help I could get. Walker had been very helpful during my first six weeks, but I couldn't exactly call him in prison every time I had a question, and

Tim was no help at all. I processed as much as I could of what Kieran was saying, wishing I had thought to bring a tape recorder.

"So you worked with Brenda Puckett before she died," he said at one point. I nodded. "She'd been bending the rules for years, you know. It's a good thing someone finally stopped her, although rather a pity it had to happen the way it did."

Having been the one to find Brenda with her throat slit from ear to ear, I had to agree.

"And quite a shame about Walker Lamont, of course." Kieran took another bite of medium-rare cheeseburger, chewed daintily and added, "He was a nice man."

A nice man who had murdered two women and would have murdered two more, myself included, if I hadn't stopped him.

"He was," I agreed. "We always got along well. Until he threatened to kill me, of course."

"Of course," Kieran nodded. "Have you spoken to him since?"

"Oh, yes. He asked to see me, so I went out to Riverbend Prison one day last week. He wanted to apologize and tell me where to find the paperwork to fix some of the illegal things that Brenda did. It's hard for me to say that Brenda deserved what she got—nobody ever deserves to get her throat cut, I think—but all the same, I can't feel as sorry for her as maybe I should."

I took another bite of my own burger and added, "People told me that real estate was a cutthroat business, but I had no idea they meant it literally."

Kieran nodded. "There are a lot of raw deals in this business, dear. The longer you stick around, the more you'll realize how true that is. Most people are out for themselves, and will step over your lifeless body to get where they want to go. Just look at the way Tim Briggs was getting his face on TV after Brenda died. Or your friend Lila, how she's using this unpleasant, criminal situation to make herself more recognizable to the public. She's trivializing a crime that involved not only her, but me as well. And my clients. They're beside themselves with grief. They lost a collection of paintings that it had taken two generations to amass."

I nodded sympathetically. I had felt the same way when Tim was getting himself in front of the TV-cameras after Brenda's death, and I knew he would probably reap the benefits in increased referrals and sales.

On the other hand, I could understand where Lila was coming from, as well. She was trying to scratch her way to the top of a very competitive business—a business that Kieran Greene, by the looks of him, had succeeded quite well in—and if she decided to use the lemons life had handed her to make lemonade, it was hardly my place to object. More power to her, even if it wasn't the choice I would have made. My mother would never have let me hear the end of it if I had.

Five

The second house that Gary Lee and Charlene wanted to see was an early ranch—anno circa 1940—with huge windows and tall ceilings. It hadn't been renovated to the degree that yesterday's Tudor had, and a lot of the old features had been maintained. The fireplace hadn't been outfitted with hissing gas-logs, but burned good old-fashioned wood, and the windows were original rather than tilt-in replacements. I liked it a lot better, with the exception of the carpets that covered all the floors. But as I explained to Gary Lee and Charlene, there were bound to be hardwoods underneath, and refinishing floors is no big deal. (Or so I gather, although I've never had to do it myself. The carpenter who refinished my mother's floors a few years ago didn't seem to think it was anything much, anyway. Messy and dusty and inconvenient for a few days, but hardly nuclear science, for all that. Rafe had managed to refinish the floors in his grandmother's house, and he had barely made it through high school before he went to jail. Mostly what it takes, I believe, is the ability to figure out how the machine works, and the necessary muscular strength to keep it upright and moving.)

My cell phone rang just as Gary Lee and Charlene were heading up the stairs to the master suite on the second floor. I checked the number and waved them on. "I have to answer this. Take your time upstairs, and let me know if you have any questions."

They nodded and giggled and kept going. I ducked out into the back yard, to the brick patio, before I answered the call. "Good afternoon, detective. What can I do for you?"

"Where are you?" Tamara Grimaldi asked, without introduction. I told her I was showing a house in the Riverwood neighborhood in East Nashville. "I'd like to see you when you're done."

"Sure," I said. "I'll come downtown as soon as I'm finished here."

"I'll meet you somewhere closer. Are you familiar with the TBI-building?"

I wrinkled my forehead. "The Tennessee Bureau of Investigations? Sure. It's just a few minutes from here. What are you doing there?"

"I'm not there. I'm just down the road from it. Brown building on the right before you get to the TBI-building. I'll be waiting in the lobby. Don't drag your feet."

I had a hard time breathing. "What's wrong? What's happened?"

"I'll tell you when you get here." She disconnected. I closed the phone with shaking hands. This didn't sound good.

Gary Lee and Charlene were still upstairs when I came back inside, and I stopped at the bottom of the stairs and started gnawing the lipstick off my bottom lip. Time passed, during which I tried to convince myself that a few minutes wouldn't make a difference, and that it wouldn't be kosher to drag them out before they were ready. After two minutes I decided I'd waited long enough, and raised my voice. "Excuse me!"

My voice cracked and I had to try again. "Gary Lee? Charlene?"

I heard something that sounded like a scramble, and then Gary Lee's voice. "What's up?" His voice sounded rusty, too. It was followed by a giggle and a low-voiced comment from Charlene.

"I'm sorry," I yelled, "but are you guys almost finished? I've had an emergency and I have to go."

"Oh." There was a momentary pause and then, "Just a minute."

"I'll be outside." I headed for the front door, and stood tapping my foot impatiently until they came rushing down the stairs. Charlene's hair was disheveled—so was Gary Lee's, although there was nothing new in that—and both of them looked rumpled and rather the worse for wear.

"I'm sorry," I said, as I hurriedly locked the door and hid the key inside the gray lockbox, "but I have to go meet someone. Something's wrong, and I have to deal with it. We can come back later, if you want."

They exchanged a look. "No," Gary Lee said, "I think we've decided that this one isn't for us."

Charlene nodded. "The master suite didn't really work for us."

"I'm sorry," I said again.

"There's another house we'd like to see. On Baxter Avenue. If you think you'll have time tomorrow—if your problem's gonna be solved by then—maybe we can go see that instead?"

"I'm certain things will be taken care of by tomorrow," I said, with no clue whether I was telling the truth or not, "but unfortunately, tomorrow is Sunday, and I'm hosting an open house from 2 to 4. Do you want to do it earlier or later, or do you want to wait until Monday?"

Gary Lee and Charlene exchanged a look. "Monday's fine," Gary Lee said.

"Great. Give me the particulars, and I'll meet you there. Same time?"

3:30 worked well for them on Monday, too, and I jumped in the Volvo and peeled rubber out of the driveway, leaving them to get into their hybrid and drive off at their leisure. Not the way a shark-like real estate professional should behave, but my priorities are thankfully not so skewed yet that I'd slaver over a pair of buyers rather than answer the summons of the MNPD.

I broke several laws and almost the sound barrier on my way to Gass Boulevard, but mercifully I avoided getting a ticket. Although I admit I almost ran off the road when I came to the brown building on the right, just before the TBI-building. Or more accurately, when I saw the discreet sign at the entrance. *Center for Forensic Medicine*, it said.

Now, I don't have much of a social life outside Todd Satterfield, so I read quite a bit (tawdry romance novels, mostly) and I watch TV. Like everyone these days, I know what Forensic Medicine means. Just to clinch it, in case I hadn't known, underneath it said *Davidson County Medical Examiner's Office*. Tamara Grimaldi had directed me to the morgue. This couldn't be good.

I managed to settle the Volvo in a parking space without dinging the cars on either side of me, and walked into the building, heart beating. Just like she had said, Detective Grimaldi was waiting in the lobby, her feet on an oak coffee table and her head leaned back with eyes closed. I hesitated, loath to wake her if she was enjoying a no doubt well-deserved nap. She looked like she could use one. Her naturally olive complexion had lightened to a drab tan, and there were circles under her eyes.

"I'm not asleep." Her eyes opened and fixed on me.

"How did you know it was me?" I took a few steps closer.

"Your smell precedes you. Chanel No 5, isn't it?"

"It's a classic. So what am I doing here?"

"I need a favor." She swung her legs off the table and stood up. She was dressed in jeans and a crisp button-down shirt today, with a gun in a holster under her arm. I avoided looking at it. Ever since Walker came after me with one, I've been a little leery of guns.

"Is this something left over from Brenda and Clarice's deaths?" I asked, referring to my recently departed co-workers.

"Unfortunately not. This is something new." She headed for a door at the back of the lobby, waving me to follow. I did, my ladylike pumps clicking fast to keep up with her long legs and short heels. She added, over her shoulder, "There's been a death. I need confirmation of an unofficial identification."

I felt the color leeching out of my face. "Oh, my God! Who died? It's not someone in my family, is it?" I'd had no idea any of them were coming up to Nashville today, but they might have driven up without telling me. "Or Todd? He hasn't called me, but sometimes he likes to show up unexpectedly." To surprise me, he says, although sometimes I wonder if it isn't so he can make sure I'm alone. "Or... it's not Rafe, is it?"

The way he drove, like a bat out of hell, it wouldn't be surprising. And I didn't suppose he really had a next of kin who could identify him. His parents were both dead; Tyrell before Rafe was born and LaDonna this summer. And his grandmother, poor old Mrs. Jenkins, went in and out of knowing who he was, thinking he was her son, or someone she didn't know at all.

Or was it Mrs. Jenkins herself...?

But no, then Grimaldi would call Rafe to do the honors, wouldn't she?

"It isn't Mr. Collier. Nor anyone else you mentioned. I would tell you who we believe it is, but I don't want to prejudice your identification."

She pushed the call button for the elevator, and we waited in silence. My mind was spinning. I'll admit to being relieved when she sent the elevator up rather than down. On TV, the dead bodies are usually kept in the basement, and I was cowardly happy that we weren't headed that way.

Upstairs, she led me to a small, friendly room that looked more like someone's sitting room than an office at the Forensic Science Lab. It looked out over green trees and the spiky satellite and cell phone towers on top of the TBI-building. A manila folder was holding pride of place in the middle of the table, and she waved me to it. "I thought it'd be easier for you to look at pictures rather than the corpse itself. Just glance at the first two photos, if you don't mind. There are some others in there—crime scene photos—that I doubt you'll enjoy. Take your time."

I took a couple of shaky steps toward the table. She added, "I'm going to go to the soda machine. Do you still prefer Diet Coke?"

"Under the circumstances, I'd prefer a stiff drink, but Diet Coke will do." She turned to go, and I added, belatedly, "Thank you."

"No problem. Have a seat at the table, and when you're ready, open the folder. I'll be back in a minute."

She disappeared. The door shut behind her with a soft click. I eyed the manila folder as if it were a snake preparing to bite me.

I don't enjoy being involved in violent crimes. Finding Brenda's butchered body had been the grossest experience of my life, and the thought of it still had the power to turn me woozy and nauseous. I was brought up to be a lady. I'm delicate and squeamish and sensitive, and the sight of blood—especially that much blood—bothers me. I wasn't looking forward to whatever the folder had to offer.

Better get it over with. I sank onto the chair and pulled the folder across the table toward me. This didn't involve a family member; the detective had said so. And if it wasn't Todd, and it wasn't Rafe, exactly how hard could it be?

Taking a deep breath, I opened the folder and looked at the first picture. And felt the room start to spin slowly while colored confetti began raining down in front of my eyes.

When Rafe and I had found Brenda, I had taken one look at her and promptly passed out. Rafe had had to carry me outside. This wasn't quite as bad. No blood, for one thing. Or none I could see. Still, good call on Detective Grimaldi's part to make me look at pictures rather than the real thing. If I had come nose to nose with this bloated, discolored face down in the morgue, I would have collapsed on the spot. And while Detective Grimaldi might be more capable than most men, she was no match for Rafe.

"Here." She had come in without my hearing her through the buzzing in my ears, and now she placed an ice-cold can of Diet Coke on the table in front of me. I popped the top and took an unladylike swig. My stomach objected, and then settled a little.

"Do you recognize her?" Tamara Grimaldi sat down on the other side of the table with her own can of Dr. Pepper.

"Who'd recognize *that*?" I responded, hoarsely.

"Try again. Look at the other picture."

I glared at her, but slid the first photograph out of the way so I could see the second. It showed a hand, brown, with long fingers and long nails, and what looked like abrasions around the wrist. The nails were painted with tiny flowers, each set with a rhinestone chip. I put the picture down.

"Lila Vaughn."

My voice was flat. Detective Grimaldi eyed me. "Are you sure?"

"Those are her nails. They were painted like that yesterday. Or whenever it was I saw her."

"Can you manage to look at the other photo again? Just to make sure? I can't accept a positive ID based on fake nails, even from a professional such as yourself."

I was too far gone even to object to this jab at my previous job behind the make-up counter at the mall. Instead I steeled myself and looked at the picture, fighting the nausea that was rising in my throat. This second look didn't last more than five seconds, but it was enough. I shut the folder with as much of a bang as a manila folder can make, and pushed it across the table toward the detective. "It's Lila. The hair, the face shape, the nose... God, what happened to her?!"

"From the evidence," Detective Grimaldi said, "she was strangled."

"No kidding?" I'm no detective, but even I could have figured that out. Lord!

I took another long drink of soda and leaned back, closing my eyes. Now I understood why I had found Detective Grimaldi in that same position down in the lobby. Strange as it sounds, it helped me to keep from regurgitating the salad I'd had for lunch.

"I need a formal statement from you regarding everything Ms. Vaughn said during your lunch the other day," the detective said, from far away. I opened my eyes.

"Why?"

"In the event that she said anything that could shed some light on what happened to her."

"She didn't. All we talked about was business. And what happened on Sunday, of course." I paused as a thought struck me. "Oh, my God! You don't think…?"

"We're considering the possibility. Whoever did it, tied her to the bed first."

I felt myself blanch. "And raped her?"

"There's some evidence of trauma," Detective Grimaldi said, her voice even, "but not so much that it couldn't have been consensual. Some people like rough sex."

"Not this rough, surely?"

"There have been cases of death during autoerotic asphyxiation."

I must have looked blank, because she added, "Some people practice self-strangulation during masturbation. They say it enhances orgasms."

"Yikes!" I was fighting not to blush. In the circles where I travel, people don't throw words like "masturbation" and "orgasm" around, let alone "autoerotic asphyxiation."

Tamara Grimaldi shrugged. "Not something you've ever been introduced to, I daresay."

I shook my head. Mercy, no. "My ex-husband was pretty traditional in bed. Not that I'm complaining. He was an adulterous jerk, but at least he never suggested we try something like that. That's just nasty. Although this… um… auto-asphyxiation wasn't how Lila died, was it?"

Grimaldi shook her head. "She had a partner. One she let into her apartment. There was no sign of forced entry, so she must have opened the door for him. Either that or he followed her home and pushed inside before she had a chance to lock the door."

Scary.

"Of course, there's the possibility that whoever she had sex with wasn't the person who killed her," Grimaldi said judiciously. "However, our theory is that one man did both, and that it's connected with the robbery. That's why I need you to go over your conversation with her again, in detail. As much of it as you can remember. Anything, however little, may help us find the person who did this."

I nodded. "Of course. Anything I can do."

"I'm going to tape you, if you don't mind. That way, I can get someone to transcribe the tape later, and I won't have to worry about taking notes now. I don't want to miss anything."

"Sure," I said. She pulled out a small recording device, pushed a button, told it her name and the date and time, and asked me to introduce myself. "Interview regarding Vaughn, Lila Jeanette. Case H-5927694. Go ahead, Ms. Martin. Tell me about your lunch with Ms. Vaughn. I'll interrupt if there's anything I want to clarify; it not, just keep going."

I took a sip of Diet Coke and a breath, and threw myself into it. "I had lunch with Lila two days ago, at Fidelio's Restaurant..."

An hour later, we were still going strong. Detective Grimaldi had made more interruptions and repeated more questions than I would have thought possible, making me answer different variants of the same thing in different ways—I guess to see if my answers changed—although there was no denying she covered all the bases. Her detailed questioning kept my mind occupied, too, and I was grateful. I wasn't looking forward to being alone with my thoughts. Already, the numbness was starting to wear off and I was beginning to shake.

At the end of the interview, Detective Grimaldi shut off the recorder. "I'm sorry to put you through that, Ms. Martin."

"That's OK. Lila was my friend. I want to help." I swallowed and added, reluctantly, "I feel like this is my fault."

She leaned back. "How can it be your fault?"

"I told her not to worry," I said wretchedly. "I didn't think she was in any danger."

The detective arched a brow. "That doesn't sound like you, Ms. Martin. I would have expected you to tell her to be careful."

"I did! I mean, I did at first. But then…"

I trailed off. There was a thin line here, and it was one I wasn't certain I wanted to cross. Of course I wanted the detective to know anything that might help her find Lila's killer, but telling her that I suspected Rafe of being involved in the robberies surely wouldn't make a difference when he couldn't have killed Lila. And he couldn't have. He just couldn't.

"You know, Ms. Martin," Detective Grimaldi said as she handed me a tissue, "it's always better to tell the truth. The whole truth. And let us worry about what's important and what isn't. It's our job."

She sat back in her chair and started taking notes on a yellow legal pad. I sniffed into the tissue a few times before I mopped my eyes.

"It's not that I didn't tell you. I did. Just now. I just didn't…" I just hadn't spelled it out. I hadn't wanted to. But now I felt like I should. "It's about the man Lila met. The one she propositioned."

"Let me guess. You've realized the description sounds a lot like someone we both know."

It wasn't a question. And she wasn't looking at me, but kept her eyes on the legal pad, where she was doodling something. From the other side of the table and upside down, it looked like a hanged-man in the game that little children play. *Gimme an R*, I thought, *gimme an A, gimme an F*…

When I didn't answer, she added, with a glance at me from under her own lashes, "Did you ask him about it?"

I grimaced. "Yes."

"I don't suppose you'd care to share his answer with me?"

"He said that if the open house robbers show up at my open house tomorrow, I shouldn't tell them the same thing that Lila did."

"A threat?" Detective Grimaldi said interestedly.

I shook my head. "Just a joke. You know Rafe. He never tells the truth if a lie will do, and there's no telling what the truth is in this case. There are a lot of men out there with brown eyes. Every black, mixed-race, or Hispanic man in Nashville has dark eyes, and most of them have long, thick eyelashes, too. At least a few hundred must be over six feet tall, and I'm sure a lot of them call women darlin'. This is the South, after all."

"True." She didn't say anything else. I waited until I couldn't handle the silence any longer.

"So is that it? Can I go?"

"Unless you'd like to look at the rest of my crime scene photos. Or you've remembered something else. Or have any questions. Or you'd like to try again to convince me why Mr. Collier couldn't have strangled Ms. Vaughn."

She looked up, her eyes like knives slicing right through me. I shook my head. I had questions, but none that couldn't wait. Right now, I just wanted to get out of this place, with its crime scene photos and dead bodies and bad memories. I'd save my breath for later, when it might do more good.

For the record, I didn't think Rafe had strangled Lila. There was a time, not too long ago, when I'd been worried that he might strangle *me*; but he didn't, and I wasn't about to suspect him of strangling anyone else. If he had managed to control himself under the circumstances I'd put him in, he would have managed to control himself with Lila. But if I tried to convince Detective Grimaldi of that, I'd probably only make him sound worse than he was. It wasn't difficult to do. As Todd Satterfield's paranoidal background check a few weeks ago had revealed, Rafe didn't have a job, didn't have any visible means of support, didn't own property or borrow money or pay taxes; he hadn't even had a verifiable address before he moved in with his grandmother. It all added up to someone living slightly below the radar, which—considering his history—probably meant that he was involved in something illegal. If Todd could come up with that information, chances were the police could do even better. And although I didn't think Detective Grimaldi was the type to arrest someone without the necessary proof, I might be wrong. Better to wait until then to argue my case.

Six

As soon as I was out of the Center for Forensic Medicine parking lot, I made a beeline for Potsdam Street. My hands were shaking and I wanted nothing more than to go home and curl up and cry, but there was something I had to do first.

101 Potsdam is a run-down Victorian house on a couple of acres in what isn't the best part of town. It's also Tondalia Jenkins's house, where Brenda Puckett was killed a few weeks ago. As I had explained to Kieran Greene yesterday, Brenda had taken advantage of old Mrs. Jenkins's dementia to con the woman into selling her home. Brenda signed Mrs. Jenkins to an illegal net-contract, under which Mrs. J would receive a paltry $100,000, with the rest of the profit from the sale going to Brenda. Who then listed the property for sale for three or four times what Mrs. Jenkins was due. Walker was aware of it, but it wasn't until Rafe showed up and started asking questions, that Walker decided that Brenda had been a liability long enough. After the murders and Walker's arrest, and with Steven Puckett's help, it had been a fairly easy task to have the property returned to Mrs. Jenkins. Rafe had moved her

out of the nursing home where Brenda had stuck her, and had hired a full-time nurse for her. This was the person who answered the door when I knocked, with a glare and an unfriendly greeting.

"What *you* want?"

Marquita and I had met before. We had gone to high school together, for one thing, although we hadn't had any contact that I could remember. But she had been hanging around Rafe ever since he came back to Middle Tennessee, so I'd encountered her on a few occasions lately. She was a black woman a year or two older than me, with breasts the size of watermelons and a derriere that strained the fabric of the hot pink nurse's scrubs she had on. She was fiercely possessive of Rafe, whom she had known (and wanted) since they were both teenagers, and she didn't like me because she thought he was paying me too much attention. It didn't seem to have crossed her mind that I would never, ever view him in the light of a potential boyfriend and thus wasn't a threat to her plans of snagging him for herself. (Although I have to admit I haven't always been above yanking her chain.) I wasn't surprised at her tone of voice, or her aggressive stance, with hands on her hips and her chins jutting out.

I smiled sweetly. "Hello, Marquita. So nice to see you. You look lovely today. That bright pink is a good color for you."

She folded her massive arms across her super-sized chest and scowled. "What you doing here?"

So much for softening her up. "I'm looking for your employer." I glanced past her ample shoulder into the dusky interior of the hallway. She moved to block my gaze.

"He ain't here."

"And you wouldn't tell me if he was. When do you expect him back?"

Her shrug was eloquent.

"Well, when was the last time you saw him?"

"He ain't been here much lately," Marquita said grudgingly.

"Surely he comes home to see his grandmother?"

Marquita shrugged again.

"It's important that I talk to him," I said. "When you see him, would you tell him I'm looking for him? Someone's dead, and the police are going to want to talk to him. Believe me, you don't want him to get arrested so he can't pay your salary. I know you don't like me, but really, it would be best to tell him that I was here and what I said."

Marquita didn't answer, just took a step back and slammed the heavy oak door in my face. I thought she'd taken my point, however. Especially the one about her salary. I felt reasonably confident that I'd hear from Rafe at some point during the evening.

In all the hoopla, I'd forgotten that tonight was Saturday night and that I had a date with Todd. By the time I remembered, it was too late to head him off. I didn't feel much like going, but he had reserved a table for dinner, and bought tickets to the theatre, and was probably already on his way up from Sweetwater, so I didn't have much choice. Mother would never let me hear the end of it if I stood him up. And it might just help to take my mind off things. I rushed home and got ready in record time. In black, as a tribute to Lila. (And also because black is quite slimming and goes well with my blonde hair and pale skin. Not to mention how easy it is to accessorize.) I pulled my favorite little black dress over my head, threw on a pearl necklace and some matching earrings, pulled my hair back in a sleek (and easy) chignon, and stepped into strappy sandals. When Todd knocked on the door at 5 o'clock sharp, I was touching up my lipstick in front of the hall mirror.

We ended up at Fidelio's again, of course. I don't know why Todd kept insisting on bringing me there, but I've been too well brought up to inform a gentleman that I don't like his choice of restaurant. I went along without demur. If nothing else, I could always count on the cuisine to be first-rate. No telephone calls interrupted the peace of our meal this time, and Todd was suitably sympathetic about Lila's death and my interrogation by the big, bad detective.

"And they think her ill-advised remark last Sunday is to blame?"

"They think there's a connection between the robbery and the murder, yes. That the murderer was one of the robbers, or maybe someone she told about the remark she made."

"Or someone they told," Todd suggested.

I nodded, even as the chicken piccata turned to sawdust in my mouth. "I've certainly told enough people, and there's no telling whom they told. Gosh, I hope I didn't inadvertently give someone the idea to kill her...!"

"Who did you tell?" Todd wanted to know.

I answered without thinking. "First there was you, of course, and Detective Grimaldi, and Rafe Collier, and Kieran Greene..."

Todd fixed on the only name in the litany that interested him. "When did you see Collier?"

I could have kicked myself, but I did my best to make my own voice sound calm and even. "The same night I spoke with you."

Todd's eyes narrowed. "I brought you home at ten o'clock!"

"I know you did," I said.

Todd's eyes narrowed further, and he started breathing through his nose. "Did he spend the night?"

"No, of course not." I sighed exasperatedly. "My goodness, how stupid do you think I am? And how many times do I have to say it? There's nothing going on with Rafe and me. We just talk once in a while, that's all."

"About what?"

I put my fork down. The conversation had made me lose what little appetite I had started with. "This and that. Life. Small-talk. Nothing in particular, mostly. This time I told him about my conversation with Lila, because it was on my mind."

"And what did he say?"

I rolled my eyes. "That I shouldn't make the same suggestion Lila did if the open house robbers stop by during my open house tomorrow."

"Hmph!" Todd said. I shrugged. "You don't suppose he might have had a hand in either the robbery or your friend's death, do you?"

"No," I said firmly, "I don't." And I was only answering the second part of the question, not the first; although of course Todd didn't know that. "I refuse to believe that someone I know is capable of strangling an innocent woman."

"There's not much I'd put past Rafael Collier," Todd said darkly.

"I'm sorry to hear that," I answered, in much the same tone, "but he's never laid a finger on me, and I've never heard of him forcing himself on another woman, either. Frankly, I don't think he has to. I've seen the way women react to him."

I stopped, wondering what the hell had compelled me to add that last sentence, and to Todd, of all people, who couldn't be trusted to know a bit of lighthearted humor if it jumped up and bit him in the nose. He flushed to the roots of his sandy hair. "When have you had occasion to see how women react to him? I didn't think you spent all that much time together."

"We don't. But I saw the women at Brenda's funeral, and the staff at Mrs. Jenkins's nursing home, and Marquita Johnson, and Detective Grimaldi, and Tim..."

"Tim?"

"Timothy Briggs. He's gay. Look, I'm sorry I mentioned it. I just don't like the idea that someone I know is capable of something like this. Until I have definite proof to the contrary, I'd prefer to believe that Rafe is innocent of anything worse than misrepresenting his income for tax-purposes. OK? I see him occasionally, and it would make me feel better to believe that he's harmless."

"All right," Todd said. But he didn't sound like it was. It wasn't long after that he asked me if I was ready to leave, and we headed for downtown and the performing arts center.

I wish I could say that I enjoyed the show, but honestly, I was too busy running things over in my head to hear the music at all. I watched the Phantom's preoccupation with Christine and wondered if perhaps someone had had a similar obsession with Lila. A friend or boyfriend, or coworker or neighbor, who had heard about her remark to the robber last week, and who had decided to take advantage of it. The death might not even have been premeditated; the sex could have become rougher than Lila wanted, and she might have objected, and the murderer was trying to keep her quiet and went too far.

I was quiet myself on the way home, pleading over-stimulation after the spectacle we'd just seen. Todd was remarkably understanding; in fact, he was pretty quiet himself. Maybe the music and colors had affected him, too. As soon as we turned onto Main Street, I started looking around for Rafe's motorcycle. He hadn't called—and this time I'd wanted him to!—so I figured he'd turn up in person sooner or later, like he was wont to do. I didn't see him outside the building, but I kept an eye out as we walked upstairs. Todd looked around, too, warily. And when he kissed me goodnight outside the door, I had to consciously tell myself to close my eyes instead of trying to peer past his ears into the shadows further down the hallway.

Todd left, frowning slightly, and I went into the apartment. I stopped just inside the door, without turning on the light, and waited. But there was no sign of life; no breathing, no foreign smells, no electricity in the air from another human body. Nevertheless, I turned on every light in the apartment and went through it, room by room. It was empty.

I fully expected to hear a knock on the door as soon as Todd had pulled away from the curb, but none came. After a suitable interval of waiting, I decided I might as well sit down. I couldn't take my dress off, of course—the idea of receiving a strange man, especially Rafe Collier, in my nightgown was unthinkable—but I removed my contacts and kicked my heels off and curled up on the sofa. And there I stayed, watching late-night reruns of 'The Cosby Show'—'CSI' cut too close to the bone—until I fell asleep.

When I woke up it was morning, and the sun was shining through the balcony doors. I was still alone, not that I'd expected otherwise. I was finally able to get out of the cocktail dress, which would be going straight to the cleaners to have the wrinkles removed, and then I spent the morning at home, just so Rafe could find me if he wanted to. But either he didn't want to, or he couldn't, because he didn't show up. At a few minutes before noon, the phone rang, and I flung myself across the coffee table to snatch it up.

"It's about time you called!"

"Gee," a male voice said, "I didn't know you were waiting."

I blushed. Oops. "Sorry. I thought you were someone else."

My brother's voice was dry. "You don't say? Would you like me to guess, or do you want to tell me?"

My brother Dixon is two years older than me, and a typical big brother. He worries about the men in my life and enjoys picking on me. He is not, however, in the habit of calling for no reason. We're not that close. Or rather, we're just as close as most brothers and sisters, but we don't live in each other's pockets. We see each other every few weeks, when I drive down to Sweetwater for a visit or—more rarely—when Dix has business in Nashville, and we talk when there's something on either of our mind's, but not usually otherwise.

"Neither," I said firmly. "What's wrong?"

"Nothing. If by wrong you mean illness or accident befalling one of our family members. Sheila is fine, and so are the girls. Catherine and her brood seem OK, and mom's... well, mom."

"So what is it?"

"Can't you guess? I saw Todd at church this morning, and he told me that you're still seeing Collier."

I rolled my eyes. "I'm not *seeing* Rafe. I just see him once in a while. Haven't we already been over this?"

Dix said we had. "And I thought we settled it then. Until Todd told me you had a date with him at ten o'clock one night this week."

"First off," I said, flushing irritably, "it was not a date. I needed to talk to him about something, so I left him a message, and instead of calling back, he showed up on my doorstep. I was the one who had asked to talk to him, so I couldn't very well turn him away. He only stayed for about fifteen minutes, just long enough to drink a glass of iced tea, and then he left again. And secondly, where does Todd get off spreading my personal business around to everyone he knows?"

"I'm hardly everyone," Dix said reasonably. "I'm your brother, and his best friend; it's only natural that he would confide in me."

I had to concede his point. Not because I wanted to. "Maybe so. What's not natural, however, is that none of you believe me when I say I'm not seeing Rafe. I don't understand why everyone believes Todd, but you won't believe me."

"We know you," Dix said. I resisted the temptation to stick my tongue out at the phone and then decided that since he couldn't see me anyway, I might as well.

"What do you mean?" I said self-righteously when my tongue was back inside my mouth. "I don't usually lie; everyone knows that."

"Only because you're the worst liar in the world," Dix retorted. "You blush, you fidget, you play with your hair... Everyone can see right through you, and you know it, so you don't even bother to try anymore."

"But you figure that since you can't see me now, I'm lying to you? Todd could see me when he asked. Why doesn't he believe me?"

"He's jealous," Dix said. "He was in love with you in high school, but then you married that jerk Ferguson in college, and Todd married Jolynn because she reminded him of you. Then Ferguson divorced you, and Todd divorced Jolynn, and now he wants to be with you again. But he's afraid that after what happened with Ferguson, you're feeling so undesirable and unwanted that you'll let yourself be swept off your feet by some slick operator like Rafael Collier, who's only after one thing."

I wasn't sure whether to laugh or swear. "Todd actually said that?"

"I read between the lines," Dix answered. "We're guys, sis. We don't talk like that."

"Right. For the record, I was the one who divorced Bradley, not vice versa. You know that. I'm sure he would have gotten around to it eventually, considering how quickly he tied the knot with Shelby after our divorce was final, but at the time, he seemed perfectly content to be married and sleeping around on me. You may want to reacquaint Todd with that fact. And I don't actually feel that undesirable. Between Todd gearing up to propose and Rafe doing his best to talk me into bed, I'm feeling wanted all over the place."

"He's doing what?" Dix said.

"Todd is thinking about proposing and Rafe is trying to talk me into bed."

"The bastard!"

I hid a smile. "Bob and Pauline Satterfield were legally married when Todd was born."

"Funny," Dix grumbled. "I'm not talking about Todd, as you very well know. And you can't say the same thing for your other boyfriend, can you?"

"He's not my boyfriend. Neither of them is. But no, I can't."

Like every other girl in Sweetwater, I had grown up hearing the story of LaDonna Collier. My mother, a delicate Southern beauty who could trace her antecedents back to the War Between the States and beyond—that's the Civil War to those of you born north of the Mason-Dixon Line—had lowered her voice when she spoke of it. "That poor girl. Just fourteen when it happened."

"When what happened?"

Mother leaned closer to me. "She got herself in the family way. By a *colored* boy."

"Oh," I'd said, disappointed. I had envisioned something more titillating than a mere pregnancy.

Mother had nodded, and added pensively, "I knew LaDonna slightly. She was a few years younger than me, of course, and common as dirt, so we didn't associate." She'd smoothed a manicured hand over her impeccably styled, blonde hair.

"Of course not," I'd agreed. In the throes of that romantic stage every girl goes through in her teens, I must admit I had harbored sneaking sympathy for LaDonna Collier. In my juvenile mind, the story had a hint of Romeo and Juliet about it, and although I'm sure it hadn't been romantic for LaDonna, pregnant at fourteen with a baby whose father was nowhere to be found, I hadn't known any better.

"It wasn't Tyrell Jenkins's fault that he was shot before he could get around to marrying LaDonna," I said now. "And Rafe can't help who his parents were any more than you or I or Todd can."

"He can help that he's thinking of nailing my sister!" Dix said in a muted roar. I suppressed a giggle. My brother is always so perfectly proper—a true Southern gentleman, as mother would say—that it was fun to listen to him lose his cool. Nevertheless, I felt I had to set him straight.

"He's a man, Dix. Of course he's thinking of—as you so elegantly put it—nailing your sister. It's what men do. Todd's probably thinking about it, too; he's just not ill-bred enough to come right out and say so."

"So you agree that he's ill-bred?"

"Of course he's ill-bred," I said. "He grew up in the Bog, for God's sake. How could he not be? And it's not like I'm thinking of agreeing to it, you know."

"So you're not involved with him? Not even a little?"

"No, of course not. I'm not in love with him. I'm not sleeping with him. And I've only kissed him once, and don't want to do it again."

"That's good," Dix said, in a strangled voice. I hid another grin. "But it was him you were waiting for to call, wasn't it?"

Busted. "Yes, it was."

"Why?"

I took a steadying breath. "A friend of mine died yesterday. Lila Vaughn; the girl who was on the news last week, after that second open house robbery."

"Todd told me," Dix said. "What's her connection with Collier?"

I took another breath. Dix is absolutely correct regarding my talent for prevarication. Or my lack thereof. I'm a bad liar, and this was coming too close to lying for comfort. "I believe they... um... met once, and I wanted to tell him about it before he read it in the paper. I left a message for him yesterday afternoon, but he hasn't gotten in touch yet. When the phone rang, I assumed it was him."

"Sorry," Dix said, not too sincerely. I gathered he didn't think Rafe's feelings were worth sparing.

"No problem. I'm always happy to hear from my favorite brother."

"I'm your only brother."

"That's probably why you're my favorite. Incidentally, did mom hear what Todd told you? Or did he have enough sense to tell you in private, so she wouldn't have a heart attack?"

"You're off the hook," Dix said, and added ominously, "for now. It was just him and me when he blurted it out. Although I wouldn't count on that lasting. If Todd thinks that telling mom will make her lean on you, he's not above using her. He knows we all rush to obey when mom speaks."

"I would have thought, in your boys-together sort of way, you'd stick up for Todd and chew me out."

"It doesn't sound like you've done anything I can chew you out for," Dix said, a little grudgingly. "I'd prefer that you had no association with Collier whatsoever, but if you're not sleeping with him, or in love with him, there's not much I can do. I'm not your keeper. I can't lock you in your room and refuse to let you out until you agree to marry the suitor I choose. Believe it or not, sis, all I want—all we all want—is for you to be safe and happy."

"Thanks, Dix," I said, touched, "that's so sweet."

"Of course, I think you'd have a much better chance of both happiness and safety if you chose someone like Todd, who wouldn't lie and cheat and break your heart, but that's up to you."

"Don't worry," I said, "after Bradley, the last thing I want is another liar and cheat. Next time I pick a boyfriend, if there is a next time, I'll make sure that he's the faithful sort, at least."

"That's good to know," Dix said. "I guess I should go."

"That might not be a bad idea. I'm hosting an open house at 2 o'clock, and I have to get ready."

"You'll be careful, won't you?"

"Of course I will," I said. "I'm sure the open house robbers have more important things on their minds today than robbing another house, but even if they do show up, I'm pretty sure I don't have anything to fear from them."

"They killed your friend Lila," Dix said.

"No, they didn't."

"I read the paper. The police are clear about the connection."

"Nevertheless, I don't believe they did. I just... don't."

Dix's voice radiated disbelief. "Well, be careful anyway, sis. OK?"

I promised I would, and we hung up.

Seven

W hen I left my apartment an hour later, I was dressed, made up, and blow-dried to the max, presenting to the world the very image of the polished, professional Realtor. I fully expected to find Rafe lounging against my front fender when I got down to the parking lot, but I was wrong. He also wasn't inside the car, nor anywhere on the street. I inserted myself into the Volvo and pulled out of the lot lamenting my bad luck or more accurately, bad judgment. Obviously I had overestimated the impact my threats had had on Marquita. She couldn't be trusted to pass my message on to Rafe after all.

You may wonder why I didn't just call and leave another message with Wendell. It had worked last time, after all. Well, the reason is really very simple. If Rafe was involved in the robberies—or the murder, although I didn't really believe that—then chances were that Wendell was involved as well. That would explain the changing identities of the businesses he ran, from car lot to pawn shop to storage place. I'd only met him once, and he'd seemed to be practically personality-less, but I hadn't been too chatty that evening myself. Rafe had sent him to pick me up for that date-that-wasn't-a-date last week, instead of coming to get me on his Harley-Davidson, and I'd been nervous about having dinner with Rafe and nervous about going anywhere with Wendell and just plain nervous in general because two of my coworkers had been murdered in the span of a week... and to make a long story short, I hadn't taken the opportunity to get to know Wendell. Now I wished I had. But anyway, under the circumstances I thought it was better not to call his number looking for Rafe. By now Rafe had probably heard the news about Lila on his own, at any rate.

The house that Tim had assigned to me was located a whole quarter mile from the house where Lila had been robbed—in the same subdivision, no less—and no more than a half mile from Kieran's listing, in a development just up the road. I was so close to both that I had to resist the temptation to stop in and have a look around. But I didn't really have the time, and both were occupied, anyway, so if I wanted to go inside, I'd have to schedule appointments first, to give the owners time to clear out. I made a mental note to do so tomorrow, since I didn't have anything else to do until I met Charlene and Gary Lee at 3:30.

Who knew, maybe I'd pick up on some connection the police had missed.

Like both the other two, my open house was a typical McMansion, built sometime within the past five years by someone with delusions of grandeur and the money to indulge their whims. It was a pseudo-French Chateau in honey-colored stucco, on a postage-stamp sized lot in the middle of an upscale development of similar houses. A black Mercedes SUV was idling in the circular drive, and just as I pulled in behind it, a woman came out of the house and down the stairs. When she saw me, she slowed. "Can I help you?"

"I'm Savannah Martin," I explained, extending a hand. "I work with Tim Briggs. He asked me to host the open house this afternoon."

"I see." She looked me over from head to toe and back. I waited. My mother dresses with the best of them, and Bradley had expected me to keep up appearances as well, so I wasn't worried. I may not be able to afford the cream of the runway on the salary I make these days, but I can still dig enough designer duds out of the closet to impress the pickiest of Brentwood matriarchs. Which this woman wasn't. She couldn't have been much older than me—either that, or she employed the best plastic surgeon in the country—and she was flashily dressed in purple suede pants and a striped shirt, with Manolo Blahniks on her feet.

I must have passed muster, for after a thorough look, she took my hand. "I'm Connie Fortunato, and this is my husband Perry." She indicated the car. I ducked my head to smile at Perry, who was middle aged and non-descript, with curly hair just starting to go thin on top. He didn't seem to find any fault with my appearance, either; especially the way my blouse gaped open when I bent over to greet him.

"Nice to meet you both," I said politely, straightening up. Connie sent a frowning glance at her husband, who immediately looked away and put the car in gear. She slid into the passenger seat. "We're off to the races. Have fun, Savannah." She waved a languid hand with purple talons. For just a moment I was reminded of Lila's long nails with flowers and tiny chips of gemstone, and then it was gone.

"No doubt," I said to the tailpipe of the Mercedes. And just for the record, I didn't envy the Fortunatos their 4,000 square foot McMansion or their Mercedes or their afternoon of leisure. The only thing I envied them was their bank account, but only because my own bottom line was so depressing that if I didn't sell a house soon, I'd be defaulting not only on the payments on the Volvo, but on my rent, my utility bills, and my Saltines and ketchup. Money can't buy happiness, something my short marriage to Bradley had brought home with a vengeance, but it can buy a whole lot of other things. Like food on the table and a roof over one's head.

But I digress. I waited for the Mercedes to leave the driveway, and then I headed up the wide front stairs and let myself in through the fifteen-foot high doors into a formal foyer with a chandelier that must have cost as much as my car. Off to either side were formal sitting rooms, one with a black lacquered baby grand piano and the other with something I could have sworn was a genuine Georgia O'Keeffe in a frame on the wall. Beyond the entry was a hallway, which culminated in a grandiose family room with a massive stone fireplace that took up one entire 15x15 wall. There were genuine Kashmiri rugs on the floors, genuine art on the walls, and genuine antiques everywhere. If the open house robbers came here, they'd throw their backs out hauling valuables to the truck.

In both Lila's and Kieran's cases, the robbers had waited until the open house was almost over before they appeared. Surely the time when I needed to start worrying, would be around 3:30 or so; not before. Not now. And if there were people here, browsing, when 3:30 rolled around, any hypothetical robbers probably wouldn't bother coming in at all. They couldn't tie us all up, after all. And they were probably busy trying to deal with the fallout from Lila's murder, anyway, whether they'd had anything to do with it or not. For the next hour and a half at least, I ought to be able to relax and do my job without worrying about being tied up and subjected to sweet nothings by a man with a sexy drawl and hot, dark eyes.

I spent the final five minutes familiarizing myself with the house, just so I'd know what I was talking about when I gave people directions to the master bedroom, game room, or music room, and then I stationed myself at the front door, with an uninterrupted view of the circular drive, and got ready to greet all comers. "Good afternoon. My name is Savannah Martin. Welcome to our open house. There are refreshments in the kitchen, as well as some fliers with information about the house. If you have any questions, please don't hesitate to ask; it's what I'm here for. And before you leave, if you wouldn't mind signing the guest register so I can keep track of how many visitors I have...?"

For the first hour, hour and a half, traffic was slow but steady, with no less than three people in the house at any time. At around

3:30 it started slowing down, and I was just beginning to think about worrying when a small, dark blue Honda turned into the driveway. I arched my brows.

A minute later the Honda's doors opened, and Gary Lee and Charlene Hodges came up the stairs, clinging to each other and giggling. "Hi," I said brightly. "Welcome to our open house. How are you?"

Gary Lee allowed as how they were fine. "Since we couldn't go look at that house we wanted to see today, we figured we'd just come see this one instead."

I nodded. "No reason why not; that's what an open house is for." I used to go to them all the time before I got my real estate license, just to see what they were like. It's fun, pretending to be living in someone else's house. Especially when one's own house, and one's own life, isn't so great.

Charlene giggled. "So where's everything at, Savannah? You know, bedrooms, bathrooms, kitchen... master suite?"

I pointed out the locations of the various highlights, and watched the two of them walk down the hall as closely entwined as Siamese twins.

Another five or ten minutes went by, as I wandered into the kitchen to count entries on the log to see how many visitors I'd had so far. With Gary Lee and Charlene there were seventeen; Tim ought to be pleased with the turnout. Idly, I wondered if Lila and Kieran had kept track of the people who had visited their open houses, and if so, if the police had taken charge of the lists, just in case someone had noticed anyone hanging around outside, waiting for everyone else to leave, or perhaps if even one of the robbers had stopped by earlier to case the place.

I was still in the kitchen, looking at my list of names, when I heard the sound of an engine pulling up outside. The oven clock said 3:50 right on the dot, and my heart started beating faster. The rumbling was replaced by silence, and then I heard the sound of heavy boots on the flagstone steps. The door knob turned just as I hurried into the front foyer. The door opened and a man came in. He was tall and dark, with broad shoulders under a black leather jacket, and long legs encased in faded denim. His skin was the color of coffee with plenty of milk, a warm golden tan, and the eyes that scanned the room before landing on me, were as dark and melting as those on a Cocker Spaniel, and surrounded by a thick fringe of long, sooty lashes. They were also rimmed by a smudgy bruise of fatigue, a mute testament to a long and mostly sleepless night. When I didn't say anything for a second, just stared at him, he flashed a grin. "Cat got your tongue, darlin'?"

My vocal chords were galvanized into cooperating as my cheeks turned pink. "You took your time getting back to me."

He quirked a brow. "I didn't know you'd called."

"I didn't call," I said. "I left word with Marquita."

"I ain't been over there for a while." He wandered closer to me, assessing the O'Keeffe, the baby grand, and the antiques along the way. "Your kind of place, ain't it? All this old stuff."

I shook my head. "The house is too modern. When you grow up in an 1839 mansion on the Antebellum Trail, a brand new house, no matter how ostentatious, just doesn't cut it."

Rafe didn't answer, but he smiled. I flushed, feeling stupid. He had spent his childhood in a trailer in the Bog, surrounded by leaning walls and a leaking roof, so this place probably looked like a palace.

Then again, Mrs. Jenkins's house on Potsdam Street, where he lived now—at least from time to time—wasn't anything to sneeze at, either. Circa 1889, it was a three-story Victorian with a ballroom on the third floor and a circular tower on the southeast corner. It needed a ton of work, some of which he had done, some which he hadn't gotten around to yet, but it had all the personality this cookie-cutter McMansion lacked.

"So what's been going on," I asked, "that you haven't been over to see your grandmother lately?"

"I spent the night with Tammy Grimaldi." His voice was so even that it took a moment for the words to sink in. Just as the realization of what he'd said sucker-punched me in the stomach, he added, "So what is it you want, darlin'?"

"Want?" I repeated blankly.

"If you went toe to toe with Marquita, you gotta want something. What is it?"

"Oh. Right. Sorry." I grimaced. "I wanted to tell you that Lila Vaughn was dead. But if you spent the night with Tamara Grimaldi, I guess you already know that."

His eyes were opaque. "The subject came up, yeah."

"Pillow talk?"

Try as I might—and I wasn't trying that hard—my voice came out sounding snippier than I wanted it to. His lips curved.

"Never mind," I added, with what little dignity I could muster. Goodness, how humiliating! I wouldn't blame him for thinking I was jealous.

His voice was easy. "You're giving me too much credit, darlin'. Women like Tammy Grimaldi don't look twice at somebody like me."

"You haven't heard the way she asks questions about you," I answered.

He laughed. "That ain't cause she likes me, darlin'. She probably thinks I'm doing something I shouldn't be."

"And are you?" The words just fell out of my mouth without conscious thought, and Rafe chuckled.

"I'm sure I'm doing plenty of stuff I shouldn't be."

"Like what?"

"You sure you wanna know, darlin'?"

I hesitated. For just long enough to make it difficult to say yes. "You said you had things to do this afternoon," I said instead. "What happened?"

He shrugged. "Change of plans."

"Well, if you didn't speak to Marquita and get my message, how did you know I wanted to talk to you?"

That was easy, he didn't.

"So what are you doing here?" I asked.

"Maybe I just came by to pick up where we left off last week." He grinned, and I took an immediate step back, fetching up against the nearest piece of antique furniture with a bump that sent the elegant console-table knocking against the wall. He laughed. "Relax, darlin'. After Tammy told me what'd happened to Lila, I wanted to make sure you were all right."

"I see," I said. "That's really quite nice of you, to take time out to check on me. Do you want to go back to her, now that you've seen that I'm all right?"

He laughed. "What exactly d'you think we were doing, darlin'? I spent the night in jail. She hauled me in for questioning around 8 o'clock yesterday, kept at me till one in the morning, let me sleep for five hours, and came back to work at seven. Then we kept going in circles till one, when she finally let me leave. I had to tell her you were waiting for me before she'd let me out of her sight. She's probably outside right now, making sure I'm doing what I said I was gonna do."

"So you're only here because you told her you would be?"

He shrugged, looking around. "You alone?"

"No, actually. There's a young couple around somewhere. They went back that way, to look at the master suite..." I pointed, "it must be ten minutes ago now."

And they hadn't come back yet.

Maybe Gary Lee and Charlene had overheard our conversation and decided to make themselves scarce until we had finished. Or maybe they'd exited from the master suite out onto the deck, and had gone around the house to their car that way. Maybe I really *was* alone. Except for Rafe, who was making me feel just a touch apprehensive. "Why do you ask?"

"Just wondering. Busy day?"

"Not too bad. Seventeen visitors, eighteen with you. I've seen worse."

"You sure you shouldn't check up on your couple? If you ain't heard a noise for ten minutes, they could be up to all sorts of trouble. Going through the medicine cabinets, pocketing the silverware, strangling one another..."

I shook my head. "They're nice kids. Newlyweds looking for their first house. I met them two weeks ago at your grandmother's open house, and I've shown them a couple of homes since then. They have another they want to see tomorrow. They're not doing anything wrong."

"It's almost time to close up, though. You don't wanna leave nobody behind."

I glanced at my watch. "If they're not out here in two minutes, I'll go look for them. Just out of curiosity, why are you being so helpful? You don't have a moving truck on standby outside, do you?"

"After what happened to Lila? No, darlin'. I ain't that stupid."

"Good to know," I said, wondering whether he really had just admitted that he'd been involved in the open house robberies or if my imagination was running away with me.

"Course, if you've got a hankering for being tied up, I could oblige just to make you happy."

"After what happened to Lila?" I said. "No, thanks. I'm not that stupid."

"Good to know," Rafe said with a grin, which faded when he added, "I'm sorry about your friend. You all right?" His dark eyes were probing.

I could feel tears prickling at the back of my own eyes, and deliberately made my voice crisp to keep them at bay. "As well as I can expect to be. We hadn't known each other long, but I liked her a lot. I hope they catch whoever did it."

Rafe opened his mouth to speak, but just then Gary Lee and Charlene appeared, hand in hand and giggling, and he closed it again. "Sorry, Savannah," Gary Lee said. "We got... um... tied up."

I grimaced. Bad choice of words under the circumstances, but of course they didn't know that. "No problem. If it was just us, I'd let you stay as long as you wanted, but the owners will be back soon, and we should be gone by then."

"Sure." They nodded, glancing curiously from Rafe, standing in front of the O'Keeffe, hands in his pockets and face inscrutable, to me. Charlene contemplated him with her head tilted, much the same way he contemplated the O'Keeffe; like a connoisseur assessing a work of art. Gary Lee was watching me. "Um... Savannah?"

I nodded.

"You OK?"

"Fine," I said. "Why...?"

He glanced over at Rafe.

"Oh," I added, as I realized that he was worried about me. "This is Rafael Collier. He's an... um... old friend."

Rafe's lips curved. Charlene giggled.

"Right," Gary Lee said. "None of my business. C'mon, babe." He steered Charlene toward the door, telling me over his shoulder, "We'll see you tomorrow."

"I'll be there," I promised. "Three-thirty."

"If you can't make it, just call," Charlene said. "If, like, something comes up." She giggled.

I grimaced. Gary Lee looked embarrassed.

"Comes up," Charlene added. "Get it? Comes up!"

I nodded. "I got it. Thanks, Charlene. If I can't make it, I'll definitely call." Although I knew, as she obviously didn't, that the chances of something coming up, in the way she meant, were slim indeed. Or rather, if something did come up, it wouldn't make me late for our appointment. Whatever came up would come down on its own, with no help from me, and that was all there was to it.

Eight

"So," Rafe said when they'd left, "that's the happy couple."

I nodded. "Aren't they cute? I remember being that young and happy once. Then I married Bradley."

"I didn't peg you for a cynic." He started wandering again, looking around.

"Who, me?" I followed, wondering where he was headed. "Only when it comes to marriage. Or remarriage. Todd was telling me the other night that I need a husband, and I felt like he had punched me in the stomach."

"Depends on the husband, don't it?" He peered into the dining room, with its custom-made chandelier and glass topped table.

"I imagine it might," I admitted. "In this case, I think Todd was thinking of himself."

Rafe took time away from his inspection of a Japanese vase to glance at me. "Proposed, did he?"

I shook my head. "Not exactly. He just hinted. Although I suppose he might have come out and said something specific if I'd given him some encouragement."

"Something to remember for next time."

Rafe moved on, in the direction of the kitchen. My heart started beating faster as he slipped through the door. This could be it. I could be on my way to being tied to one of the chairs, like Kieran and Lila.

"You know," I said, lingering in the doorway, "Todd's still going on about how dangerous you are, and how I need to stay away from you. I keep asking him what you've done that's so bad, but he just makes ominous noises and says there are things about you I don't know."

"No kidding?" He zeroed in on the breakfast bar with its four leather-topped bar stools. I kept an eye on his hands, just in case he planned to pull a coil of rope out from under his jacket and lasso me.

"No. So what is it about you I don't know?"

"Most everything, I'd say." He stopped behind the bar, where I'd placed the informative brochures and a guest register. I wondered if he was waiting for me to sit down across from him, and that's when he'd be whipping out the rope.

"Why don't you tell me something, then." I stayed right where I was, at a safe distance both from him and the chairs. Connie and Perry wouldn't find *me* trussed like a turkey when they came home.

He squinted at me, twirling the pen between his fingers. "Something...?"

"Something about you. Like, you secretly read poetry. Or you're a Cordon Bleu cook. Or you make your living as a motorcycle mechanic. Or you've got an ex-wife and four kids somewhere."

He stared at me in silence for a second, pen forgotten between his fingers. "I don't read much of anything. Don't like sitting still. I don't cook. I don't have a wife, current or ex, and if I've got kids, nobody's bothered to tell me. I've tried to make sure I don't, seeing as how I know what it's like to grow up without a daddy."

I nodded. Tyrell Jenkins had been shot dead before Rafe was born, and the closest thing to a father he'd had growing up, was his grandfather Jim, who was the person who had shot Tyrell. Not exactly the best situation to grow up in. I didn't blame him at all for not wanting to inflict that same fate on another innocent. Of course, he could have avoided the problem by settling down with someone and raising whatever kids he sired with her, but he obviously didn't consider himself the settling-down kind, either.

He continued blandly, "As for the mechanic thing, it ain't how I make my living, though I've been known to get my hands dirty on occasion."

"Somehow I'm not surprised to hear that."

He grinned and lowered his eyes to the counter. As I watched, he scribbled his name on the bottom of the guest register and put the pen down on top. I forgot myself and wandered into the kitchen. "What are you doing?"

"Ain't that what I'm supposed to do? Sign this paper?"

"If you're a visitor, sure. But..."

"I'm here, ain't I? You want I should have a look around while you pack up your stuff? Just to make sure nobody's hanging around?"

I squinted at him, suspiciously. "You won't open up a window or door so someone can come in later and rob the place, will you?"

"Would I do that to you?"

"I don't know," I said. "Would you?"

"You're just gonna have to trust me, darlin'." He headed for the door, and I jumped out of his path. He arched a brow, but didn't comment, just continued on past me. I watched him walk away, to make sure he was really leaving the room and wouldn't suddenly turn around and hog-tie me like a recalcitrant calf if I let my guard down.

By the time he came back, I had gathered my guest list and all my paraphernalia – pens, paper, silver-plated cookie tray, scented candles, and fancy napkins – and put it all together in a bag, which I was dragging toward the front door. Rafe grabbed it out of my hand and lifted it easily. "I got it."

"Thank you. Why are you being so nice to me today?"

"I'm always nice to you," Rafe said, holding the front door open. I rolled my eyes and stepped through, only to come face to face with Connie Fortunato, who had just ascended the steps.

She looked rather the worse for wear, her eyes puffy and her make-up smeared, and she was brought up short when she saw us. For a second, it seemed as if she might turn and run. However, she made an effort to pull herself together and do the proper thing.

"Oh, Savannah. I didn't realize you'd still be here."

"I'm sorry," I apologized, with a discreet glance at my wrist. "We had some late visitors, and then it took time to pack up and make sure all the doors and windows were secured."

She nodded, but distractedly, like my words hadn't really registered on a conscious level. "And who is this?" Even under the circumstances, with her mind clearly on something else, she couldn't help but respond to Rafe's rock'em, sock'em sex-appeal by lowering her eyelashes and looking at him from below.

"Hired muscle," I said.

Rafe grinned. "I'm her bodyguard."

"Lucky girl." Connie glanced over at me and back to him. "Might you be available to guard *my* body sometime?" She managed a passable smile.

"If you two would like to be alone," I said, "I'd be happy to leave now."

Rafe grinned. "She doesn't like to share her toys."

He winked at Connie and put his free arm around my shoulders. I stuck my tongue out at him, and he laughed out loud. Connie looked at me down the length of her sculpted nose. Now that I saw her again, up close, I put her age closer to forty than thirty. Of course, the downward turn of her lips and the tear-tracks on her cheeks didn't help. It's difficult to look one's best after a good cry, or—as in this case—a bad one.

"Are you OK?" I asked, my better self taking over.

"Fine." She pressed her lips together. After a moment she added, reluctantly, "I just received some bad news."

I nodded sympathetically. "I've had some of that lately, too. Is there anything I can do?"

She shook her head. "Nothing, thank you. I've just discovered that a friend of mine has passed away. There's nothing anyone can do."

"I'm sorry to hear that," I said. "A friend of mine passed away recently, too. I know what you're going through."

Connie's pale blue eyes filled up with tears. "Thank you. I'm going to miss her."

I nodded. "I'm going to miss Lila, as well."

"Lila?" Connie repeated. I gave her Lila's full name and saw her eyes light with recognition. It seemed we hadn't both lost friends this week; we'd lost the same friend.

"How did you know Lila?" I asked.

"We did volunteer-work together." Connie dabbed at her own eyes with a tissue.

"She told me she was volunteering somewhere." And how helpful it had been to her career, because it allowed her to meet people. Rich people. People with expensive houses they might want to sell. "I suppose, now that she's gone, you'll be short-handed. I'd be happy to take her place, if you think I would be of help."

Connie sniffed. "We meet on Monday nights at 6:30, in the small drawing room at the Cheekwood Museum and Gardens. If you're not busy tomorrow, I'm sure everyone would love to have you."

"In that case," I said, "I'll be there."

Connie dabbed at her eyes again and excused herself to go inside, with one last look at Rafe. We started down the steps, only to be brought up short by the appearance of Perry, coming toward us from the direction of the garage. He must have gone to stable the car. "Oh, Savannah," he said, with considerably more enthusiasm than Connie, "you're still here."

His voice changed, "And you invited a friend." His tone indicated that I'd overstepped my rights.

Rafe grinned. "Rafael Collier," he said, extending a hand. Perry took it, but with the expression of a man palming a dead fish.

"It was Tim's idea," I explained. "He wanted to ensure that I had somebody with me who'd be able to protect me if something went wrong. Because of the robberies and the murder, you know."

"Very considerate of Tim," Perry said. I nodded. Rafe didn't speak, but the two of them stared at each other like two dogs in an alley. I'd seen Todd do the same thing when confronted with Rafe, so it must be some innate male thing. Alpha-dog staring, or something.

"Well," I said finally, into the awkward silence, "I guess we should get going."

Perry nodded. "Thank you for coming, Savannah. It was a pleasure to meet you." He captured my hand and lifted it to his lips. They were moist and lingered just a fraction of a second too long. Rafe didn't speak, but his eyes narrowed.

"Thank you, Mr. Fortunato," I said politely, retrieving my hand. Before either of them could say anything else, I started down the stairs, leaving Rafe to follow. The door closed with a substantial thump by the time we'd descended a few steps.

"What was that all about?" I asked in a low voice while Rafe deposited the bag he'd been carrying in the trunk of the Volvo. "Did he see the way his wife was looking at you, do you think? Is that why he was squaring off like he wanted to fight with you?"

Rafe shrugged. "Don't know, don't care. Don't like the way he looked at you."

"Funny," I said lightly, "that's exactly what Todd says about you."

He smiled. "Why d'you think I don't like it?" He glanced up at the sun, hanging low over the treetops, and added, "How about some dinner?"

I hesitated, squinting up at him. "Are you asking me out?"

He arched a brow. "You don't want me to ask you out?"

I shook my head. Definitely not.

"In that case I guess I ain't."

"I wouldn't mind having dinner. Just as long as we're not going on a date."

His lips quirked. "I'm sure that makes sense to you."

"Look," I said. "My family will disown me if it gets back to them that I went on a date with you. *Another* date with you. I'm still getting backlash from the first time. But if we're just having dinner together, as business associates or what-not..."

He shrugged. "Whatever works for you. Where do you want to go? Fidelio's again?"

God, no. I shook my head. "Somewhere where no one will know who I am."

Rafe grinned. "I know just the place." He threw a long leg over the seat of the black Harley-Davidson parked behind the Volvo, and revved the engine. I slithered into my car and, when he had pulled around me, followed him down the driveway. As we turned onto the main road, I glanced back at the house and caught sight of someone standing by the window in what I thought must be the music room. But before I'd had a chance to determine whether it was Connie gazing longingly after Rafe, or Perry watching both of us drive away, the person had disappeared from view.

NEAR THE REAL ESTATE OFFICE, there's a neighborhood hangout called the FinBar. It's a young, hip watering hole where young, hip professionals hang out after work and shoot the breeze and watch extreme sports and golf on big-screen TVs. The place Rafe took me also called itself a sports bar, but that was where the resemblance ended. The Shortstop was located off the beaten path, on a back road off Nolensville Pike in South Nashville, and people shot pool there, but not the breeze. From the outside, the small cinderblock building looked like a dive, and the inside was no better. There were TVs, true, but they weren't big-screen and they didn't show golf. There was NASCAR on one and pro wrestling on the other.

The FinBar has mood-lighting and ceiling fans and lots of ferns and polished wood; the Shortstop's mood was considerably darker, with Formica-topped tables and discarded kitchen chairs. I was afraid to lean back for fear of what might adhere to my dress, and when the gum-chewing waitress came to take our order, I had a hard time making out her features in the gloom. "What can I get you folks?" She was addressing both of us, but looking at Rafe. Nothing new there; every woman I'd ever met reacted the same way. Rafe opened his hand in my direction, indicating I should go first.

"I don't suppose you have any Sauvignon Blanc?" I inquired, without much hope.

"Come again?"

"Wine? White, preferably?"

She turned to Rafe. "Where d'you find her, hon? Buckingham Palace?" She guffawed. I rolled my eyes.

"She'll have sweet tea," Rafe said. He was lounging in his chair, long legs stretched out under the table and one arm hooked over the back corner of the chair. "I'll have a beer. Thanks, darlin'."

"Sure thing." The waitress stuck the pencil she'd been holding through her bouffant hairdo and popped a bubblegum bubble before she walked off. I looked around.

"Horrible place."

He shrugged. "You said you wanted someplace where nobody'd recognize you. The food ain't bad."

"I'll take your word for it. Although you told me once that after spending two years in prison, most food tastes good to you."

"Prison'll do that. Among other things."

"I hope Detective Grimaldi fed you this morning. By the way, you never told me what she was questioning you about."

He arched a brow. "Can't you guess? She asked me to provide an alibi for Friday night."

"Friday?" I blinked. I'd assumed she'd been questioning him about the robberies, not the murder. "Surely she doesn't suspect you of killing Lila?"

"Ain't that long ago you suspected me of killing Brenda Puckett," Rafe pointed out.

"You had a good reason for killing Brenda. She had cheated your grandmother out of her house. And I changed my mind about that, anyway. I no longer think you'd kill anyone."

He didn't answer, just quirked a brow. I wasn't quite sure what that signified, but I decided I'd rather not ask. Sometimes, ignorance really is bliss.

I continued, "You had no reason to kill Lila. Unless Detective Grimaldi can prove otherwise, you never even met her."

"She can't."

The waitress arrived with our drinks, and he nodded his thanks. I narrowed my eyes. Not '*I didn't*' but '*she can't*'...?

"You eating?" the waitress said.

Rafe nodded. "I'll have a cheeseburger and fries. Medium-rare." He turned to me. "What about you, darlin'?"

I hesitated. If I asked for something I liked, they probably wouldn't have it. "Why don't you order me something you think I'll enjoy? You seem to know the menu by heart."

Rafe grinned. "She'll have what I'm having."

The waitress nodded and sauntered off. I turned to Rafe, incredulously. "Do you know how many calories are in a cheeseburger and fries?"

His voice was easy. "I ain't worried about gaining weight."

"I know *you're* not," I said, eyeing his flat stomach and hard biceps straining against the sleeves of the white T-shirt, "but I could stand to lose a few pounds." The viper he had tattooed around his left arm was looking at me. I tore my eyes away from it and added, "I've already had my share of red meat and French fries for this week. Couldn't you have ordered me a salad or something?"

"Ain't nothing wrong with the way you look, darlin'." He lifted the beer bottle and toasted me before he drank.

"Easy for you to say," I said. "You haven't seen me without clothes on."

I nearly bit my tongue in half when I realized what I was saying, but it was too late. He smiled. "Not yet."

"Not ever," I corrected firmly.

The smile widened. "You don't mean that."

"Yes, I do."

He shook his head. "No, you don't. You just think you do."

"No, I really..." I realized I sounded like a petulant five-year-old, and stopped. "We were talking about Lila. What makes Detective Grimaldi think you had something to do with her death?"

"I assumed I had you to thank for that."

"And you're still talking to me?" I shook my head and took a sip of tea. It was passable, if a little too sweet. "Sorry. So could you give her an alibi for Friday night?"

Rafe shook his head. "After about ten o'clock or so, ain't nobody who can prove where I was."

"And was Lila killed after ten?"

He shrugged. "Tammy didn't say. But why else would she ask?"

The burgers arrived shortly thereafter, and to my surprise, they really weren't bad. Not quite as good as Rotier's, but better than I'd feared. Not too greasy, and with a bun that didn't disintegrate between my hands. I even ate a few fries, which were salty and just crispy enough. At the same time, Rafe polished off his burger, his fries, and what was left of mine. Plus an order of onion rings he decided he needed. After dinner, he insisted on having apple pie, a thick slab of which he ate with every sign of enjoyment while I watched surreptitiously, nursing my cup of black coffee and feeling as if the lard in the pie crust was applying itself directly to my thighs just from watching.

A hand landed on Rafe's shoulder, and we both looked up. I saw a tall, black man with a shaved head and eyes of a melting brown. The two of them spoke softly, and the noise level was too high for me to hear what they were saying, but they exchanged a complicated handshake, and then the other man indicated the pool tables. Rafe shook his head, saying something, and the man glanced over at me. His eyes may have been pretty, with long lashes and rich color, but the expression in them was too bold for my taste. I looked away and he said something else to Rafe, accompanied by what I interpreted as a congratulatory fist to the shoulder. All in good fun, although it didn't appear that Rafe found the joke quite as humorous as did his friend. His reply was short and succinct, and stopped the conversation dead. A beat followed, until the man lifted his hands and stepped back fractionally. He said something else, and Rafe turned to me and raised his voice. "Excuse me a second, darlin'? Something I gotta do."

"Of course," I said politely, not at all sure I meant it.

"Don't worry. I'll keep an eye on you."

"Thank you," I said, with all sincerity, and was rewarded by one of his rare, genuine smiles.

"No problem. Ain't no hardship looking at you." He winked and got up. I watched him follow the other man across the floor, over to the pool tables, where yet two more men were occupying themselves playing a game. They all exchanged the same complicated handshake, and got into a conversation. From the looks on the men's faces, it concerned something serious. Rafe took part, but as he'd promised, he kept his eyes on me. And not in the protective, brotherly way I had hoped for, either.

A few weeks earlier, during that date-that-wasn't-a-date at Fidelio's, one of Rafe's looks had flustered me to such a degree that I'd had to ask the waiter for ice water to cool down. He had been sitting across the table from me at the time—Rafe, not the waiter—and I had convinced myself that the proximity was part of the reason for my overblown reaction. Now I discovered I'd been wrong. He could still pack a punch from all the way across the room. I squirmed uncomfortably as those dark eyes snagged on my lips, my throat, the top button of my blouse, and then followed my legs from hem to floor and back. Twice.

By the time he returned to the table, I'd had time to pull myself together (with the help of what was left in the iced tea glass), and it was a good thing, because his greeting wasn't designed to help my mental peace. "Nice legs."

"Thanks," I managed. "I hope you weren't planning to ask when they're open."

He laughed, tendons moving smoothly under the golden skin of his throat. "I wouldn't be that crude, darlin'."

The waitress gazed raptly at him, and the three men over at the pool table turned around to stare, as well. The bald one who had come over to the table to fetch Rafe earlier, gave me a leisurely once-over, and I turned away from the boldness of his gaze.

We left shortly thereafter; or I guess maybe I should say that I did, because I think Rafe went back inside after he walked me out to the car.

I unlocked my car door and turned to him. "Thanks for dinner."

He grinned. "My pleasure."

"Did you... um... have a particular reason for asking? We didn't talk about anything in particular." And he hadn't hit on me, either. Much.

"Maybe I just like spending time with you, darlin'."

My wide-eyed expression made him laugh, and he waited a few seconds before he added, "Or maybe it's all part of my master plan to get you in the sack. Maybe if I just keep acting like I'm a nice guy, one of these days you'll relax enough to let me have my way with you."

"Don't hold your breath," I retorted, but I admit that as a brush-off it wasn't very effective, mostly because the idea of Rafe having his way with me made me lose my breath for a moment. In terror. He chuckled softly, and it was the kind of noise that made all the little hairs on my arms stand up at attention.

"All the same it's gonna happen one of these days, darlin', so you may as well prepare yourself."

I found I didn't have anything to say, so I got into the car and, after a few tries, managed to fit the key into the ignition and turn it over. My hands were shaking when I drove out of the graveled lot and into the road, and when I looked in the rearview mirror as I started back toward town, he was still standing there watching me drive away.

Nine

Monday morning found me back in Brentwood, visiting the houses where the two robberies had taken place. Snooping.

The police must have been over the crime scenes after the robberies, gathering fingerprints and DNA and such, but when I'd called to set up the appointments, there hadn't been any problem with going to see the houses, and there was no sign of any cops now. No yellow crime-scene tape across the doors, or anything. Everything was back to normal inside, neat and clean, and both houses were crammed with nice stuff, albeit with obvious holes where the missing objects must have been. What was left behind gave me a good idea of the quality of the things that had been taken. Whoever had planned these robberies, had known what they were doing. They must have had previous knowledge of what was here, in order to be able to pick and choose so accurately.

It begged the question of how they had known. There was a possibility that they simply had a truck on standby, and spent every Sunday afternoon visiting open houses until they came across one they liked. It would be a brilliantly simple way of committing robberies.

Considering the price range of the houses in this area, the chances were better than 90% that each and every one of them had something in it worth taking, and keeping the selection random would ensure that they didn't get caught, because there was no real common denominator, and no trail of clues for anyone to follow.

If the houses weren't chosen at random, that meant that someone had picked them deliberately. (Obvious, I know, but sometimes it helps to state the obvious.) If the same person had picked both houses, that meant that out there somewhere, there was someone with a connection to both.

I ran over likely possibilities in my mind, starting with the truly basic and working my way down from there. The same listing broker—no. Kieran Greene worked for Re/Max, Lila (and her colleague whose listing it was) for Worthington Properties.

A selling broker who had seen both houses, with or without clients in tow? Possible, but the police would be better equipped to check that than me. I would suggest it to Detective Grimaldi the next time I spoke to her. Just to cover all the bases, however, I wrote down the names of all the Realtors who had left their business cards at both houses. There were a few names that appeared twice, but that wasn't really surprising, when both houses were in the same area and the same price range, and a buyer looking in this area and price range would probably want to see both. As for Timothy Briggs, who had left his nicely laminated card in both houses, he had probably just wanted to see how they stacked up to his own listing, the Fortunatos' house. Checking out the competition is common practice, and I would have thought less of Tim if he hadn't.

The police would also have to check all the potential buyers who had come through with agents, and there would probably turn out to be a lot of them, as well. Moving right along, I considered the possibility of a shared home owners insurance agent. An insurance agent would have a detailed list of all the valuables in the house. It could be a case of insurance fraud, maybe, if the owners had decided to burgle their own houses and sell their property on the black market, while at the same time getting their money back from the insurance company. Something else I could suggest to Grimaldi, to take her mind off Rafe. If the houses were insured with different companies, I could point out that the owners wouldn't necessarily even need an insurance agent to be in on the scheme; they could have hatched the plot between them. From family photographs and personal items left in both houses, I gathered that the Worthington property was owned by a family with two children; boy and girl of about 16 and 14, respectively, with a pretty, dark-haired mother and a tall and handsome, balding father. Kieran's listing belonged to a gay couple with a penchant for leopard and zebra prints. Between the two families, they had enough tall males to make up a foursome, and in ski-masks and coveralls, it would be impossible to tell whether the men were young or old, gay or straight. The boy had inherited his mother's dark eyes, and one of the gay men was brown-eyed also, although I personally wouldn't have asked either to tie me to the bed. There's no accounting for taste, however, and Lila had clearly been more impressionable than I.

If the families had friends in common, the scheme could have been orchestrated by someone who knew them both and coveted their possessions, but I couldn't help but think that there had to be a connection to real estate somewhere. If it was just a matter of robbing the houses, a friend wouldn't have waited until the houses were on the market before he/she acted. Much safer and easier to just break in some night when the family was out. It seemed as if the fact that these houses were on the market and open to the public had some significance. Which pointed to either a Realtor or someone else involved in the business; someone who wouldn't have had access to the houses if they hadn't been for sale.

After Brenda's murder and Walker's arrest just a week or two ago, and the new crop of reality TV-programs painting all Realtors as greedy, immoral, unethical sharks, our profession really didn't need any more bad press. There didn't seem to be any way to avoid it, however. I would have to call Detective Grimaldi and tell her my conclusions, and let the pieces fall where they may. If nothing else, at least she'd have to focus on someone other than Rafe as a suspect. And there was always the possibility that the robbers were posing as buyers, checking out the open houses first, and then coming back to do the actual robberies.

Tamara Grimaldi answered on the first ring, and after telling her where I was and what I was thinking, I hesitated for a moment. I wanted to control myself, but I wasn't able to refrain from adding, "I hear that you and Rafe spent the night together on Saturday."

Her voice sounded amused. "Is that what he told you?"

"At first. It took me a minute to figure out that he didn't mean what I thought he meant."

"That must have been a relief."

I decided not to dignify that remark with a response. "You let him go again, so I guess I can assume he's cleared?"

"Hardly." The detective's voice turned serious. "I didn't have enough evidence to keep him, but that doesn't mean I've forgotten about him. Believe me, I'm going to keep a close eye on Mr. Collier from now on. You can pass that on to him if you want."

"I'm not sure when I'll have the opportunity," I said, "but I'll be happy to. Wouldn't that defeat your purposes, though, if I tip him off that you're watching?"

"Just tell him to watch his step," Detective Grimaldi said, as if through gritted teeth, and hung up in my ear before I had the chance to say anything else. I arched my brows. Had it been something I said?

I was in the process of locking the front door of the French Chateau when a bright blue Mini Cooper with white racing stripes zipped into the driveway and stopped at the bottom of the stairs. A young man jumped out. He looked to be in his early twenties, and was devastatingly handsome, in that glossy way that soap opera actors and matinee idols (and gay Realtors) are. His skin was luminous and as poreless and smooth as a baby's bottom, his soft, brown hair flopped over his forehead in shining waves, and his eyes were midnight blue bordering on black and surrounded by lashes almost as luxurious as Rafe's. "Hel-*lo*, beautiful!" he caroled when he saw me, his teeth shining with the radiance of a toothpaste ad. I smiled politely.

"Hi."

He stuck out a hand. "I'm Beau. The house boy."

"The what?"

"House boy. Here." He dug into the inside pocket of his leather jacket and pulled out a business card, which he handed to me. I caught quite a load of skin at the same time, because Beau—an awfully appropriate name, and one I doubted was legally his own; it was just too fitting—was bare-chested beneath. His jeans hung low on his hips, exposing a taut, tanned stomach and admirable musculature all the way around.

I looked away, down to the business card, blushing. Way to go, Savannah; ogle the gay guy, why don't you?

Beau Riggins, the card said, *House Cleaning*, followed by a phone number. *Feeling Dirty?* the slogan underneath said, *Call the House Boy!*

"I'm sorry," I apologized, "I'm sure you are who you say you are, but I really can't let you into the house."

"That's OK, gorgeous. I've got my own key." He pulled it out and dangled it in front of my face, something which necessitated another display of skin. "Mr. Givens will be here any minute himself, I'm sure. He always comes home for lunch on Mondays. To watch me work." He winked.

"I see," I said. "Um... not that it's any of my business, but wouldn't it be better to wear a uniform of some kind? What if you spill bleach on yourself or something?"

Beau ran a hand down his chest and stomach. It was as manicured as the rest of him. Whatever he was doing to the house, didn't involve chapping his hands in hot water and ammonia. No calluses on Beau. "This is a bona fide, genuine tan, sweetie. The real thing; I was in Acapulco just two weeks ago, working on it. Bleach won't take it off. And wearing a shirt would totally ruin everything. Nobody's gonna pay me $100 an hour to vacuum the floors while I wear clothes."

"You clean in the nude?" I said. "For $100 an hour?" Truthfully, I wasn't entirely sure which was more shocking.

"I clean in a pair of Wonderjock," Beau corrected, unconcernedly pulling down his zipper to show them to me. They were bright blue, the same color as the car, and fit him like a second skin. The waistband identified them as *Property of Australia* in bright red and white letters. I stared in horrified fascination, although I still felt like I was missing something.

"I'm sorry. Wonder... what?"

"Wonderjocks," Beau repeated, with a fond look down at them. Or himself. "They work the same way as that bra you're wearing." He demonstrated on his own well-developed pectorals. "The Wonderjock lifts and separates, too."

"Lifts and separates what?" I asked. "No, don't tell me. I don't want to know."

Beau grinned. "They're wonderful, aren't they? Boosts the appeal of even the smallest guy, and for those of us who are OK on our own, they take us out of the merely average and give us a little something extra. And $100 an hour is my starting price. It goes up from there."

"Good Lord," I said reverently, not quite sure whether I was reacting to Beau's price or the briefs. They were the first pair of men's undies I had seen since my divorce, and Bradley's tighty whities sure hadn't looked like this.

Beau chuckled. "I do just fine, darling. Nashville is full of rich gay men and bored housewives who'll pay through the nose to watch me swing a feather duster. It's a dirty job, but someone's gotta do it." He winked.

Just at that moment, a dark sedan pulled into the driveway and saved me the trouble of coming up with a response. A well-dressed, older man got out and came up the stairs. "Good afternoon, Beau."

"Hi, Mr. Givens," Beau grinned. Mr. Givens, Beau's employer—and audience for the next hour or two—turned to me.

"Hello." It was less a greeting than a request for me to explain who I was and what I was doing there, distracting his entertainment.

"Hi," I said. "I'm Savannah Martin with Walker Lamont Realty. Previewing the house. I was just leaving."

Mr. Givens nodded, but didn't answer. His gaze had already returned to the beautiful Beau. "Did you lose your key, Beau?"

"Not at all, Mr. Givens," Beau said, brandishing it. Givens's eyes glazed over at the display of skin, and Beau's dimple made a brief appearance. "I was just shooting the breeze with Savannah. But now that you're here, I guess I should get to work."

Mr. Givens didn't answer, just turned toward the front door. It was answer enough. Beau winked at me and followed.

I WAS HALFWAY HOME WHEN THE cell phone rang. I glanced at the display before I answered, hoping that it would be Detective Grimaldi calling to apologize for hanging up on me and maybe to share some new and thrilling tidbit of information. It wasn't, and I had to talk myself into doing the right thing and answering the call.

"Savannah? Todd here. I was wondering if you were available for dinner tonight?" The query was unusually abrupt, without any of the usual introductory small talk. Most of the time, I could count on Todd to behave with better manners.

"Unfortunately not," I said.

"Another date with Collier?" His voice held an undertone I didn't like, and I had to tell myself sternly that there was no way he could have known I'd had dinner with Rafe the night before. Todd was just being his usual paranoid self.

"Planning meeting for some charitable event or other. I forgot to ask what. I'm taking Lila Vaughn's place, since she can't be there."

My voice caught, but Todd didn't comment. He hesitated for a moment, regrouping. "How about tomorrow?"

"Tomorrow's fine."

"Would you mind driving down to Sweetwater to meet me? I have an early meeting on Wednesday morning."

I moved the phone away from my ear for a second and stared at it. Usually, Todd drove to Nashville to take me to Fidelio's, and sometimes we'd have dinner at the Wayside Inn if I was going to be in Sweetwater anyway, but he'd never before asked me to make the trek there just for him.

"I suppose I could do that," I said hesitantly. "I have to be back in Nashville by Wednesday afternoon, though."

"Date?" Todd wanted to know, with the same strained note in his voice.

"Funeral. Lila's memorial service is Wednesday at 2 pm."

"Oh," Todd said.

I waited a moment, but when he didn't say anything else, I added, "Is everything OK? You sound—I don't know—strange?"

"Everything's fine," Todd said. "There's just something I want to talk to you about. Something important. But it can wait until tomorrow. 6:30 at the Wayside Inn?"

I said I'd be there, and we hung up, me with the gravest misgivings. Lately, when Todd says he has something important to talk to me about, it means that he's freaking out over my imagined relationship with Rafe. In this case, however, there was no way he could have known about yesterday. I had made sure we went somewhere where no one would know me—and with the Shortstop, I was convinced I had succeeded—and furthermore, if any of 'our' people (as mother would say) had been there, they would have stood out like a sore thumb, the way I had done. So Todd couldn't possibly have known. But if this wasn't about Rafe, what was it about...?

And then it hit me, and I almost drove off the road. What if Todd was planning to propose? He'd been hinting last week, with his comments about my needing a husband, and I had pretended I didn't understand what he was getting at. What if he'd decided to just come right out and ask, so as not to give me any wiggle-room? And Good Lord, if he did, what would I say?!

Ten

In the worry over Todd's phone call and everything else that was going on, I almost forgot that I had promised to show Gary Lee and Charlene another house. In fact, I was so late that by the time I got there, they were getting back into their car again. I jumped out of mine.

"Sorry. I'm so sorry. Something came up and I totally forgot the time."

Charlene grinned. "I told you that if something came up, you could call and cancel, Savannah."

Oh, Lord! I flushed. "Not that! I just got a phone call from a friend, that's all."

"Ooooh!" Charlene giggled. "Phone sex."

"That's quite all right, Savannah," Gary Lee said with a quelling look at his wife. "We've still got time."

"Thank you. Let me open the door for you, and you can have a look around. I've got... um... another call to make, so I'll just stay out here."

"OK." They bounded into the house like eager squirrels, all bright-eyed and bushy-tailed, leaving me on the porch. I pulled out the phone and dialed my mother.

"Hi, mom? It's Savannah."

"Hello, darling," mother said. "How are you, dear?"

"Just fine, thank you. Listen, Todd just called and asked me to dinner tomorrow."

"Did he?" Mother sounded like she was smiling.

"He wants me to drive down to Sweetwater to meet him. I wanted to make sure it would be OK for me to stay the night with you."

"Of course," Mother said. "Why wouldn't it be?"

"No reason. I just didn't want to assume." It would be impolite, and believe me, if I'd shown up unannounced, Mother would have told me so.

"No, darling, of course you can stay with me." Mother hesitated for a moment before she added, "As a matter of fact, we'll probably be seeing the two of you at the Wayside Inn. I'm having dinner with the sheriff."

"You don't say?" What were the odds? "That's quite a coincidence, isn't it?"

And it made it all the more likely that Todd was planning to propose, if both our parents were going to be present, ready to jump up and congratulate us after I'd said yes. And of course I'd have to say yes, if Mother was sitting right there, waiting. Brilliantly reasoned on Todd's part.

"Well, it *is* the only four-star restaurant in the county," Mother pointed out. "I mean, darling, you can hardly expect the sheriff to treat me at Beulah's Meat'n Three, now can you?"

"I suppose not," I admitted grudgingly. "I'll try to stop by the house first, but if I get a late start, I may just go straight to the Wayside Inn."

"Whatever you need, darling," Mother said. "I'll see you tomorrow."

She hung up. I did the same, gnawing the remaining lipstick off my bottom lip.

Gary Lee and Charlene came wandering out of the house after another few minutes, and notified me that this wasn't the house of their dreams, either. The master bedroom just hadn't blown Charlene's skirt up. But they had another house they wanted to see; this one a renovated craftsman bungalow in the Potsdam Street area, near where Rafe's grandmother lived. Personally, I didn't think they would enjoy living there—that particular neighborhood was still a bit too much like the Wild West for my taste, with desperados and guns behind every bush—but first-time buyers have been known to fall in love with unsuitable houses before, and I certainly wasn't about to deprive Gary Lee and Charlene of the opportunity to do so. We agreed to meet the next day at the same time, and Gary Lee went to the car to make a phone call of his own. Charlene stayed on the porch making small talk while I locked the door and hid the key inside the lockbox hanging from the door handle. "That was quite a house yesterday."

"The Fortunatos house? It's OK, if you like the type."

"Great bedroom." She smiled reminiscently. I shrugged. Perry and Connie Fortunato's master suite had toe-curling shag carpeting and mirrors all over the ceiling. Personally, I couldn't imagine a worse mood-killer than having to watch my own imperfect body slide across those black satin sheets, but maybe Connie was made of sterner stuff. And of course Charlene had the nubile body of someone just out of her teens, and nothing whatsoever to worry about. As a matter of fact, she was showing more of it than I'd realized earlier. Her blouse was misbuttoned, and showed her midriff. I was just about to point it out when she added, "That guy that you were with... was he your boyfriend?"

I shook my head. "Just a friend. He came by to make sure I was all right, what with the robberies the past two weekends and the murder last week."

"Oh." Charlene dug her tiny, white teeth into her lip. "I assumed, with the way you were looking at him..."

I hadn't been aware of looking at Rafe in any particular way. Other than that I was afraid he was thinking of tying me to a kitchen chair, I suppose. "What do you mean, the way I was looking at him? I wasn't looking at him any way." I would never *look* at Rafe. Not that way.

"Whatever you say, Savannah," Charlene giggled. "See you tomorrow. If something comes up, whether it's big or small, don't hesitate to cancel."

She skipped down the steps to rejoin her husband, still laughing and with her misbuttoned blouse flapping. And just for that parting remark, I decided not to tell her about it. Walking into society looking like she had just rolled out of bed and put on the thing nearest to hand was no more than she deserved for making me think—even for a second—about the extent of Rafe Collier's private parts.

By 6 PM, THOUGH, ANY THOUGHTS of Rafe or his body parts were banished from my mind, safely tucked away as if they'd never existed. I was on my way to Cheekwood: historic home, art museum, botanical garden, and special events center. And also the setting for the planning committee meeting for whatever charity Lila had been involved with.

Back in the early part of the 20th Century, a Nashville man named Joel Cheek developed a superior blend of coffee, which was marketed through the finest hotel in Nashville at the time, the Maxwell House. In 1928, General Foods purchased Cheek-Neal Coffee for a whopping forty million dollars, and in the process made Joel and all the other Cheeks obscenely wealthy.

Joel's cousin Leslie and Leslie's wife Mabel used some of their money to buy 100 acres of woodlands in West Nashville for a country estate. They hired New York architect Bryant Fleming to handle the project and gave him total control over everything, from landscaping to interior furnishings. The result was a 30,000 square foot limestone mansion in the style of an English country-house, surrounded by extensive formal gardens. The Cheeks moved in in January 1933. Leslie died just a few years later, but members of the family occupied the mansion until the 1950s, when Huldah Cheek Sharp and her husband Walter offered the property as a site for a museum and botanical garden.

I'd visited Cheekwood before—most Nashvillians stop by occasionally, to smell the flowers or admire the artwork or lunch in the Pineapple Room restaurant—and I had no problem finding the small salon where the meeting was set to take place.

When I walked in at 6:25, the room was abuzz with voices. Mostly female, although the occasional male stuck out like a sore thumb here and there. After a minute or two, I spotted Connie Fortunato on the other side of the room, and started weaving my way through the crowd toward her. When I came closer, I saw that she was deep in conversation with a redhead in a brown suede jacket, and I hesitated just out of hearing, loath to interrupt what looked like a fairly personal exchange. But the redhead looked up and saw me, and nudged Connie, who also turned to me.

"Oh," she said after a second, "Savannah."

"Hi, Connie." I smiled brightly. "I'm sorry to interrupt, but I saw you from the door and thought I'd say hello. You're the only person here I've met before."

Connie hesitated, but the redhead stuck a hand out. "Hi, I'm Heather Price."

"Savannah Martin." I took the proffered hand and shook. "Your name sounds familiar. Have we met?"

"I don't think so," Heather said. "Although I've heard of you. Connie said you might be stopping by."

I nodded. "Lila Vaughn was a friend of mine. If this benefit was important to her, I'd like to help out."

"That's very kind of you," Connie said.

"It seems the least I can do. I just can't believe she's gone, you know. It's just a few days since I saw her—Thursday—and she seemed so alive, and happy…"

"Just goes to show we should be careful what we wish for," Heather said darkly.

I looked from one to the other of them. "I guess she told you what happened last Sunday?"

They both nodded, and Connie said, "I imagine she told everyone she knew. The way she went on about this man, he must have been a veritable Greek god."

I nodded, and then stopped myself. "He certainly sounds that way. Of course, he may not have been her killer."

Heather glanced at me, and something came and went in her eyes, but she didn't speak. Connie snorted in polite disbelief. "Who else could it be?"

I shrugged. "I haven't known her very long, so I don't know a whole lot about her. She doesn't—didn't—have a boyfriend that I know of, but there was an ex-husband, at least."

Lila and I had shared divorce stories over coffee one night at school. She had gotten married fairly young, like me, but unlike Bradley, who had cheated on me with Shelby and then married her once our divorce was final, Lila's husband had been devoted to the point of obsession, always accusing her of sleeping around on him. He didn't want her talking to other men, didn't want her looking at other men, didn't want her leaving the house, cut her off from watching TV because she was watching other men. When she threatened to leave, he beat her senseless and told her he'd kill her if she tried. One of the neighbors called 911 once, when things got especially bad, and that's when she finally got rid of the guy. Arrest warrant, restraining order, the whole nine yards.

Heather nodded. "Bastard," she said succinctly. "But you know, that's not a bad idea. I wonder if the police are looking into that nasty piece of dog doo-doo." (She used a stronger word, one of the sort my mother had warned me would make me sound common. I won't repeat it.)

"I'm sure they are," I answered. "When someone is murdered, the husband or wife or significant other is always high on the suspect list. I'll…"

I stopped on the verge of saying that I would ask Detective Grimaldi the next time I spoke to her. It might make Connie and Heather feel uncomfortable to know that I was in pretty regular communication with the police. People tend to be a little leery of folks who can rat them out to the law, even when they don't have anything to hide.

"How long did you two know Lila?" I asked instead, looking from one to the other of them.

"Only a couple of months," Connie said. Heather nodded. "Since the planning for the Eye Ball started in July."

"The Eye Ball?"

Heather giggled. "That's the nickname for this event. The Vanderbilt Optometry Department's Benefit Gala. An Eye Ball."

"Funny," I said. "I guess you wouldn't know much about the men in her life, then, if you haven't known her long."

They exchanged a look. "Other than this guy on Sunday, she's mentioned very few," Heather said. "We always go—used to go—out somewhere for drinks after the meetings on Monday nights, and she was very pretty, you know…"

"And not attached, like me and Heather," Connie shot in. Heather nodded. So did I. Lila had been very pretty. A brief impression of her face in the picture Detective Grimaldi had shown me flashed in front of my eyes, and I swallowed hard and forced my attention back to the conversation. Heather continued.

"She wasn't above flirting with some of the men who caught her eye, but I don't remember her ever leaving with any of them."

"And she never mentioned any of them again," Connie added. "I'd ask once in a while—did so-and-so ever call?—but she never said anything about getting together with any of them later. And she wasn't promiscuous. Her husband was crazy; she didn't cheat on him."

"I've never heard her rave about anyone the way she did about this burglar," Heather said.

Connie nodded. "By the way, Savannah, that boyfriend of yours wasn't exactly hard on the eyes, either."

"He's not my boyfriend," I began.

"He said he was her bodyguard," Connie explained to Heather, "and seeing the way he was looking at it, I think he was telling the truth."

Blushing, I explained, "He's a friend of mine. Because of the robberies and Lila's murder, my boss suggested that we all be extra careful this weekend."

Connie added, "If Lila's guy looked anything like Savannah's guy, I don't blame Lila one bit for asking him to take advantage of her. This guy could take advantage of me any time he wanted."

"A pity he's spoken for," Heather remarked, with a glance at me.

"Oh, yes," Connie said, "they made that very clear. Both of them."

She winked. I blushed. But before I could say anything the meeting was called to order. We took our seats around the table, and the conversation was shelved as centerpieces, napkins, and tablecloths took over as the main topics of conversation.

THE HOUSE NEAR POTSDAM STREET that we visited on Tuesday afternoon didn't turn out to be Gary Lee and Charlene's dream home, either. They went inside and spent a good, long time there, but when they came back outside, they told me that no, this wasn't it.

"OK," I said, figuratively taking the bull by the horns. "Maybe it's time we set some parameters. You've seen a few houses by now. Are you able to narrow down what you're looking for just a little bit? Is it a certain style of house? A certain age? A certain area? Are there special features you're looking for, like a fireplace or a Jacuzzi tub?"

They exchanged a look. "Not really…"

"How will you know you've found it?"

"Um…" They looked at each other again.

"I guess," Charlene said, "we'll know when we see it. Or experience being in it."

Gary Lee nodded. "We're looking for something that'll blow Charlene's skirt up."

I arched my brows. "I see. OK, then. If you can't give me anything more definite, I guess we'll just continue the way we've been going. I can't show you anything tomorrow—I'll be in Sweetwater in the morning, and then I have a memorial service to go to in the afternoon—but I'm sure you have something you want to see on Thursday?"

"Um…" They glanced at each other and then down, sheepishly. "Not really."

"I see," I said, breathing through the nose. After all this, they were just going to fall off the map? I was going to have wasted all of this time for no commission?

"I think we need to… um… reassess where we stand," Gary Lee spoke up. "Process what we've learned. Decide on the next logical step."

It seemed to me that the next logical step was to make an offer on a house they wanted to buy, but of course I didn't say so. "Fine," I said instead, my voice strained. "You have my number. When you've reassessed where you stand and decided what you want to do, give me a call."

They said they would and scurried into their car, peeling rubber pulling away from the curb, as if they couldn't get away from me fast enough. I allowed myself the satisfaction of kicking the steps of the house, with nothing to show for it but bruised toes.

Eleven

Because of Gary Lee and Charlene and the totally wasted hour I spent with them, I got a late start on the drive to Sweetwater, and ended up in the worst crush of rush-hour drivers, speeding home to the southern suburbs from their jobs in the city. That slowed me down even more, and then there was the three-car pile-up just before the off-ramp at Peytonsville Road. I didn't have time to stop by the house on my way, and as it was, I arrived at the Wayside Inn ten minutes late, to find Todd drumming his fingers on the tabletop and watching the door. Mother and Sheriff Satterfield were already halfway through their meal, and I stopped beside their table on my way to say hello. The sheriff stood up to greet me, and leaned in to peck me on the cheek. "Evening, missy. Having a bite with my boy, are you?"

"I am, Sheriff. If that's OK with you."

"Course, darlin'. Course. Couldn't be happier." He sank back down at the table. Mother beamed.

"It looks like he's waiting, so I guess I should get over there. Enjoy your meal. What's left of it."

"Oh, we'll be outta here in just a few minutes," the sheriff promised. "Don't wanna interrupt the boy's plans." He winked at me. I smiled back, politely, while my heart sank all the way down to the floor.

Todd looked very handsome in his dark suit and tasteful tie, and I found myself wishing I'd taken the time to change into something different myself, even if it would have made me even later than I already was. Not that there was anything wrong with what I was wearing. If there had been, mother would have let me know. My outfit of tangerine top and pale blue skirt was flattering and appropriate, although I suppose it could have been less wrinkled. I had, after all, been wearing it all day. I had spent the downtime on the road touching up my make-up in the rearview mirror, however, so at least my face looked dewy-fresh.

Todd rose as I approached—he has beautiful manners—and kissed my hand. "Good evening, Savannah." He handed me into my chair and walked back around the table to his own.

"I'm sorry I'm late. I hit traffic, and then there was an accident..."

Todd waved his hand dismissively. "I'm just glad you could make it. Drink?"

"Please."

"White wine?"

I nodded, and Todd turned to the waiter and ordered a glass of Sauvignon Blanc for me, and a glass of Merlot for himself. The waiter withdrew, and Todd turned back to me. "I hope your open house on Sunday went well?"

"Very well, thank you," I said. "Seventeen visitors—no, eighteen— and no robbers. Or at least none that made themselves known to me."

"That's good," Todd said. He glanced around, over at our parents, who were now enjoying dessert. "And how did your committee meeting go yesterday?"

"Fine, thank you. We decided on using the waterfall design for the folded napkins, and since the event is taking place just a few days before

Halloween, we're discussing the idea of a costume ball. I met a couple of women who knew Lila, although they didn't seem to know anything about what happened to her. Other than what was in the paper, I mean."

Todd nodded. He slid another glance in the direction of our parents.

"Is something the matter?" I asked.

He turned back to me. "Pardon?"

"Are you worried that your father is going to fall prey to my mother's gold-digging charms, or something?"

"Of course not," Todd said, his fair skin flushing all the way to the roots of his blond hair. "I'm just... um... it's difficult to talk about anything important while they're there."

"We have all night," I said kindly, and then wished I hadn't. "I mean, until dinner is over. Or even later, if you wanted to take a drive or something afterwards."

"I suppose," Todd said, but he lapsed into silence and didn't come out again until the waiter arrived with our drinks. Then he roused himself for long enough to ask me what I wanted for dinner, and to order for both of us, before he lapsed back into insignificant small talk.

When our parents walked out of the restaurant about halfway through our meal, he thawed a little bit, but it wasn't until the waiter had removed our plates and Todd had ordered dessert—cheesecake for him, black coffee for me—that he deigned to get to the reason for asking me to meet him.

"I wanted to talk to you about something, Savannah."

"OK," I said.

"Something important."

"All right."

"Just a moment. I have something to show you." He avoided my eyes as he bent over to rummage in the briefcase leaning against his chair leg. My heart started beating faster.

I expected him to surface with a small jeweler's box, or maybe just a ring, but he didn't. What he held, was a plain manila envelope. It didn't bulge, and I started breathing easier. Until he removed a stiff piece of paper and glanced at it for a moment before sliding it across the table to me. I picked it up, and so unprepared was I, that it took me a second to realize what—or whom—I was looking at. But then all the blood left my face and pooled somewhere in the vicinity of my stomach; or at least it felt that way.

"Where did you get this?" My voice was uneven, and deteriorated further when I added, incredulously, "Are you having me followed?"

Todd hesitated. I wish I could say I thought he was quailing under the onslaught of my righteous indignation, but I'm afraid not. He was just weighing his options and deciding how much to tell me. "Not you," he said finally. "Him."

I had to take a breath before I could continue. "Why is the district attorney's office interested in Rafe Collier?"

"They're not," Todd said. And added ominously, "Yet."

"So you're doing this on your own? Why?"

Todd glanced again at the photograph I was holding, and seemed to draw some sort of strength from it, because he met my eyes straight on. "Isn't it obvious? Look at yourself, Savannah! Look at the way you're looking at him. Can you blame me for worrying about you?"

I looked down at the photograph again. And it was mostly to avoid Todd's accusing eyes, not because I wanted to inspect it in any more detail. Because, believe me, I'd seen enough.

Oh, it wasn't that I looked bad. Quite the opposite, in fact. I looked pretty darned good, if I do say so myself. Maybe even a little too good. Usually, I'm not crazy about the way I look in photographs. The extra ten pounds the camera adds, coupled with the extra ten I'm carrying myself, tend to make me look tubbier than I like. In this case, however, I had no cause for complaint. I looked great. My eyes sparkled, my skin glowed, my smile was radiant, and my cheeks were becomingly flushed. Even my hair looked good. My only consolation was that I was not, in fact, doing what Todd was accusing me of. "What do you mean?" I demanded. "I'm looking down, not up at Rafe."

"But you're smiling," Todd said coldly. "And blushing. And flirting."

"I'm not flirting. *He's* the one who was flirting!" That's why I'd been blushing.

"But you don't look like you minded," Todd shot back, accurately. I could feel another blush creep into my cheeks, and thanked the Lord it was dark in the restaurant. Maybe Todd would mistake my heightened color for temper rather than embarrassment or residual memory.

"What did you expect me to do," I demanded, "slap his face?" And what a photograph *that* would have made!

The idea of it made me smile, and allowed me to calm down sufficiently to add reasonably, "You're being silly, Todd. Rafe flirts with everyone, even Timothy Briggs. It doesn't mean anything."

"He doesn't have to flirt with *you*!" Todd said petulantly.

I shrugged. "Well, of course he doesn't *have* to." Although flirting seems to come as naturally to Rafe as breathing, so maybe he did have to. It wasn't something I planned to put to the test, since his flirtation didn't bother me the same way it did Todd. For the most part I enjoyed it. I didn't want it to go any further than it had, but I didn't mind what he'd done so far.

Thankfully, the waiter chose this moment to appear with Todd's cheesecake and my coffee, and by the time he had left, I had gathered myself enough to be able to ask, quite calmly, "So is this it, or do you have any other pictures in that envelope?"

Todd nodded. "Plenty. Have a look." He pushed the envelope across the table toward me. I reached in and pulled out a sheaf of other photographs, starting with Rafe outside Police Plaza at 1:20 pm Sunday afternoon, in the process of putting on his sunglasses. Then there was Rafe and I talking to Connie Fortunato on her front steps at 4:13 pm. He had a proprietary arm around my shoulders, and I didn't look as uncomfortable as I thought I had. Then Perry Fortunato and Rafe squaring off at 4:16. I hadn't noticed it at the time, but they were almost of a height, both tall and dark, although Perry was a good ten years older and fleshy rather than muscular. He did his best to make up for it by looking at Rafe down the length of his Roman nose, but the attempt failed because Rafe had him beat by an inch or so in height. Perry had to tilt his head back, which rather ruined the effect.

Then there was a shot of Rafe grinning at the waitress and another close-up of me at the table in the Shortstop, with a half-eaten hamburger in my hand and my mouth open. Not so flattering to me, that one. After that came one of Rafe and his friend talking at the table, and another of all four of them in conversation over by the pool tables. The light was nice and sharp over there—the better to see the all-important game of pool—and the pictures were crystal clear and detailed. It was followed by close-ups of all three men.

Todd had been watching me across the table. "Those are criminals," he said.

I glanced up. "How do you know?"

"The investigator I hired told me. The information is written on the back. They've all been arrested several times, for things like burglary, check fraud, grand theft auto..."

"Nice," I muttered, reading the back of the photographs. Ishmael Jackson, A. J. Davies, and Antoine Kent, and their assorted crimes, beginning in their teens and carrying through to now. Todd allowed himself a tiny smirk. Usually, he has an appealing smile, one that crinkles the corners of his gray-blue eyes and shows off his even, white teeth. Not now. At this moment he just looked smug and self-satisfied. The temptation to knock him off his high horse was almost irresistible. "So what did your tame P.I. have to say about Rafe? Anything I haven't heard already?"

Rafe's criminal history wasn't written on the back of the photo, and I had a nagging feeling that it might be because it was too extensive to fit.

Todd flushed. "That he's been in trouble almost as long as he's been alive. That he was arrested at eighteen and spent two years in Riverbend prison for assault and battery. That while he was there, he was recruited by a crime organization in Memphis, and when he was released, he moved there and went to work for them. A couple of years later, when the Tennessee Bureau of Investigations arrested the leaders, he managed to stay out of jail by the skin of his teeth."

"Good for him," I said.

"After another couple of years, the TBI cracked down on the organization again, and made what almost amounted to a clean sweep. Except for Collier, who disappeared before anyone could catch up with him. He resurfaced six or eight months later in Knoxville, with a group of guys who were hijacking tractor trailers and fencing the contents. That lasted a few months, and then the TBI wiped them out, too. They nabbed him, and held on to him for as long as they could, but eventually they had to let him go for lack of proof. He moved on to Chattanooga and Jackson, and then to Clarksville, where he had something to do with thefts from the military base. Earlier this year, he showed up in Nashville. Where he was on the scene when Brenda Puckett was murdered."

"He was on the scene 45 minutes later," I corrected. "We've talked about this, Todd. He didn't have anything to do with killing Brenda. Or Clarice Webb."

Todd ignored me. "And two weeks before that, my dad suspected him of having had a hand in doing away with his mother."

"Your dad had no proof that anyone was involved in LaDonna Collier's death," I protested. "If he did, he would have arrested someone by now."

"Just because there's no proof, doesn't mean Collier didn't do it," Todd said.

Just because Todd wanted Rafe to be guilty, didn't mean he was, either, but I had no time to say so. Todd added, "All it means is, he's very good at covering his tracks."

"I'm not so sure about that," I answered. "Doesn't it seem more likely that he's just not a very good criminal? Everything he's ever gotten involved in has been shut down by the police after a month or two."

Todd shrugged. We sat in silence for a moment or two while Todd ate his cheesecake and I drank my coffee.

"So is that it?" I asked eventually, keeping my voice level. "Because it's interesting, but not really surprising. I already suspected that he had an alternate source of income. One that wasn't entirely legal."

Todd looked at me. I could see the wheels ticking behind his eyes. He was debating whether to tell me something, and he wasn't sure. But was it because he wanted to keep it in reserve for next time, or was it because he wasn't entirely sure it was accurate...?

Eventually he decided. "There's more. Do you remember Elspeth Caulfield?"

I wrinkled my brows. "I can't say I do, no. Who is she?"

"She went to high school with us. You, me, and Collier. My year. Her father was a preacher for some little fundamentalist sect west of Sweetwater."

A glimmer of a memory was beginning to come to me. "Petite, blond girl? Very quiet? Had some sort of nervous breakdown, and never came back?"

"Her parents took her out of school before senior year, just after you and I started dating."

I nodded. I remembered now. Vaguely. I hadn't had anything to do with Elspeth and wasn't sure I'd recognize her if she walked through the door right now. "What about her?"

"There were rumors at the time that she was pregnant and they were taking her somewhere to have the baby so no one would know."

I tightened my stomach muscles. I've heard it can help someone beat a lie detector test, and I could really use some help in not showing my reaction right then. I had a feeling I knew what was coming, and I didn't want Todd to guess that I knew, or more accurately, that the idea bothered me.

Todd smirked knowingly. "Would you care to speculate as to whose baby it was?"

"Not Rafe's," I said. "I asked him just the other day if he had any children, and he said no." None he knew about.

"Maybe he doesn't know," Todd said, playing right into my secret worry. "He was in jail by then. Or maybe she had an abortion. It's not difficult to get rid of an unwanted pregnancy."

His attitude said, very clearly, that any child of Rafe's would be unwanted by any woman in her right mind. I didn't answer. I'm not sure I could have spoken even if I'd tried. It's not something a lot of people know, and Todd certainly didn't, but at one point during my short and ill-fated marriage to Bradley, I'd had a miscarriage. It had happened very early in what was an unplanned pregnancy, almost before I knew I was expecting, albeit not before I'd had time to get over the initial shock and start looking forward to the happy event. In retrospect, considering the way things turned out between Bradley and me, it was probably just as well it had happened the way it did. Our simple, uncontested divorce would have been a thousand times messier had there been children involved, and a child would have tied me irrevocably to Bradley for the rest of my natural life. All in all, I couldn't really regret the way things had fallen out. Still, there were times like now, when I was reminded, that I mourned the loss.

"Have you spoken to Elspeth about this?" I asked when I could trust my voice again.

Todd looked shocked. "Of course not. I can't pry into her personal life."

The fact that he'd pried into mine, not to mention Rafe's, didn't seem to have occurred to him.

"So how do you know she was pregnant? Maybe it was just a rumor."

"Everyone knows what happened," Todd said. "But you don't have to take my word for it. Talk to Cletus Johnson. He was there; he'll tell you."

"Marquita's ex-husband? That Cletus Johnson?"

"Deputy Sheriff Cletus Johnson," Todd said.

"The same Cletus Johnson who gave Rafe a black eye a couple of weeks ago? And I would trust his word because...?"

Todd flushed. "Just go talk to him, Savannah. He'll tell you."

"Fine," I said coldly, "maybe I will."

Or maybe I'd talk to Rafe instead. Someone who'd actually be in a position to tell me something definite, and not just rumors and speculation and innuendo and sour grapes.

Twelve

For a few moments after leaving the Wayside Inn, I thought seriously about driving back to Nashville rather than facing mother. But it was late and in spite of what I'd tried to show Todd, I was upset by what he'd told me, so I turned the car toward the Martin mansion after all. And was rewarded by not seeing Mother. Her bedroom door was closed and the lights out, and by the time I got up the next morning, I was alone. If it had been anyone but my mother, I would have suspected that she'd spent the night elsewhere, because her bed showed no evidence of having been slept in, but knowing her as I do, I didn't think anything of it. She's obsessively concerned with appearances, and had just put her bed in apple-pie order before heading out to the spa or hair-dresser or breakfast, that's all.

I was happy to avoid her. I didn't want to discuss my dinner with Todd. I didn't want to ask Cletus Johnson about Elspeth Caulfield, and I was reluctant to look for Elspeth herself. So I did the only thing I could do, and visited the one member of my family who was, at least provisionally, on my side.

The law offices of Martin and McCall are located on the town square, in a turn-of-the-(last)-century brick building with a green canopy. The company was started by my great-grandfather back when the country was young, and my father worked there his entire adult life. Currently, the resident Martin is my brother Dix, while Jonathan McCall, our sister Catherine's husband, makes up the other half of the company. Catherine also has a law degree, but she doesn't practice much these days. For the record, I'm the only Martin of my generation who didn't finish law school. Instead, I dropped out to marry Bradley, and never went back.

Jonathan—bless him—was closeted with a client, but Dix was available to talk to me. When I walked into his office and closed the door behind me, he looked up from the paperwork on his desk and squinted. "You look horrible."

"Nice to see you too," I answered, sitting down in one of the worn leather chairs in front of the cherrywood desk that had belonged to my father and his father before him. Dix leaned back in his swivel chair and folded his hands on top of the manila folder on the desk.

"Late night?"

"Not with Todd. Just with worrying."

Dix sighed. "What's going on now?"

"Didn't Todd tell you what he's been doing? Let me show you." I dug in my purse and fished out the photograph of myself and Rafe that had started the conversation yesterday. "Look at this."

Dix looked, and shook his head sadly. "When are you going to learn, sis?"

"I had dinner with a friend," I said angrily. "It wasn't even a date. If I sleep with him, or—God forbid!—fall in love with him, then you can give me a hard time, but not for having a meal." Unless it was breakfast in bed, but we wouldn't go there. Literally or in discussion.

"Fine," Dix said. "I won't give you a hard time. Although mother would, you know."

"Why do you think I made Todd give me the picture? I know he can probably get another copy, but at least this way, he won't be showing it to her right away."

Dix shrugged. I added, "You have to make him stop, Dix. You're his best friend; he'll listen to you. He has to understand that he can't hire private investigators to follow civilians around. I know that he's worried about me, but Rafe will have a fit if—when—he finds out. And if he gets upset, there's no telling what he might do."

"Do you plan to tell him?" Dix asked.

I bit my lip. "Todd brought up some things I'd like to ask him about. If I do, he's going to ask me who told me about them, and how that person found out."

Plus, it wasn't fair to let Rafe go about his—probably nefarious—business with a private eye dogging his footsteps, when I knew about it and could warn him.

"And you can't just let it go?" Dix wanted to know.

"I might, if I could get the answers I want without having to ask him. Do you by any chance remember Elspeth Caulfield from high school?"

"Just barely," Dix admitted. "Didn't she drop out early?"

I nodded. "Although, according to Todd, she didn't drop out so much as was taken out by her parents, either because she had a nervous breakdown, or because she had gotten herself in the family way and they wanted to hush it up."

Dix nodded. "I remember now. Quiet girl, but very intense. One of those 'still waters' types. A lot going on underneath the surface."

"Todd intimated that she was pregnant, and that the baby was Rafe's. Do you remember hearing anything about that?"

"I remember hearing all sorts of things," Dix said. "But now that you mention it, I think I may have heard something about that, yes. It was years ago, though, so it's difficult to remember the details."

"Todd said that Cletus Johnson would know."

"So why aren't you asking Cletus?" Dix wanted to know. "Afraid of what he'll say?"

"Of course not," I denied quickly. "I just don't want to cause any more gossip. Cletus Johnson is a deputy sheriff, and if I call him and start asking questions about Rafe, he'll tell Sheriff Satterfield, who'll tell mom, who'll ground me for the next hundred years. I'll be like Sleeping Beauty, locked in a tower away from everyone. Except when I get out, I'll be 127, and no one will look twice at me."

"At 127 you'll be dead," Dix said. "So what do you want me to do? Call Cletus myself?"

"Would you? He might be more inclined to tell you rather than me. All you have to do is give him that same old excuse: that you're worried about your sister getting involved with Rafe."

"Excuse?" Dix muttered, but he didn't say it loudly. "All right. For you. I'll give him a call later on today, and let you know what he says."

He saw my mouth open and preempted my protest. "No, I'm not going to do it now, while you're sitting here. It's too early in the morning, and I don't want to have to worry about what you hear. I want to filter the information I get first."

"Just don't leave anything out," I warned, getting up to go.

"Not to worry, sis," Dix answered dryly, "I won't."

I CONSIDERED—I REALLY CONSIDERED—DRIVING OVER AND knocking on Elspeth Caulfield's door, but in the end I decided against it. Not only would it be rude to show up unannounced, but it was probably better to hear what Cletus Johnson had to say first, not to mention Rafe himself. Or Marquita. If Cletus knew something, maybe Marquita did, as well. Although, just as Cletus was firmly anti-Rafe these days, Marquita was pro-Rafe, and I wasn't sure I could trust her testimony any more than I could trust her ex-husband's. It just goes to show that one should always attempt to get the dirt right from the horse's mouth, and even then, take everything with a grain of salt.

LILA'S MEMORIAL SERVICE TOOK PLACE in the ballroom at the downtown Sheraton, without Lila herself. Lila's mother had taken her daughter's body back to Detroit for burial, and this was just an excuse for the rest of us to get together and eat, drink and be merry, speeding Lila on her way in a manner of which she would have approved. I did my best to keep a smile on my face, although I admit it wasn't easy. A huge photograph of Lila, blown up to many times life-size, hung on the wall above the banquet table, and every time I looked up at it, a new wave of guilt swamped me. The food looked and smelled exquisite, but I couldn't choke down more than a few carrot sticks. Leaving my plate behind, I started circulating instead, and after a few minutes I came across Tamara Grimaldi, who was standing with her back against the wall near the door, dressed in the same boxy business suit she'd worn to Brenda Puckett's funeral a few weeks earlier.

"You know," I said as I stopped beside her, "I always knew there would come a time when I'd be reading the obituaries looking for the names of friends who had passed away, but I didn't think it would happen so soon. This is the third funeral I've been to in less than a month, and it's freaking me out."

"There's been a veritable open season on Realtors lately, hasn't there?" Detective Grimaldi agreed. "You're being careful, I hope?"

"You sound like my mother. Yes, I'm being careful. I've even considered buying myself a weapon of some sort, to keep in my handbag. Just in case."

"That might not be a bad idea," Grimaldi said, "although you did a fine job of apprehending Mr. Lamont with your lipstick."

"I couldn't have shot him with it, though. But I don't think I want a gun. Carrying a gun is an invitation to shoot someone, don't you think? I'd rather have something nice and safe and girly, like defense spray."

"I'll give you the name of a store," the detective said. "It might not be a bad idea to take some self defense lessons, too, while you're at it. If nothing else, you'll learn never to open the door to strangers."

"I already know that," I said and lowered my voice. "Are you any closer to finding out who killed Lila?"

A shutter came down over her face. "We're working on it. An arrest is not imminent. Although we've found a witness who saw what we think was the murderer come out of Lila's building in the early hours on Saturday morning. Wearing coveralls and carrying a black duffel bag."

"Really?"

"Really. The next time you see Mr. Collier, maybe you'll be so good as to tell him to hold himself in readiness for a lineup?"

I swallowed. "Sure."

"Thank you."

"No problem. So... um... are any of your suspects here?" I looked around the room.

"You know I can't tell you that," Detective Grimaldi said. "Although there are people here I've spoken to. That's the victim's ex-husband over there, in the yellow. Malcolm Rodgers. He was the one who found her."

"I've been meaning to talk to you about that," I said, diverted, while I looked at Malcolm. He was a flashily good-looking black guy with his hair in cornrows, dressed in a too-spiffy mustard-colored suit. "Malcolm, I mean. You're looking into him, I'm sure. He used to beat her, you know."

"No," Detective Grimaldi said, "I didn't know. I'll have to look into that."

"He put her in the hospital once. After that, she filed for divorce and got a restraining order, I think."

Grimaldi nodded. "Mr. Rodgers says he got a phone call from Lila sometime on Friday night—not a message, just her number on caller ID while he was out—and he waited for her to call back. When she didn't, and she didn't answer her phone in the morning on Saturday, he decided to stop by. When he got there, he found her dead."

"He probably thought she wanted him back," I said. He looked like the type who would.

Detective Grimaldi shrugged. "He has a record for petty theft and drug dealing. It's some years ago now, and he swears he's clean, but she might have thought he knew something about the robberies."

"Or maybe," I said slowly, "she recognized him. Maybe that was why she didn't seem as distraught as Kieran Greene about what happened. And maybe she threatened to expose him, and he killed her, and then pretended to find her."

Detective Grimaldi smirked. "Have you ever thought of writing thrillers, Ms. Martin?"

"God forbid," I said piously. If I were to write anything, it would probably be a steamy romance novel, since that's what I tend to read. "Anyway, Kieran was scared out of his mind, and I would have been too, but Lila didn't seem too worried, did she? She even managed to flirt with one of the burglars. Which makes sense if he was her ex-husband and she recognized him. He even has pretty, brown eyes."

We both looked at him.

"That's true," Detective Grimaldi admitted. "He's tall, too. Not as muscular as I expected from the witness descriptions, but in padded coveralls, possibly muscular enough. Although, if Lila recognized him, do you think she'd have described him accurately?"

"I guess that depends on how much she wanted to keep him out of jail," I said. "Or how afraid she was of him. Kieran Greene saw him too, and the descriptions match."

Tamara Grimaldi nodded. "I think I'll have another talk with Mr. Rodgers. Find out if he has an alibi for either robbery. If he has a history of spousal abuse, that's going to count against him. By the way, the medical examiner estimates time of death between eleven and midnight. Your boyfriend doesn't have an alibi."

"My boyfriend," I said sourly, "doesn't need one. If you're talking about Rafe, he's not my boyfriend. And he didn't kill Lila. Come on, Detective. You've met him. Do you really think he has it in him to rape and then strangle someone?"

"They don't pay me to think," Detective Grimaldi said, and relented, "It doesn't matter what I think, because on the evidence, he does. He has a conviction for assault and battery, and he's been a suspect in quite a few other violent and non-violent crimes. Just because he wasn't charged, doesn't mean he didn't do them."

"It doesn't mean he did, either."

She looked at me for a second. "I try very hard not to arrest the wrong person, Ms. Martin. It looks bad, and opens us up for nasty lawsuits. If I arrest Mr. Collier, it will be because there is compelling evidence against him."

"I'm not sure that's helpful," I muttered. She shrugged. "So is there compelling evidence against him?"

Her voice and face were smooth, giving nothing away. "As of right now, not enough. He fits the description of one of the burglars, and he has no alibi for the time of the murder, or for the time of the robberies. His background indicates that this is something he might be involved with. He has a rudimentary understanding of the real estate business— that would be through you, Ms. Martin—and it certainly wouldn't surprise me to hear that someone had suggested that he tie her up and have his way with her. However, it's all circumstantial. And whereas I could probably get permission to arrest and charge him, based on circumstantial evidence, I probably wouldn't get a conviction."

"Good to know," I said. And then added, repentantly, "I'm sorry you're not making progress as fast as you'd like. We all want you to get whoever this guy is off the streets."

"No problem. I'll find him. And when I do..." Her smile was so cold I could hear the ice cubes clinking together, and I felt a chill creep down my back. Tennessee is still a death-penalty state, and I knew that when she caught him, she'd recommend he swing. Or fry. Or die by lethal injection, which I guess is the way they do it these days.

She added, looking around, "I don't see Mr. Collier."

I looked around too, automatically. "Did you expect him to be here?"

"He was at Mrs. Puckett's funeral."

"That was mostly because he wanted to talk to me, I think. He was still trying to find his grandmother then, and he might have been hoping that she'd be there."

While showing up here would only reinforce the idea that he'd had a connection to Lila, and he was much too smart to do that.

"Why, hello, Detective!" a syrupy voice said, tearing me out of my reverie. "And Savannah, too. How... surprising, to find the two of you together again."

I turned my head and saw Tim, who was standing in front of us, bouncing on the balls of his feet and beaming. Without the calming influence of Walker to remind him to dress down for the occasion, he was kitted out in skin-tight pants, a shimmery satin shirt open halfway down his beautifully tanned chest, and a blazer. All of it was unrelieved black, and it set off his coiffed blond hair and veneers wonderfully, but of course it was hideously inappropriate, even so. As was his demeanor, not that there was anything unusual in that.

Heidi Hoppenfeldt was standing behind him, with a plate piled high with hors d'oeuvres in one hand and a glass of punch in the other, chewing. "Hello, Heidi," I said politely. "I didn't expect to see you here. I didn't think you knew Lila."

Heidi shrugged, causing her voluminous tent-dress to sway. She had probably come for the food.

"Lamont, Briggs and Associates wanted to be supportive," Tim said smoothly, "so we came out in force."

"Lamont, Briggs and Associates?"

He smirked. "Walker agreed that a name-change was in order. Under the circumstances, it seemed like a good idea. I've already notified the NAR, the TAR, and the GNAR."

"Great," I muttered. It had been just over a month since I'd received my first batch of business cards with 'Walker Lamont Realty' on them, and now I'd have to toss them all in the trash and start over.

"And how have you been, Detective?" Tim turned his 200 watt smile on Tamara Grimaldi, who smiled back, though not as brightly.

"Very well, thank you, Mr. Briggs."

"I suppose you're here in your official capacity? Lila's misfortune was your gain, so to speak, in that you get paid to find her murderer." Tim's baby-blue eyes were bright and malicious. Detective Grimaldi's official capacity didn't seem to worry him overmuch, or at least not so much that he curbed his tongue. However, Tamara Grimaldi wasn't the gal to take any of Tim's nonsense lying down.

"Much the same way Mrs. Puckett's and Mrs. Webster's misfortunes were your gain, Mr. Briggs," she answered smoothly. "I wasn't aware that you knew Ms. Vaughn. It appears I've been amiss. Would you mind if I asked you a few questions?"

Tim looked like he minded, but under the circumstances, there wasn't a whole lot he could do. He had clearly let himself in for the extra attention. I made my excuses and left them alone, resisting the urge to pat Detective Grimaldi on the back to congratulate her on a superb job of getting under Tim's skin.

Heidi drifted back to the buffet table, and I continued my circuit of the room, saying hello to people I knew and offering my condolences to people who looked like they had known Lila. About halfway around I came across Kieran Greene, who was conversing with the vice-president of the local association of Realtors. Unlike Tim, Kieran was somberly dressed in a beautiful, charcoal gray suit and pale pink ascot, and he was clearly in an absolute tizzy over something. When I came closer, I saw that he had buttonholed the vice-president to tell her that but for the grace of God, it could have been him lying on a cold slab in the morgue. Or rather, by now, six feet under in Detroit. The vice-president looked haunted, and I took pity on her and cut Kieran smoothly off in mid-sentence. The vice-president escaped, with a grateful nod at me, and I turned to Kieran. "How are you?"

That simple query turned the torrent of words on me instead, and I smiled politely and let them wash over me, like water off a duck's back. I've spent many an interminable hour sitting through less scintillating conversation, with my back straight and an expression on my face that said I was hanging on every word. My mother had made sure I could do it in my sleep. I could also mouth the appropriate platitudes without even thinking about what to say. "I know what you're going through, Kieran. I blame myself too. But she has gone to a better place."

Kieran lowered his voice. "I saw you talking to the detective, and now she's talking to Tim Briggs. Does he know something about what happened?"

"As far as I know, nothing at all," I answered. Kieran looked disappointed. I was just about to explain that Tim and Detective Grimaldi had gotten off on the wrong foot during the investigation of Brenda Puckett's murder, when someone else spoke.

"Hi, Savannah. I didn't realize you knew Kieran."

It was Heather Price, who stuck her arm familiarly through Kieran's and kissed him on the cheek.

"I didn't realize *you* knew Kieran," I answered.

"Oh, sure." She grinned. "He's kind enough to send me business once in a while. I return the favor when I can, although it's not often. His clients sometimes have use for my services, but my clients usually come to me with a real estate agent already attached."

"Although Heather's boyfriend has been quite helpful in decorating my humble abode," Kieran said, smiling demurely.

"I'm sorry," I apologized. "I don't know what you do. Are you involved in some aspect of real estate, too?"

"I'm a stager," Heather said. A stager, for those of you not in the know, is a special kind of interior decorator who comes on the scene when a house is ready to go on the market and stages it to show to its best advantage. Something like a make-up artist for houses. Some stagers fill empty houses with stylish furniture they keep on hand for the purpose, while others just go through what's already there and put it together in better ways. Most people have way too many knick-knacks and personal items sitting around, and a stager is adept at cutting through the clutter. Tchotzkes and family photographs disappear into drawers, along with throw-rugs and refrigerator magnets, until what's left looks like a glossy magazine page.

"Did you stage Kieran's clients' house?" I asked. "The one that got robbed three weeks ago?"

Heather bit her lip, nodding. "Poor Paul and Simon. They lost all the paintings that Simon's family had spent so long gathering. I felt so bad for them."

"It was terrible," I agreed. "Although compared with what happened to Lila..."

"Oh, of course," Heather said quickly. "Paintings are just things; they can't compare to someone's life. Still, it was a terrible loss."

"I'm sure."

I was gearing up to ask if she had also staged the other house, the Worthington property where Lila had encountered the robbers, when an interruption occurred. This was the first time I had noticed Connie Fortunato being present, but here she was, standing at my elbow, talking past me. "You know, Heather, I've been meaning to talk to you about your work. Our house has been on the market for three weeks now, with no offers, and I thought maybe you'd be able to come by and give me some pointers on what to do to make it more appealing."

Personally, I had found the Fortunatos' house plenty appealing, except for the mirrored ceiling in the master bedroom. I also didn't mention that in a market where average days on the market are one hundred and twenty, three weeks isn't much at all. Far be it from me to keep another struggling young woman from making a living. Heather lit up. "I'd love to! When?"

"How about tonight? Perry is going out of town, and I was just planning to open a bottle of wine and take it easy. I'd love some company."

Heather hesitated. "Julio and I were planning to get together after he gets off work, but I suppose I could call and cancel..."

"Oh, no-no-no!" Connie shook her head. "I wouldn't dream of depriving you of an evening with that handsome Latin boyfriend of yours." Kieran giggled. "Tomorrow will be fine. Or the next day. I'm not in that much of a hurry."

It was Heather's turn to shake her head. "Julio never wants to stand in the way of my career. Maybe I can meet him early, and then come by your house later."

As they started talking about specific times, I excused myself to wander off, leaving the two of them and Kieran together.

It was just another few steps later that I came across another familiar face. Beau the beautiful house boy was here, in his jeans and leather jacket, although with an Oxford-shirt shielding the rest of his gloriousness from view. He was engaged in an animated conversation with several Realtors—all of them gay men; the profession attracts more than its fair share—and he flashed me a grin and a finger-wave, but didn't stop discoursing to say hello. I could hardly blame him for the omission; the Realtors were hanging on every word that fell from his delectable lips, and I felt certain he'd pick up more work than he could handle from this appearance. Of course it's horribly gauche to ply one's trade at a funeral, but Lila would have approved; had she been alive, she would probably have done the same thing.

Thirteen

The party—excuse me, funeral—broke up shortly thereafter, as all the Realtors—and Beau—ran off to their next appointments. I headed out myself too, although I didn't have an appointment to go to. Before I went, I looked for Detective Grimaldi, to share what I had just found out about Heather Price, and to suggest that she look into the background of Beau Riggins, whom I knew swung his feather-duster in the house where Kieran had been robbed, and who, considering he'd been present at Lila's funeral, might have a connection with the Worthington property as well. But the detective was nowhere to be found. When I tried to call her, her voice-mail picked up. I hoped her disappearance meant that she had caught a break in the case and was on her way to arrest someone for Lila's murder, but in actuality, it probably just meant that someone else had dropped dead, and her focus had shifted from Lila onto some other unfortunate victim. I left my information on the voice mail and went home.

I didn't have any plans for the rest of the evening, so once there, I did like Connie Fortunato and made myself comfortable on the sofa with a bodice ripper novel and a glass of white wine. But no sooner had I gotten to the first love scene, than the phone rang. The number on the display was familiar, and I felt my heart start to speed up. It took effort to keep my voice steady. "Hiya, Dix."

"Do you want the bad news or the worse news first?" my brother answered.

I arched my brows. "I'm not sure. If you're telling me both, I don't suppose it matters."

"And it isn't like you care what anybody says about Collier anyway," Dix said.

I pretended I couldn't hear the sarcasm. "I prefer to make up my own mind. So you've spoken to Cletus?"

"I've listened to Cletus," Dix corrected. "Cletus spoke to me."

"I see," I said.

"No," Dix told me, "you don't. I called him and said I wanted to check up on a story that Todd Satterfield had told me about Rafe Collier, and that was all I got out, because Cletus started raving. Is it true that Cletus's ex-wife is living with Collier?"

"She's taking care of Rafe's grandmother," I said. "They needed a nurse, she needed a job, and I don't think Rafe's there a whole lot, so I guess she has to live in. At least that was how he explained it to me."

"It isn't how Cletus explained it to me," Dix said.

"Marquita is 300 pounds and has all the cuddliness of a Rottweiler. I'm sure Rafe can control himself."

Dix didn't answer. "He went on and on for hours—at least that's what it felt like—but eventually he cooled down enough that I could ask him about Elspeth Caulfield."

"And?"

"And he confirmed that there was something between them in high school."

"Between Elspeth and Rafe?" Stupid question—the answer was obvious—but it gave me a few extra seconds to think.

"Of course between Elspeth and Rafe."

"Damn," I said. "Darn, I mean. I didn't want it to be true."

"Sis..." Dix began, and his voice was worried, like he was waiting for the other shoe to drop.

"Oh, get real, Dix. How often do I have to tell you I'm not interested in him that way?"

And even if I were, what he was doing twelve or fourteen years ago wouldn't be any of my business anyway.

"But," I added, "it's awfully difficult to imagine Elspeth having anything to do with him, isn't it? He's not so bad now, but back then, he was nothing but trouble, and if I remember correctly, Elspeth was a prim and proper preacher's kid."

"So you're thinking that if something happened between them, she was forced?"

"Maybe not forced, exactly. I don't think he would force himself on anyone. Coerced, maybe. Prevailed upon." Teenage boys can be very persuasive when they want to be, and Rafe could probably be more persuasive than most. "Didn't Cletus tell you what happened? According to Todd, he was there when whatever it was, did."

But Dix said that Cletus hadn't gone into detail. "All he said was, there was something between them back then. It was during his and Collier's last year at Columbia High—your first year, my third. The next fall, her parents took her out of school and she never came back."

"Rafe was in jail by then," I said. "That fight with Billy Scruggs happened during the summer."

"And that didn't have anything to do with it?"

Not as far as I knew. "Rafe said Billy Scruggs had beaten LaDonna black and blue, and when she refused to report him, Rafe decided to show Billy how it felt. He didn't say a word about anyone else being involved."

"In that case," Dix said, "I'm sure no one else was. Elspeth could have been four or maybe even five months pregnant by August or September, which would put whatever it was back to April or May."

"If she was pregnant at all," I reminded him. "And the only person who'd know that, is Elspeth."

"And Collier," Dix said.

I shook my head, even though he couldn't see me. "He'd know whether she'd had the opportunity to have gotten pregnant, at least by him, but she's the only one who'd know if she did. He'd only know if she told him. And that is if she told him the truth."

Dix conceded my point. "So what does that mean? You'll have to talk to Elspeth?"

I grimaced. "It may come to that. My main concern isn't actually with whether she was pregnant or not. That's personal, and none of my business. Although if she did have a baby and it's out there somewhere, Rafe ought to know."

"But surely it isn't your place to tell him," Dix protested.

He was probably right. Although someone should. "Todd intimated that whatever had happened back then, didn't reflect well on Rafe, and if she can accuse him of rape, that's not going to help his case with Detective Grimaldi at all."

"I see," Dix said. He didn't say anything else, but I could hear his thoughts loudly and clearly.

"I love you, Dix," I said. "Don't worry, OK? If I thought he was dangerous, I wouldn't have anything to do with him."

"That's good to know," Dix said in a half-choked voice. "Are you out of your mind, sis? He *is* dangerous, and you know it; you just refuse to acknowledge it."

"Let me rephrase," I said. "If I thought he was a danger to *me*, I wouldn't have anything to do with him. But he's not. He won't hurt me. On that score, at least, you can relax."

"I'm not sure that's possible," Dix said and hung up. I made a face and did the same.

And then I tried to get back into the bodice ripper, but found that the token struggles of the petite, blond heroine left me cold. More than that, chilled. Somehow, she ended up looking a lot like Elspeth Caulfield—a glorified Elspeth, since I couldn't remember her well enough to picture her features—while the dark and dangerous rogue in whose arms she was swooning, had Rafe's face and physique. I closed the paperback with an irritated snap and tossed it across the room. I meant for it to land on the other chair, really I did, but somehow it smacked against the wall instead. Hard. Quite unintentionally, of course.

I got to my feet. It was still early; maybe I could get hold of Rafe and ask him what had happened. If nothing had—nothing illegal, immoral or embarrassing—maybe he wouldn't mind telling me.

The house at 101 Potsdam Street was mostly dark, except for a flickering light in the kitchen window. I knocked on the door and waited.

"Oh," Marquita said when she saw me, "it's you again. Rafe ain't here."

"I assumed as much," I said, "seeing as there's no motorcycle. When will he be back?"

Marquita shrugged. She was wearing turquoise scrubs today, and they undulated gently whenever she moved. I glanced across her shoulder into the semidarkness of the house.

"Is Mrs. Jenkins around?"

"She's sleepin'," Marquita said, in a tone that dared me to do something about it. Of course I didn't, not only because the poor old dear needed her sleep, but because there wasn't anything she could tell me. She hadn't known Rafe when he was in high school.

"Would you mind if I asked you a question?"

Marquita blinked, and I could see that she was weighing her options. Refuse outright, or play along while retaining the right to refuse later? "What?"

"You knew Rafe in high school, right?"

"Sure," Marquita said.

"Do you remember a girl named Elspeth Caulfield?"

"Bitch," Marquita said.

I blinked. "Excuse me?"

"Why you wanna know 'bout Elspeth Caulfield?"

"Your ex-husband told my brother that Elspeth and Rafe had... um... been together in high school. I was just wondering if it was true."

Marquita folded her massive arms across her even more massive chest. Dolly Parton, the queen of cleavage, has nothing on Marquita. "You gonna stop chasin' him if I tell you it's true?"

"I wasn't aware of chasing him," I answered, with dignity. "But you know what? You don't have to tell me. I'll just ask someone else instead. Like Rafe. Or Elspeth."

Marquita muttered something. It sounded like a repetition of that word that rhymed with witch, so I decided not to ask her to elaborate. Instead I just added sweetly, "Don't bother telling Rafe I here. I'll probably see him before you do. He knows where to find me when he wants me."

Marquita's only comment was to slam the door in my face. I wasn't surprised; in her position, I would have done the same thing. If I could have. The door must have weighed almost as much as she did, and Marquita managed to close it with a no doubt satisfying bang.

It was way too late in the day to drive down to Sweetwater to track down Elspeth, but that was OK. Common courtesy dictated that I should call ahead to tell her I was coming.

Or maybe not; maybe it would be better to take her by surprise. It's horribly ill-bred to show up uninvited and unannounced, but mother would never know, and the surprise might make Elspeth more inclined to talk. If I called first, she might try to put me off, or make sure not to be there when I arrived. I didn't have any plans for the following day, now that Gary Lee and Charlene had cooled on the house-hunting, so maybe I could just get up tomorrow morning and head for Elspeth's house. I could be there by ten and back home by one, without anyone being the wiser.

That settled in my brain, I looked up Elspeth's address online and printed out a MapQuest so I'd know where to go, and I then went back to my book again. This time I skipped the love scene and went on from

152 | Jenna Bennett

there, not wanting to tempt fate again. But no sooner had I got into the action, than the phone rang once more.

"Ms. Martin?" Tamara Grimaldi's voice was terse, and my heart started speeding up. What had happened now?

"Yes, Detective? What can I do for you?"

"I got your message. I'd like to talk to you a little more."

"Sure," I said, settling into the sofa.

"Could you come by my office in the morning?"

"Oh. I suppose."

"Thank you." She made to hang up, and I yelped. She added, impatiently, "What?"

"Is something wrong? You sound strange."

"We'll talk about it tomorrow." This time she really did hang up. I went back to the book, but gave up after ten or fifteen minutes, when I realized that I'd just read the same page over and over, and I still had no idea what it said.

NASHVILLE POLICE PLAZA IS LOCATED in downtown, in a modern brick building across the street from the municipal offices and the newly renovated courthouse. Detective Grimaldi's office is on the second floor, and she was waiting for me when I got there at a few minutes after nine. "Come in, Ms. Martin. Have a seat."

There were two chairs in front of her desk, one piled high with a leaning tower of folders, the other conspicuously empty and free from dust. She must have cleaned it off before I came.

"Thank you," I said, touched and a little uneasy. She sat, too, folding her hands on top of the desk. She looked horrible, with tight lips and dark rings under her bloodshot eyes. I added, with a mounting sense of dread, "What's wrong?"

She looked at me in silence for a moment. "There's been another murder."

"Another...? A murder like Lila's, you mean? Who died?"

"Not a realtor this time. The owner of a house in Brentwood, that was also on the market. She must have surprised a burglar when she came home yesterday afternoon, and he killed her. Her jewelry is missing, and so is a priceless painting that was hanging on her wall. She was found by a friend who came by to spend the evening with her while her husband was out of town."

"Oh, my God!" I said, wild-eyed. "You're not talking about Connie Fortunato, are you?"

This may sound like a giant leap of deduction, but in actuality, it wasn't so big. Connie owned a house in Brentwood, which was for sale. I had seen the priceless Georgia O'Keeffe on her wall. Her husband was out of town, and I had heard her arrange with Heather Price that Heather would come by last night.

"You know Mrs. Fortunato?" Detective Grimaldi asked.

"Of course I know Mrs. Fortunato! I spent Sunday afternoon at her house, hosting an open house for Tim. I saw her again on Monday night, at the planning meeting for the Eye Ball—she's another of the volunteers—and she was at Lila's funeral yesterday. She asked Heather Price to come over to her house last night, to give her advice on staging it."

"Ms. Price was the person who called us," Detective Grimaldi said. "Which is why I called you, because I knew, from the message you left me, that you know Ms. Price."

Silence reigned for a moment, while I tried to catch my breath and get my brain around the fact that another woman I knew had been murdered. Detective Grimaldi started talking, more to give me time to gather myself than because these were facts I needed to know.

"When Ms. Price left the funeral yesterday afternoon, she drove to East Nashville, where her boyfriend has his home and his business. They had an early dinner together, and then she left and drove to Brentwood, to the Fortunatos' house. She got there around 7:30. When there was no answer to her knock, she tried the door. It was locked, but she carries one of those digital key-code boxes that Realtors have..." I nodded, "...and she used that to get the extra key and open the door. Mrs. Fortunato didn't answer when Ms. Price called her name, and Ms. Price thought it was strange, seeing as Mrs. Fortunato had told her she'd be home alone all evening. Also, Mrs. Fortunato's car was parked in the garage."

"And when Heather walked into Perry and Connie's bedroom, she found Connie?"

Detective Grimaldi nodded. "Tied to the bed and strangled, just like Lila Vaughn."

"Oh, my God!" I said, burying my face in my hands. "What's going on? Who is doing this?"

"If I knew," Tamara Grimaldi said, "I'd be arresting him, not sitting here talking it over with you. There was no sign of forced entry, and so far, we've gathered a surprising amount of physical evidence—hairs, fibers, fingerprints—which isn't so surprising after all, if you hosted an open house there this weekend. Do you keep a list of the people who visit those things?"

I nodded. "I can keep in touch with them until they either buy something, or die of old age. Would you like a copy of my list?"

Detective Grimaldi said she would, and gave me her fax number so I could fax it to her when I got home. I wrote it down, and then I hesitated for a moment before facing the music. "I may as well tell you. Rafe Collier's name is going to be on that list. He showed up at the Fortunatos' house after you finished with him on Sunday afternoon."

"You don't say?" Tamara Grimaldi said.

"He told you he would, didn't he? Anyway, I'm sure, once you get around to matching your physical evidence, you'll find his fingerprints all over the place. Along with a lot of other people's, of course. There are eighteen names on the list, if I remember correctly. And then there are all the other people—prospective homebuyers and their agents—who have been visiting the house in the three weeks it's been on the market."

"I don't suppose you have any idea where Mr. Collier was yesterday afternoon or early evening?"

I hid a grimace. "I'm afraid not. He wasn't with me."

And he hadn't been home, either. Unless Marquita had lied. Which was certainly possible; she'd never made a secret of wishing I'd stay the hell away from Rafe.

"If you should happen to speak to him today," Grimaldi said, "let him know I'd like another word, would you?"

"You're not arresting him, are you?"

She looked up at that. "No, Ms. Martin. Not yet. I'll need more evidence before I can arrest anyone. I just want to know if he can provide an alibi for yesterday."

"If I see him, I'll let him know," I said.

She nodded her thanks, and then, just before I left the room, she did a Columbo. "By the way, Ms. Martin, since you're here... Here's the information about that store we discussed, where you can purchase defense spray. Tell them I sent you. This seems like an excellent time to arm yourself, if you'll forgive my saying so."

I took the business card she handed me and beat it out of there.

Fourteen

Elspeth Caulfield lived on the northwest side of Sweetwater, in a little community called Damascus. It was closer to Nashville but further from the interstate, so it took me as long to get there as it would have to go to Sweetwater. With everything I had on my mind, though, the drive flew by, and before I knew it, I was standing in front of a run-down Queen Anne Victorian badly in need of a paint-job. Four big, black Labrador Retrievers were barking and slavering at me from inside the fence, and I was considering my next move carefully. If I opened the gate and walked in, they'd jump on me and knock me to the ground, and then they'd either maul me or lick me to death. And even if I got away with my life, my silk blouse and linen skirt would be beyond help. On the other hand, if I didn't open the gate and go in, I wouldn't be able to see Elspeth.

I was still standing outside the fence, dithering, when the front door opened. A petite blonde came out. Looking at her, I realized I did indeed remember Elspeth Caulfield.

A few weeks back, Todd had told me I didn't look a day older than when we'd dated in high school. It was a blatant lie, and I was well aware of it. Elspeth, however, really didn't look any older. She was still just a fraction over five feet tall, and her figure hadn't developed much in the past ten or twelve years, either. In her oversized denim shirt and with her hair pulled up into a pony-tail, she looked like a little girl playing dress-up in her daddy's clothes. She had wide, unblinking, very pale blue eyes, and a smooth face totally devoid of make-up. Even her voice was girlish, high pitched and breathy. "Can I help you?"

"I hope so," I answered. "My name is Savannah Martin. You probably don't remember me, but we went to high school together. For a year or so. Before you... um... left."

"Of course." She looked like she didn't actually remember, but was too polite to say so. Mother had brought me up to do the same thing. There's nothing more galling to a man's ego—to anyone's ego, I suppose—than to be forgotten.

"I hope you don't mind my stopping by without calling first? I was in the neighborhood."

"Of course not," Elspeth said. Politesse dictated that she invite me in, but she didn't, just waited for me to continue. I looked around, at the house and overgrown yard, searching for something to say. Something complimentary, to break the ice and ease into what I really wanted to talk about.

"Nice place."

"Thank you." She glanced around at it.

"Did I mention that I'm a Realtor now?"

"It must have slipped your mind. Although I'm afraid I'm not interested in selling."

"Oh, I didn't think you were," I said. "Although, if there comes a time, I hope you'll keep me in mind." I took a breath. "So how have you been? I haven't seen you since... um..."

"High school," Elspeth supplied.

I nodded. "What are you doing with yourself these days? How long have you been back in town?" *And where did you go, anyway? And more importantly, why…?*

"I work from home," Elspeth said.

"I see. Um…" I looked around, vaguely. "Would you like to go get a cup of coffee or something? It's almost lunch time." I had passed Beulah's Meat'n Three just a few miles down the road.

"I should probably get back to my computer," Elspeth said. "It was nice to see you again, Savannah." She started to turn away.

"Wait a second!" I exclaimed. "I actually came to ask you something."

"Really?" Her tone was politely inquiring, but nothing more. Neither curious, nor even especially interested. Surely it wasn't possible for someone to be so completely, utterly, unfailingly polite all the time? I mean, God knows I try, but I've got a long way to go before I stop putting my foot in my mouth on a regular basis, and even Mother has her moments of really quite astonishing rudeness. Deliberate ones, usually. Elspeth's measured responses made me want to shake her to try to get some other kind of reaction from her, but of course I couldn't do that. She was on the other side of the fence, for one thing, and for another, the dogs would probably hurt me if I did.

However, I watched her closely as I asked, "You remember Rafael Collier, don't you?"

If I hadn't been watching, I'm not sure I would have caught it. Her expression changed for just a tenth of a second, and then it was back to being smooth and bland. "Naturally."

"Have you seen him lately?"

Elspeth shook her head. "Not for years."

I hesitated. "I understand you two hooked up once back in high school?"

"Oh…" She laughed, a tinkly, little laugh. "I wouldn't say we hooked up, exactly. 'Hook up' is such an unattractive expression, don't you think?"

"I suppose," I said, although it had never struck me as such. There are certainly a lot of uglier words one could use for a couple of teenagers having sex, if one were inclined. "But you were... um... together, right?"

"I knew him," Elspeth said.

I resisted the urge to roll my eyes. She was approximately as easy to pin down as... well... Rafe. "So did I." Although not in the Biblical sense. The way Elspeth supposedly did.

"I don't want to talk about it," Elspeth said.

"I understand. And I hate to ask. But what happened to you might have some bearing on a criminal case—a rape and murder—that happened in Nashville recently."

Someone else might have looked shocked or appalled. Elspeth just looked suspicious. "Are you working for the police?"

"Not exactly."

"For him?"

I shook my head. "As I told you, I'm a Realtor. The woman who died was a friend of mine. I'm trying to find out who killed her."

"And you think he might have done it?"

The way she kept saying *he* and *him*, but never Rafe's name, was interesting. If I had specialized in psychology instead of law in college, it might have been even more interesting. As it was, I assumed she had been traumatized by whatever had happened to her, and avoiding his name was helping her keep the memories at a distance. I was getting a bad feeling about this.

"Actually," I said apologetically, "I'd be very surprised if he did. But the police think he might have."

"So you're trying to help him?"

Admitting to trying to help Rafe would probably be a bad idea. "Not really. I'm just trying to find out who killed my friend. But she knew him. And I thought, if what happened between you two back then could shed some light on whether he'd be capable of doing something like this now..." I trailed off.

Elspeth nodded. "I'm sorry, but I can't help you." she said.

I stared at her. "Excuse me?"

The dogs were rooting around in the yard, and now one of them stuck its enormous snout through two pickets and put its cold nose on my leg. I jumped.

"I'm sorry," Elspeth said again. "But surely you can understand why I can't talk about it. About him. You're a lady, and we don't discuss things like... that."

Well, no. We didn't. Not usually. But even I made exceptions in dire straits. And as long as I felt fairly certain my mother would never hear about it.

Elspeth turned to walk away. "I'm sorry you had to drive all the way down here for nothing."

It wouldn't have been for nothing had she just had the—pardon me—balls to overcome her ladylike vapors, but there didn't seem to be any sense in pointing that out. All I could do was watch, with my hands curled into frustrated fists, as she walked away with all four hounds on her heels. The ornately carved door closed behind her with a thud.

I ENDED UP GOING TO BEULAH's Meat'n Three by myself. It was on the way back to the interstate, I was hungry, and frankly, I was so angry I had a hard time seeing straight. A break for some food and time to gather myself might do me good. So I pulled into the graveled lot beside the cinderblock building, and walked in.

Beulah's Meat'n Three has been a fixture for longer than I've been alive. Nobody named Beulah has anything to do with the place anymore, or has for as long as I can remember, but when I sat down at a table by the window, I saw another familiar face.

Yvonne McCoy was someone else I'd gone to school with, but whom I'd barely known. Like I'd told Lila that last time we'd gotten together, my mother had been particular about the schoolmates

Catherine, Dix and I were allowed to associate with. Rafe was unacceptable because he was a Collier, with all that that embodied, as well as because he was a handful in his own right. Drinking, fighting, joyriding... he'd been in trouble with Sheriff Satterfield practically from the moment he could walk. Elspeth was unacceptable because her father was a weird, fundamentalist preacher, while the Martins and the Calverts—mother's people in Georgia—were good old-fashioned Southern Baptists. And Yvonne had been unacceptable because she was, not to put too fine a point on it, common as dirt, and a tramp to boot. Not that I'd ever considered the possibility of becoming friendly with any of them. Rafe was three years older than me, and Trouble with a capital T. Even at the tender age of fourteen, I had been aware of that. Elspeth had been so quiet and unassuming that I'd barely noticed her existence, and Yvonne was her total opposite. There was nothing shy and retiring about Yvonne. She was loud, raucous, and fun-loving, with flaming red hair and the dubious distinction of having had the biggest breasts at Columbia High. She was also, in her own way, a decent person who'd never take advantage of another human being or deliberately hurt anyone. And at the moment, she was exactly the person I needed. I greeted her with a brilliant smile.

"Hi, Yvonne."

She squinted at me for a moment or two, or even longer, before she seemed to recognize me. Not the sharpest tool in the shed, Yvonne. "Hiya, Savannah. It's Savannah, ain't it? Dix Martin's little sister?"

I nodded. "I didn't realize you knew my brother."

Yvonne grinned. "Not as well as I'd like. We were in the same class in school, but he'd never look twice at somebody like me. How's he doing?"

"He's fine," I said. "Married, of course. He and his wife have two little girls. Abigail and Hannah. They live just outside Sweetwater, in that new subdivision. Copper Creek."

Yvonne nodded. "Shoulda known he'd be married. How 'bout you? I remember your wedding. Never saw such a to-do. How's your hubby?"

"Remarried," I said succinctly. "You?"

"Oh, I'm single again. Can't seem to keep a boyfriend to save my life. But you don't wanna know 'bout that. What can I get you, sugar?"

Actually, I did want to know about that, so I ordered quickly— "Water with lemon and a Chef Salad, please,"—and returned to the previous subject. "Would you mind if I asked you a question?"

"Shoot," Yvonne said, without hesitation.

"You remember Rafe Collier, right?"

"Who could forget?" She said it with what I can only describe as a lascivious grin.

I smiled. Just as I'd hoped. "How about Elspeth Caulfield?"

"Sure. Saw her just a coupla weeks ago, down at the post office. Mailing a book or something to New York City."

"I just came from her house," I said. "I was trying to find out what happened between them back in high school, but she wouldn't tell me."

Yvonne squinted at me. "Between Rafe and Elspeth?"

I nodded.

"Hang on a second." She turned and walked away. I watched her walk across the floor and go behind the counter, where she placed my order on the little wheel in the kitchen window. Then she filled up a glass with water and popped in a lemon wedge and carried it back to me. "What d'you wanna know that for?" she asked, as if she'd never left. "You thinking of getting involved with him?"

"Lord, no!" I said.

"I didn't think so. So why?"

I took a breath. "A friend of mine in Nashville was raped and murdered last weekend. She knew Rafe. The police think he might have done it."

"Lord'a-mercy!" Yvonne said, and crossed herself piously, although I doubted very much that she was a Catholic, let alone a practicing one.

"Someone suggested that whatever happened between them wasn't consensual."

"You mean he raped her?" Yvonne shook her head. "Knowing him, I can't imagine he'd have to. Usually, she was the one running after him, not the other way around. Although she did keep moaning about being ruined, afterwards."

"Yikes," I said, although my mind was, regrettably, tangled up elsewhere. "When you say you knew him, do you mean…?"

Yvonne grinned. "Hell, yeah."

"You were… um… intimate?"

"Sugar," Yvonne said confidingly, "were we ever."

"Wow," I said. "So… there was no persuading necessary? For you?"

She put her head back and laughed, red curls bouncing. "Are you kidding?" A couple of the other customers turned to look at her, curiously. Yvonne didn't seem to notice. "I wasn't about to say no to him, sugar. Although Elspeth was different. She didn't sleep around. I never saw her so much as look at anybody else." She fixed me with a stare. "You sure you're not wanting him for yourself?"

"Positive," I said. "So when he slept with Elspeth—that was after you and he slept together, right?—didn't it bother you that he was with somebody else?"

She smiled, and it was a particularly patient smile, the sort of smile one gives a slow but well-intentioned student who just doesn't get it. "It wasn't like that. It was just sex. Something to do one night when nothing else was happening. He never suggested it again, and then there was the whole thing with Elspeth, and then summer vacation, and then he went to jail. I ain't seen him since. How's he looking these days?"

"Good," I said, and then caught myself. "I mean… healthy, you know?"

Yvonne nodded. "You used'ta date Todd Satterfield, right?"

I nodded.

She didn't say anything else about it. "I guess I'd better go get your salad. Unless you got something more you wanna ask?"

I shook my head. "I think that's it. Although if you remember anything else, or hear anything, would you mind getting in touch with me?" I handed her my business card. She squinted at it.

"Realtor, huh? I always figured you'd end up marrying Todd and driving a station wagon with three kids in the back. But good for you, sugar." She stuffed the card into her apron pocket, where I hoped it wouldn't get lost among the credit card slips and tips, and wandered off.

When the phone rang shortly after I arrived home, and Tamara Grimaldi's number appeared on the display, I accepted the inevitable with nary a grimace. "Hi, Detective. I was just thinking about you."

"You don't say? Do you have a minute?"

"Do I have a choice?" I muttered, and added, more loudly, "Of course. What can I do for you?"

I could hear the shuffling of papers in the background. "I just received the results of the physical evidence from the Fortunato residence."

"Anything surprising?" I asked, my voice reasonably level.

"Actually, yes. Your fingerprints are all over the place, of course—we took them back when Mrs. Puckett was murdered, so they're in our files—and so are Mr. Collier's."

"I wouldn't expect anything different," I said. "He was there, he helped me close up, and he wasn't wearing gloves, so it's not surprising he should have left prints."

"Of course." The detective's voice was smooth. "The DNA in the bedroom is the most interesting, however."

Oh, Lord! My heart stuttered for a second, or maybe it just felt that way. Maybe it was indigestion. "How so?"

Tamara Grimaldi hesitated. "We found traces of semen on the carpet in the master bedroom. It didn't match Mr. Fortunato's. Would you happen to remember anything about a young man by the name of Hodges, who visited your open house?"

I blinked. "Gary Lee? Of course. He and his wife are clients of mine. Why?"

The detective's voice was studiously unemotional. "The sample matched his DNA."

"You found Gary Lee's semen in Connie Fortunato's bedroom? But..."

And then the brick dropped, as I recalled the giggling and whispering behind closed doors, and Charlene's misbuttoned blouse and their search for the most mind-blowing bedroom in Nashville. I had to resist the temptation to thunk my head against the kitchen counter. The bump that would result, wouldn't be worth it. "Oh, God!"

"What?"

"Oh, nothing. Just damning myself for a fool. Again."

"So you can explain the semen?"

"I can try," I said, with a wholly unladylike giggle, "although you may want to give them a call yourself, and talk to them about it. They'd be more likely to come clean with you than with me, I think. But for what it's worth, here's what I think has been going on: I've spent the past week showing them houses, and I think they've been having sex in all the bedrooms."

The detective was silent for a beat or two. "I see," she said. "Why would they do that?"

"No idea. They're newlyweds, so maybe they just can't keep their hands off each other. Newlyweds do that, I hear. Or maybe they read about it somewhere and decided to give it a try. Like people having sex in airplane lavatories and elevators and dressing rooms. Or maybe there's an internet chat-room for maniacs who lead their realtors on in order to have sex in other people's houses." As I was speaking, my initial amusement was giving way to annoyance.

"I'll find out," Tamara Grimaldi said soothingly, "and have a stern chat with them at the same time."

"Thank you. By the way, how did you come by Gary Lee's DNA? Originally, I mean? Does he have a criminal record, too?" He had brown eyes, anyway, although no one could mistake his scrawny bass-playing frame for Rafe's, not even in padded coveralls.

"Someone sued him for child support. There was paternity testing done."

"And was it his baby?" I caught myself and blushed. "Never mind. It's none of my business. I was actually thinking about someone... I mean, something else."

"I see," Tamara Grimaldi said. "Is this imaginary pregnancy of yours taking on a life of its own, Ms. Martin?"

She waited politely while I ground my teeth. A few weeks ago, when I first met her, I had told the detective that Tondalia Jenkins, Rafe's grandmother, was confused as to who I was, and for that matter who he was. Some of the time she had no idea that she knew him at all. Other times she knew exactly who he was, and the rest of the time she thought he was his father. During those times when she thought Rafe was Tyrell, she also thought I was LaDonna, and that I was pregnant with Rafe. Horribly confusing, I know. Also untrue, of course, but the detective liked to yank my chain.

"No," I said eventually, when I had pried my teeth apart. "It's just that my... um... Todd told me about someone who supposedly got pregnant back when we were in high school, and there were some rumors at the time about the paternity of the child. It's on my mind, that's all."

"I see." She waited. I knew what she was doing, and I really didn't want to respond to it, but eventually I felt compelled to speak.

"Todd is worried that I'm developing an interest in Rafe. He's been telling me horror-stories. One of which concerns a girl named Elspeth Caulfield, who had some association with Rafe back in high school. She won't tell me what it was."

"She might tell me," Tamara Grimaldi suggested.

"She might. Or not. It happened twelve years ago, and I'm sure you have more important things to do than tracking down something like that. It's not like I care."

"Of course not," the detective said.

"You said you were going to have another talk with Malcolm Rodgers. With everything that's been going on, I don't suppose you've had a chance to do that?"

"Actually, I have." She shuffled some more papers. "Mr. Rodgers has an alibi for last night. He was with his buddies at a local bar, waking his ex-wife until closing time. They poured him into bed at three in the morning. He has an alibi for the robbery, too."

"Well, phooey! I liked the idea of Malcolm doing it."

"You like the idea of anyone but Mr. Collier doing it."

"No, I..." I stopped when it became apparent I couldn't even convince myself. "Well, yes. I'd rather have it be someone else. Someone I don't know. I mean, I spend time with him. I don't like the idea that he's capable of something like this."

"Understandably," Detective Grimaldi conceded. "The M.O. for yesterday's theft of the O'Keeffe was different from the other robberies. It might be the same group of people, who have decided to change their *modus operandi* now that everyone is aware of the open house threat, or it could be a copy cat, someone who decided that he or she would take advantage of the open house robberies to stage a small coup of their own. I'm looking for links."

"Like the fact that Rafe visited the Fortunatos' house on Sunday?"

"Or like the fact that Heather Price worked for both the other sellers, and was a friend of Connie Fortunato's."

"Did she really?" I said. "I started to ask her about it at the funeral yesterday, but we were interrupted."

"She did. And her boyfriend Julio is connected."

I wrinkled my forehead. "Connected to what? The robberies? The murders?"

"The mob," Detective Grimaldi said. "Or rather, since we don't have a true mafia here in Tennessee, a large criminal organization with ties to a lot of different illegal enterprises."

"You're kidding!"

"I wish I were."

"Why don't you arrest him?"

"Other than that I work homicides, you mean? And until the time he kills someone, he's none of my business?"

"Well, yes. Aside from that."

Detective Grimaldi hesitated for a moment. "It's a TBI thing," she said. "The Tennessee Bureau of Investigations. We handle local law enforcement, but they handle anything statewide, just like the FBI handles anything that crosses state lines. I'm sure they're working on it. But in the meantime, we leave him alone. Unless he trespasses on our turf, of course. If I can pin Lila's or Connie's murder on him, I'll nail him to the wall, and the Teds can just learn to live with it."

"The Teds?"

"You've heard of the Feds? It's what they call FBI-agents. A Ted is a TBI-agent."

"Oh," I said. "Funny."

"No, not really. Anyway, Julio Melendez has connections. He owns an import/export business, so he'd be able to move the merchandise that was stolen from the two houses. Maybe even the O'Keeffe, although that may be a little out of his league. Still, I'm not certain it was stolen by the same group. I think I'm going to have to have a talk with Julio."

"That sounds like it might be a good idea. Is he by any chance tall and dark with brown eyes?"

"Now that you mention it," Detective Grimaldi said, "I do believe he is. Interesting."

I nodded. "I'll talk to you later, Detective. Good luck." And I hung up, leaving the detective to think happy thoughts of putting one over on the Teds.

Fifteen

A quick check of the phone book showed me that Julio Melendez's import/export business was located not too terribly far from my apartment. I got in the car and headed out.

As I had explained to Todd a week or two ago, Historic East Nashville no longer enjoys the distinction of being the worst neighborhood in the city. People don't take their lives in their hands whenever they cross the Cumberland River anymore. At least not usually. We still have our share of murders, rapes, burglaries, and thefts, but no more than any other part of town.

Demographically, East Nashvillians are a diverse bunch. There's a high concentration of gays of both sexes, and various sorts of artists and musicians, with a growing population of young professionals and families with kids of school age. Racially, it's also a mixed bag. Old-time blacks and poor whites still cling to the neighborhood where they were born, trying to withstand the onslaught of the terminally young and hip. They're fighting a losing battle; East Nashville has been 'discovered' by the upwardly mobile, and the old guard is being squeezed out by higher property taxes and dirty looks.

Julio Melendez's business was located beyond the renovated areas, in an industrial park down by the Cumberland River. And in contrast to the picture in my head, all it was, was a warehouse. No storefront, no fancy sign, no architect-designed landscaping; just a square box with a single door and no windows. A tractor trailer was parked on the side of the building, being loaded. I pulled into the parking lot across the street—it belonged to a charitable organization—nosed the car into a spot facing the import/export business, and killed the engine. Then I slunk low in my seat and stared at the front door of Melendez Import/Export.

I was still sitting there an hour later, but I admit I was thinking about leaving. I was bored out of my skull, and beginning to be in need of a ladies' room. The door across the street still hadn't opened. Nobody had left or arrived. The same four cars were still parked in the lot. (A black Mercedes, a yellow VW Bug, a ten-year-old burgundy Dodge, and an older pick-up truck.) The tractor trailer had left, but had not been replaced by another. The loading dock door had been closed after it drove off. Nobody had come out of either building—the import/export one, or the one behind me—to ask what I thought I was doing there.

It was starting to turn darker, and I wondered if maybe I ought to go home. It wasn't the kind of neighborhood I'd want to be caught dead in after dark. Literally. But then the door across the street opened. I sat up in my seat. A middle aged woman came out, followed by a younger woman and a man. They stood for a minute in the lot, talking, before they got into their respective cars. The older lady took the Dodge, the younger woman the Beetle, and the man the truck. And then they drove off, leaving the Mercedes where it was. Neither of them looked my way. I slouched back down in the seat.

The man hadn't looked anything like a Julio Melendez—or, as Connie Fortunato (bless her heart) had put it, handsome or Latin—so I assumed my quarry was still inside. The Mercedes must be his. Maybe, if I stuck it out just a little bit longer, he'd leave work too, and I could get a good look at him.

But thirty minutes later, he still hadn't appeared, and I was *really* starting to need a lipstick break. I'd never make it on an all-night stakeout. And there wasn't even anywhere close-by I could go and beg the use of a facility. Unless I wanted to run around the corner and squat under a bush, of course, but that wasn't a possibility I wanted to entertain. My only option was to drive a mile to the nearest restaurant or grocery store and then come back, but by then Julio Melendez might have left, and I would have missed my chance to get a look at him.

I was just about to give in to the inevitable (the restaurant, not the bush) when there was a rap on the window. I sat up with a jolt and a squeak, and came close to—pardon my vulgarity—letting it all out right then and there. Under the circumstances, it would have been mortifying beyond belief.

"Open the door," Rafe ordered. I did, and he slid into the passenger seat next to me. Beyond him, I could see that monstrous Harley-Davidson he drove everywhere. I hadn't even noticed him pull up.

"What are you doing here?" I blurted, plumbing-problems momentarily forgotten in the surprise of seeing him. He arched a brow.

"Had some business to take care of. You?"

I hesitated, and then decided I may as well tell him the truth. "I'm trying to get a look at Julio Melendez."

"Why?"

"To see if he looks like you. Enough to be able to pass for you in coveralls and a ski mask."

He stared at me. "You're joking, right?"

I shook my head. "Whoever killed Lila dressed like that—someone saw him leaving after the murder—and he probably managed to fool her for long enough to get her to open the door for him. She thought he was you."

He didn't say anything, and I continued.

"Julio's girlfriend worked for both the houses that were robbed, and he has the ability to move the merchandise that was stolen, so he's a logical suspect. Plus, Detective Grimaldi says he's connected."

Unlike me, Rafe didn't need to have the word 'connected' explained to him. I waited for what seemed like a long time for him to say something, and when he didn't, I added, "I notice you're not denying that you're who he'd have to look like in order to get Lila to open the door for him."

He glanced at me out of the corner of his eyes. "No point in denying it, is there?"

"Not really," I said apologetically. "There never was much doubt, at least not in my mind."

We sat in silence for a moment or two. Then Rafe added, with another flash of brown eyes, "I didn't kill her."

"I never thought you did. By the way, Tamara Grimaldi wants to talk to you again. She said if I saw you, to let you know. And to hold yourself in readiness for a lineup."

He grimaced, but didn't comment on the news that he'd be asked to parade in front of a potential witness. I wondered if Grimaldi would bring Kieran Greene in at the same time as whoever she'd found in Lila's building, and whether Kieran would be able to pick Rafe out of a lineup. "What does she want to talk to me about?"

It was my turn to grimace. "To see if you can provide an alibi for yesterday afternoon. I hope you can."

"What happened yesterday afternoon?"

"There was another murder. Connie Fortunato was killed and her Georgia O'Keeffe painting stolen."

"The woman we saw on Sunday?"

I nodded.

He didn't say anything else for a moment. "When?" he asked finally. "How?"

"The same way as Lila. Tied to the bed and strangled. At least I assume so, although the detective didn't go into detail. And it was sometime yesterday afternoon or early evening. She was at Lila's funeral, and Detective Grimaldi said she thought Connie might have come home and surprised someone in the process of robbing the house. Apparently Perry had gone off somewhere. A woman named Heather Price—Julio's girlfriend—found her around 7:30 or 8:00."

We both watched the building across the street as if something was actually going on over there worth watching. Time passed. Quite a lot of it, while we just sat there without speaking.

"You know," I said eventually, my mouth moving without much conscious thought, "I just don't get it."

He glanced over. "Get what?"

"Nothing. Never mind." I blushed.

"You sure?"

I sent him a sideways look. It was difficult to communicate this way, side by side, when I couldn't see his face and gauge his reactions. On the other hand, it might make it easier to discuss touchy subjects. And I *did* want to know.

"I don't understand the whole tie-me-to-the-bed thing. It would never cross my mind to let anyone tie me down. Especially someone I didn't know. Yet Lila seemed to think it sounded exciting." Unless she'd been fibbing. "She did ask you to tie her to the bed, right?"

Rafe shrugged. "Some women seem to get off on it."

"Some men too, I'm sure." I hesitated. "Have you ever... um...?"

"Been tied to my bed for some woman to have her way with? Can't say as I have, darlin'. But if you'd like to change that, I'd be happy to oblige."

"No," I said, blushing, "that won't be necessary."

"You sure? Might be fun."

"No thanks. I didn't mean that, anyway. I was wondering if you'd ever... you know...?"

"Tied someone up? Not that way. I prefer to leave a woman's hands free. Things get more interesting that way."

"Right," I said weakly. And I admit it, I went a little cross-eyed at the thought.

Rafe chuckled. "Good thing you're sitting down, or you'd be passing out right about now. Relax, darlin'. I ain't fixing to seduce you tonight."

"Thank you. I mean..."

"I know what you mean. Though I don't know what the hell you're so afraid of. I ain't gonna hurt you."

"I know that," trembled on my tongue. I bit it back. I might think I knew that, but did I really?

"I saw a couple of your old girlfriends today," I said instead.

He sat back. "Yeah? What were you doing? Looking for recommendations?"

"Not exactly." Although, come to think of it, wasn't that exactly what I'd been doing?

"Who d'you talk to? And what did they say?"

I took a deep breath. "Elspeth Caulfield, for one."

"Who's she?" He sounded sincere, like he really couldn't remember. I wasn't sure whether that was a good or a bad thing.

"She was your girlfriend in high school," I said.

He shook his head. "I didn't have a girlfriend in high school."

"Fine. She was one of the many girls you dallied with."

He laughed, a genuine, amused chuckle. "Dallied? Darlin', that's a fancy word for what just comes naturally."

"Not in Elspeth's case, I think. Look it up in the dictionary sometime. Supposedly she had a nervous breakdown when you dumped her. Either that, or a baby."

His whole demeanor changed. His eyes turned sharp and he straightened up. Not an easy thing to do in the front seat of a Volvo. "What the hell?"

"Well, that's what they said, anyway."

"They, who?"

I explained what Todd had told me, and what Dix had gleaned from listening to Cletus Johnson rant. Rafe snorted when I mentioned Cletus's name.

"So I drove down to Damascus this morning," I finished, "to talk to Elspeth myself. And while I was at it, I talked to Yvonne McCoy, too."

His lips curved. He may not remember Elspeth, but Yvonne obviously rang a bell. "I bet Yvonne gave me a good review, didn't she?"

I turned sideways in my seat and watched him. "Pretty much. She said you only got together once, to pass the time, and it never happened again. She seemed disappointed."

He grinned.

"Elspeth wouldn't talk about you at all. Said we were ladies and didn't talk about things like that. Which I take to mean sex, or worse."

"Worse?"

"Well... rape."

Something dangerous flashed in his eyes. "You think I raped her?"

No. But I wasn't sure how much of that instinctive rejection was because it was what I wanted to believe, and how much was accurate. So to be safe I said, "I'm not sure what I think. Did you?"

He contemplated me for a second before he answered. "I've never forced myself on a woman in my life. Never had to."

"Not even Elspeth?"

"Least of all Elspeth. She had this thing for me. Something about saving me from myself, or something. Or maybe she just wanted to walk on the wild side. Nice, properly brought-up Southern girl and LaDonna Collier's good-for-nothing colored boy..."

His voice was hard, and who could blame him?

"Sorry," I said, inadequately.

He didn't pretend not to understand what I was apologizing for. "Ain't no big deal. I've heard it enough that I should be used to it by now."

"That doesn't make it right."

"Yeah, well, that's life, ain't it? Since when did you become so tender of my feelings, darlin'?"

"I'm not," I said, although I knew I was lying. The truth was that I'd never particularly considered his feelings before, or even considered whether he had any, but after getting to know him a little, I had gotten a glimpse of the world from his perspective, and it wasn't a pretty place. In fact, it made me feel ashamed of some of the things I had thought in the past, even if I hadn't—probably hadn't—articulated any of them. "So what happened between you two?"

He shrugged. "I'd been avoiding her. I knew what she wanted, and I knew she'd think it meant something it didn't. But she caught me one night when I was drunk and had had the crap beat out of me. I figured what the hell, she wanted it; it was her lookout."

"So you slept with her?"

He nodded. "It was her first time, and with everything that was going on, I wasn't as careful as maybe I shoulda been. I probably hurt her. But I didn't force her."

I waited a moment to see if he'd say anything else. When he didn't, I asked, "What happened afterwards?"

He put his head back against the seat and closed his eyes. His lashes were long and thick enough to make shadows against his cheeks. "She wanted more. I always knew she would. Hell, she wanted me to marry her. Kept coming at me, saying how I'd ruined her and I owed it to her."

"What did you do?" I asked softly.

He snorted. "What d'you think I did? I was eighteen. I bailed. Got myself a job working as a mechanic down in Birmingham, and spent the summer down there. Figured I might get hired on, and maybe I'd never have to see Elspeth again. Until I came home to see my mama one weekend, and found that Billy Scruggs had gone to work on her."

"And that's when you picked that fight with Billy and got yourself arrested."

He nodded. "Elspeth came and saw me in jail, and told me she'd wait for me until I got out. After I ended up in Riverbend, she kept sending me letters, but I never opened none of 'em. I just sent 'em back. And when I got out I left Nashville, and the letters stopped."

"I'm sorry," I said again.

He shrugged. "Wasn't like I cared, darlin'. Like you said, she was just another girl I dallied with."

"And the baby?"

"Don't know nothing about a baby," Rafe said. "If she was pregnant, she never told me."

In the silence that followed, another peremptory rap sounded on the window. I jumped and almost lost control of my bodily functions yet again. I'd forgotten them in the excitement of the conversation, but now the reminder was back, and with a vengeance.

It had gotten darker while we'd been sitting there, and it was difficult to see the person outside. I rolled down the window, and was greeted with a broad grin from a lined face topped by thinning ginger hair. "Evenin', Miz Martin. Mr. Collier. What're you folks doin', steamin' up the windows of this car like a couple of teenagers?"

"Good evening, Officer Spicer," I said politely, in spite of the flush in my cheeks and the—I admit it—fear in my heart. "We're not actually doing anything. Just talking."

Lyle Spicer grinned. He and I had first met a couple of weeks earlier, when I had stumbled over Brenda Puckett's butchered body inside Mrs. Jenkins's house on Potsdam Street. I'd called 911, and they had sent the nearest patrol car over to assess the situation. It had contained Officer Spicer and his partner, Junior Officer Truman, who was even now smirking at me over Spicer's shoulder. He was only about 22, and still young enough to find the humor in a situation like this. Of course, Spicer was pushing fifty and still thought embarrassing me was funny, too, so maybe age didn't have much to do with it.

Spicer cut his eyes to Rafe. "Nice seein' you again, Mr. Collier. Out and about, as it were. I wasn't sure the detective'd let you leave on Sunday."

Rafe smiled, but didn't take the bait. From Spicer's comment, I assumed Tamara Grimaldi had charged her two pet patrol officers with tracking down Rafe and bringing him in for interrogation last weekend.

"What are you guys doing here?" I asked, hoping against hope that they weren't here to do what I thought they were doing.

"Routin' out lovebirds along the river, ain't we?" Spicer winked at Truman, who grinned appreciatively. I sent a mortified glance toward Rafe, who didn't look as if the officers' jokes bothered him. Spicer added, "Actually, Herself sent us out here to invite someone downtown for a talk."

My stomach clenched. "What am I supposed to have done this time?" Rafe asked. His thoughts must have been following the same lines as my own, although his voice was remarkably steady.

"Oh, it ain't you she's after today. It's the fella across the way." Spicer indicated the warehouse on the other side of the road while I breathed out surreptitiously. "Name's Melendez. Seems like maybe he had something to do with these murders the detective's working on."

"Don't let us keep you," I said politely.

Spicer grinned. "Sorry, Miz Martin, but I'm gonna have to ask you to leave. This guy's considered armed and dangerous, and we don't want no civilians gettin' hurt. Go rent yourselves a room somewhere." He winked at Rafe, who arched a brow.

"Guess it's time for me to go." His voice was light, but the eyes that crossed mine weren't. "I'll see you around, darlin'."

"Sure," I said, as he opened the passenger side door and swung his legs out.

He slammed the door and walked to his motorcycle, his stride loose-hipped and unhurried, although it covered ground faster than I could have run. I thought I was probably the only one who'd noticed the tension that had settled over him after Spicer told us he and Truman were there to talk to Julio Melendez.

The only reason I could come up with why that would worry Rafe, was because he was afraid of what Melendez might say. Which meant that Melendez really was involved in the robberies, and he knew that Rafe was, too. If Detective Grimaldi threatened him with a double charge of murder, Melendez would probably roll on anyone he could in an effort to help himself, and if he named Rafe, Tamara Grimaldi would be on him like a flea on a dog. With Melendez's testimony, not to mention Rafe's earlier conviction for assault and his fingerprints all over the Fortunatos' house, she could make a pretty good case for Rafe having raped and murdered both Lila Vaughn and Connie Fortunato. No wonder he got on his bike and hightailed it out of there without so much as a glance back over his shoulder. I waited until the taillight of his Harley-Davidson had disappeared down on River Road, before I started my own car and pulled out of the parking lot with a jaunty wave at Spicer and Truman. And then I floored the accelerator and kept it there all the way home.

Sixteen

My thought processes were on overload with everything that had happened, so when I got back to my apartment (after I visited the little girl's room), I sat down at the dining room table with a pen and paper and tried to make some sense of everything that had happened and what it might mean.

Item 1: Rafe had finally admitted to committing the two open house robberies and to having been the person to whom Lila had made her ill-advised comment about tying her to the bed.

Item 2: He had denied killing both her and Connie Fortunato. I believed him, although I wasn't kidding myself: that might be because I wanted to believe him, and not necessarily because he was telling the truth. I had no doubt whatsoever that he could lie like a rug if it suited him, and there wasn't much doubt that he could kill, should the circumstances demand it. I didn't, however—or didn't want to—believe that he could kill like this.

Item 3: He'd had three other men with him when he committed the robberies, quite possibly the three I had seen him talk to at the

Shortstop Sports Bar last Sunday. Ishmael, A.J. and Antoine. Although that didn't necessarily follow; it could have been one or more of them, none or all three. It could have been Julio Melendez, or Malcolm Rodgers, or even Perry Fortunato; all of whom had some variety of dark eyes, and all of whom were middling to tall and would look something like Rafe in padded coveralls and a ski mask. With the possible exception of Julio, whom I hadn't seen yet, but if he was four feet tall and scrawny, surely Rafe would have pointed it out.

Item 4: Julio Melendez was involved in the robberies somehow; most likely as a fence. It hadn't occurred to me earlier, in the flush of being caught with my hand in the cookie jar, so to speak, but Rafe had probably been there tonight to meet with him. That would explain why Julio hadn't left the warehouse with his employees, as well as what Rafe was doing there in the first place. It wasn't like he'd come to talk to me; he couldn't have known I'd be there. There wasn't much else down there by the river—unless he was dropping off a donation to the Second Harvest Food Bank, which I doubted—and his tactical retreat when Spicer and Truman showed up hinted strongly at a healthy sense of self-preservation. I wondered where he'd ended up, and whether he was planning to make himself scarce until this whole thing had blown over. Maybe he was driving out of town at this very moment, to resurface three months from now in Kingsport or Bolivar or Lexington, Kentucky. Maybe, with the police sniffing around him, he was doing a bunk again, the way Todd said he'd been doing for the past ten years.

The thought was surprisingly upsetting. Or maybe upsetting isn't the right word. It wasn't like I cared, after all, so maybe annoyed would be a better description of my feelings. And I couldn't exactly blame him. If he thought that Julio Melendez would rat him out to Detective Grimaldi, it made sense to get out of Nashville while the going was good. Not to mention that he probably didn't have an alibi for yesterday afternoon, and couldn't prove he hadn't killed Connie. My issue wasn't so much with the fact that he'd gone, as with his manner of going. I mean, "*See you around, darlin'*," isn't *my* idea of a suitable goodbye. If he was planning to drop off the face of the earth for weeks or months, the least he could do was tell me.

Not that he owed it to me, exactly. As I was fond of pointing out to Dix or Todd or anyone else who'd listen, it wasn't like we were involved. I'd had my chance with him, more than once, and had turned him down. But surely we had enough of a relationship—friendship, acquaintanceship, whatever—that I deserved at least a proper explanation. Or if not that, a forthright goodbye. One that wasn't open for interpretation. *Sayonara, darlin'. It was nice knowing you. Take care of yourself. Don't do anything I wouldn't do. And since we won't be seeing each other again, at least not until we're both old and gray, how about a goodbye-kiss...?*

Infuriating, that's what it was. For him to just up and leave without a word, like I didn't deserve to be told what was going on...

But no, I told myself, I was jumping to conclusions. I had no proof that he'd actually gone anywhere. Time enough to curse him when I tried to look for him and he couldn't be found.

I went back to my list. However, the list wasn't really working out. I wasn't any closer to figuring out who'd done what to whom than when I'd started. Rafe had committed the robberies, with a little help from his friends. Julio Melendez had fenced the goods, and Heather Price had probably picked the targets in the first place. Or Julio had picked Heather's brain. But anyone could have overheard or heard about Lila's remark to Rafe and decided to take advantage of it. And as for Connie Fortunato's murder and the theft of the O'Keeffe...

It occurred to me that with everything that had been going on, I'd been remiss in my duty. Someone I knew had died, and I'd been too busy with my own problems—tracking down Elspeth Caulfield and having deep conversations with Rafe—to do the proper thing. I hadn't known Connie well, and knew her husband even less well, so I was probably exempt from dropping off a casserole, but surely I ought to have found the time to give Perry Fortunato a call with my condolences on his loss.

And what about Tim? Did Tim even know that one of his clients had passed away? The news probably hadn't hit the paper yet—if Tim even read the paper—and until Detective Grimaldi had some more time to figure out what had happened, she might want to keep a lid on it. But she had called me; surely she wouldn't mind if I told Tim...?

I decided it was the better part of discretion to ask first, just in case she *did* mind, so I dialed the detective's number, hoping that maybe she hadn't gotten around to interrogating Julio Melendez yet, and was able to talk. When I'd been pulled in for questioning last month, in connection with Brenda Puckett's murder, she'd let me sweat for what had seemed like several hours before she got around to talking to me, and I thought she might be doing the same to Julio.

The phone rang many times without an answer, and I was starting to think I'd have to hang up, but eventually she came on. "Grimaldi."

"Hi, detective," I said politely, "this is..."

"I know who it is. What do you want?"

"Oh. Um..." Rattled, I explained that I wanted to know whether it would be OK to tell Timothy Briggs about Connie's death, since I wanted to ask him for Perry Fortunato's number.

"It'll be on the evening news anyway," Tamara Grimaldi said, "so go ahead. Just don't give him any details."

I promised I wouldn't. "By the way, I saw Officers Spicer and Truman down on River Road earlier. How is it going with Julio Melendez?"

"They told me," Detective Grimaldi said. "Julio's sweating."

"Oh. Um...?"

"Yes, Ms. Martin. Officer Spicer mentioned that Mr. Collier was there, too."

"I told him you wanted to talk to him," I said self-righteously.

"I'm sure you did. I should have figured it would just make him run. Next time, I'll make sure that Spicer and Truman know not to let him get away."

I thought it best to change the subject. "So... um... has Julio said anything?"

"I haven't spoken to him yet. After another hour or two, I figure maybe he'll be annoyed enough to blurt out something he shouldn't. Especially if I hit him with a double homicide."

"Good luck," I said. "I'll just call Tim now, and get Perry's number."

"Remember, no details." She hung up without saying goodbye, and without giving me the time to do so. I grimaced and dialed Tim's number.

As Realtors, we're pretty much expected to be available 24/7. People will call at all hours of the day and sometimes the night, expecting us to drop whatever we're doing to jump when they snap their fingers. Like doctors, Realtors are always on call. That said, we do have the right to a social life, too. Tim must be indulging his, because he didn't answer. I hesitated for a moment while I waited for the voice mail to kick in, but eventually I decided this wasn't really the kind of news I should break in a recorded message. Instead, I just told him I had something to talk to him about, and I would catch up with him at the office in the morning. If he wasn't planning to be there, please give me a call.

That done, I sat back and chewed my lip, wondering whether I ought to look up Perry Fortunato's number in the phone book and call him anyway. But no, it didn't seem right to do so without having told Tim first. The Fortunatos' were Tim's clients, not mine, and although the reason for my call had nothing to do with business, it's a no-no for a Realtor to contact another Realtor's client directly. It would have to wait until tomorrow.

At that moment, the phone rang, and I jumped in surprise, and then grabbed it. Maybe it was Tim, calling back. Or detective Grimaldi calling to tell me that Julio Melendez had confessed to both robberies and both murders. Or Todd, inviting me to dinner. Or Rafe, calling to

say he was leaving town. Or Rafe calling to say he wasn't leaving town…
"This is Savannah."

"Hi, Savannah," a male voice said. I sorted through my mental file, and had just about come up with the appropriate match when the voice continued, "this is Gary Lee Hodges."

"Hi, Gary Lee," I said, trying my best not to grin. It's possible to hear a smile in someone's voice, and I didn't want Gary Lee and Charlene to think I was laughing at them. Or for that matter to think that I knew anything at all about them and what they'd been up to. Although I was pretty sure I had Detective Grimaldi and her 'little chat' to thank for this call, I rather doubted she had told them that she had told me about their DNA-samples. "How are you? And your lovely wife?"

"Fine," Gary Lee said. "Just fine. Um… Savannah?"

"Yes?"

"Would it be possible for you to meet us sometime tomorrow? There's something we'd like to talk to you about."

"Sure," I said, allowing myself a tiny smirk. Confession-time, most likely. "I'd be happy to. When and where?"

We agreed on 3:30 at the office, and I hung up with a giggle. Tomorrow, when they explained to me what had been going on, I'd most likely be blushing, but at the moment, the idea of what they had to admit to was humorous.

My list of clues and suspects was pretty well dead in the water by now, but I did my best to go back to it. My heart wasn't in it, though. I wanted to do something, not just sit here and think. Maybe I could call Heather Price and talk to her about what had happened. She must be devastated at having lost two friends in just a few days. Unless she and her boyfriend had been responsible, of course, but her shock and revulsion at what had happened to Lila had certainly seemed genuine when I first met her on Monday. And on top of the loss, she had found one of the bodies. I knew what that was like. Maybe I could even discover something important in the process of talking to her.

She had given me her card, and now I dug it out and dialed the number. (Life must have been so much more difficult before telephones...) "Heather? This is Savannah Martin."

"Oh." Heather sounded like she had a cold, but it was probably just a stuffy nose from crying. "Hi, Savannah. What can I do for you?"

"I heard about what happened to Connie Fortunato. How are you?"

She hiccupped. "All right, I guess."

"I thought maybe you'd like to go get some dinner or something. Or lunch tomorrow. Something to take your mind off things."

"Oh." She sniffed again. "That's really nice of you, but... um... I'm waiting for someone to call. I don't want to go anywhere just in case I miss it."

"Of course not," I said quickly. Waiting for Julio to call when Detective Grimaldi let him go, most likely. "I guess it's getting kind of late anyway. How about tomorrow? I have to go to the office in the morning, and I have an appointment in the afternoon, but I could meet for lunch in between, if you'd like."

Heather hesitated. I prepared myself for a rejection, thinking she was probably trying to come up with an excuse to say no. Instead she said yes, although her voice was notably unenthusiastic. "Sure. Unless something comes up."

"Great," I said, trying not to take it personally. "Do you have a favorite place?"

Anywhere except...

"I really like Fidelio's. Lila and Connie and I used to go there sometimes." She sniffed.

I grimaced, but did my best to keep my own lack of enthusiasm out of my voice. "That's fine. I had lunch with Lila there myself last week, as a matter of fact. When do you want to meet?"

We agreed to see each other at Fidelio's Restaurant at noon the next day, and I hung up, feeling a little better. At least I'd done *something*, and I had a fairly full day scheduled tomorrow, which is always helpful.

There's nothing worse than lying in bed in the morning, alone, and having nothing to look forward to but a day full of nothing.

BY THE TIME I GOT TO the office the next morning, Tim had already heard the news. When I bearded him in his den—what used to be Walker's office, the biggest and nicest in the building—he was sitting behind his (Walker's) desk, reading the paper and looking positively stricken.

"Oh," he said when I knocked on the open door, "it's you. Come in."

"I see you've heard the news." I sat down in one of the chairs across the desk from him. The headline read, *"Priceless Work of Art Missing!"* with an accompanying photograph of the O'Keeffe. It was unmistakable, with its bright pink flowers and spiky needles.

Tim nodded. "Disgusting," he said, folding the paper over to hide the picture.

I agreed. "The way they worded it in the article, poor Connie Fortunato's death seems like an unfortunate side issue to the theft. Like the painting was more important than her life. They didn't even run a photograph of her."

"And they didn't mention my name," Tim said.

"How is Mr. Fortunato holding up? Have you spoken to him?"

Tim shrugged. "I guess he's all right. After so many years, some of the gilt has rubbed off the lily, if you know what I mean."

"Really?" I wasn't surprised, considering the way Connie had looked at Rafe and the way her husband had looked at me last Sunday. What was surprising, was that Tim had come right out and said it. The Fortunatos' relationship wasn't any of my business, or his, and under the circumstances, when Perry Fortunato had just lost his wife, putting it like that seemed beyond rude and well into callous. Not that I'd expect any less from Tim, who has all the delicacy and sensitivity of a cheese grater.

188 | Jenna Bennett

He nodded. "Oh, yes. I think she said they'd been married for more than ten years, and of course she was getting a little long in the tooth, poor dear. Holding on for all she was worth, going the surgery route and everything, but when a woman's pushing forty, it's pretty much all down-hill, isn't it, darling?" He smoothed a hand over his sleek, blond head. "Everything sags; the face, the butt, the boobs... Of course, that's what the good Lord invented the Wonderbra for!" He winked.

"Or, I suppose, the Wonderjock."

Tim's eyes widened. "How do you know about the Wonderjock, darling?"

"Oh, I spoke to someone who was wearing one the other day," I said, wishing I'd engaged my brain before I'd opened my mouth. Conversations about men's underwear really make me uncomfortable. Tim lowered his voice conspiratorially and leaned closer, across the desk.

"You're not talking about the dishy Mr. Collier, I hope? Because if I found out that he has to wear a Wonderjock, that would just ruin all my favorite fantasies!"

"No," I said, feeling my cheeks burn, "I'm not talking about Rafe."

"Thank God," Tim said, looking relieved. "Because, let me tell you, darling..."

"I'd rather you didn't, if it's all the same to you." I stood up. "If you don't mind, I didn't come in here to discuss Rafe Collier's underwear. I actually just wanted to make sure that it would be OK for me to call Perry Fortunato to give him my condolences. He's your client, and I don't want to go behind your back."

"Sure. Call him. Tell him I'll be in touch later."

I promised I would, and withdrew, back to my own tiny office. But when I dialed Perry's number, he didn't answer the phone, and I was forced to leave a message, condoling him on the loss of his wife and telling him to call me if there was anything I could do. It's something one says in circumstances like these, and the words just fell out of my mouth without conscious thought, but after I'd done it, I sort of wished

I hadn't. The way he'd looked into my blouse and let his lips linger on my hand last Sunday, had made me feel uncomfortable, and I hoped he wouldn't take my remark as an invitation to call for a kind of sympathy and consolation I wasn't prepared to give.

Seventeen

Heather Price was late, and looked like she had spent a sleepless night. She was a handsome woman under normal circumstances, but today her eyes were red and swollen from crying, her face was blotchy, and she had made no effort to make herself more presentable. Her face was devoid of make-up, and her hair was flat and tucked behind her unadorned ears, while the rest of her was simply dressed in a pair of khaki pants and a green T-shirt. She looked like the 'before' part of a before-and-after makeover.

"Hi," I said when she plopped herself down across from me. "You look like you could use a drink."

"And how!" She waved at the waiter, who glided over. "Give me a scotch. Double."

"And mademoiselle?" The waiter turned to me.

"White wine, please. Thank you." I don't usually drink alcohol during the day, but I thought I should probably try to build a connection with Heather.

The waiter nodded and withdrew, and Heather leaned back on her chair and breathed out. "God, I feel like crap."

I nodded sympathetically. She looked like crap, too, but of course I couldn't say so. "I was sorry to hear about Connie," I said instead. "I only met her a few times, but she seemed like a nice woman."

"She was a peach," Heather agreed. "Much too good for that husband of hers."

From her vehemence, and her careful diction, I wondered if she might not have had a drink or two before coming here, as well. "Had you known each other long?"

Heather shook her head. "I met her this spring. We worked on another volunteer committee together. That good-for-nothing jackass Perry wasted no time hitting on me. Oh, thanks." She grabbed her scotch out of the waiter's hand and downed a third of it in a single gulp. The waiter turned to me, and his expressionless face managed to convey his opinion of her quite well as he placed my glass on the table in front of me.

"Thank you," I said politely. "I'll have a blackened salmon Caesar salad, please."

Heather surfaced for long enough to order a lunch portion of the chicken Alfredo with broccoli—comfort-food—and the waiter withdrew. I waited until he was out of ear-shot, and then I added, "So does Perry have a habit of hitting on people? I thought it was just me. Not that he hit on me, exactly; it was more a suggestion that he might if I encouraged him..."

Heather snorted. "Perry fancies himself a ladies man. One of those dashing types in the old movies. Instead, he's just a nasty piece of work with a roving eye and—if you get too close—roving hands, as well." She took another, more ladylike sip of her drink, and continued, "To do him justice, he's been discreet about it. If he embarrassed Connie publicly, I believe she'd divorce him. Or..." Her voice caught, and then she drained most of the rest of the scotch as Connie's death hit her anew. Her voice was raspy when she finished the thought, "she would have. If she hadn't been killed first."

"I remember when Brenda Puckett died a few weeks ago, I kept doing what you're doing. Talking about her as if she were still alive, and then realizing she wasn't, and feeling awful."

Heather nodded.

I added, "I found Brenda's body. I don't know if you knew that."

She stopped looking around for the waiter, probably to order a refill, and turned to me. "No, actually I didn't. I remember hearing about it on the news, but I didn't realize it was you who found her. She was horribly butchered, wasn't she?"

"Her throat was cut," I said. "It wasn't pretty. Lots of blood."

"Connie was strangled," Heather said, twisting her empty glass around and around in her hands. "There was no blood, but her face was purple, and her tongue was sticking out."

I nodded, with a suppressed shiver. I remembered the photograph Tamara Grimaldi had shown me of Lila. "I heard the same thing happened to her that happened to Lila."

"I never saw Lila," Heather said, "but I guess so. Connie was naked and tied to the bed, anyway. And dead." She shuddered.

I lowered my voice. "So who do you think did it?"

I watched her closely, hoping for some clue as to what she knew or guessed—a furtive look in her eyes, a flash of fear, worry—but I didn't see anything.

"Hell," she said, "how should I know? Some crazy person, obviously. Who else goes around and rapes and strangles women?"

"It would have to be someone who knew them both. And if the murders are connected to the robberies, someone with a connection to all three of the houses."

This time, I saw fear in her eyes. Her voice was even, albeit with just a hint of a tremor that she couldn't quite eradicate. "I staged both the houses that were robbed, and I'd been to Connie's house before, but I don't have the equipment I'd need to rape someone."

Her attempt at humor fell woefully flat.

I was planning to ask her about her boyfriend, but now the waiter arrived with the food, and we got busy eating. I let the subject rest for a few minutes while we chewed. "How is your food?"

"Great, thanks. Yours?" She sounded a little calmer, as if the carbohydrates had kicked in and mellowed her out.

"Very good. It always is. I hear the police talked to your boyfriend yesterday. How did that go?"

She stopped eating to stare at me. "How d'you know that?"

I'd already figured out my answer, and since it wasn't really a lie—just a slight truth-adjustment—I was able to get it out without looking like I was fibbing big-time. "They've been talking to a friend of mine, as well."

"Who's your friend?"

"His name's Rafael Collier," I said, keeping an eye on her to see if she'd give anything away. She didn't.

"Sorry, I don't know him." She shrugged lightly.

"That's OK. I think your boyfriend does, though." She didn't answer. "And of course Connie met him. So did they let your boyfriend go? Or are they still talking to him?"

Her voice was tight. "They're still talking to him. What about your friend?"

"They kept him for a long time last weekend, after Lila died. I'm not sure if they've managed to get hold of him again, but I know they were looking for him yesterday."

My voice, I'm pleased to say, held just the right amount of worry.

"Is he your boyfriend?" Heather asked.

I shook my head. "Not exactly. More of a... um..."

"Future boyfriend?"

"Well..."

She smiled, leaning back in her chair. "You obviously care about him."

"Well..." I said again, my cheeks pinking. And that betraying flush wasn't all pretend. I did care, at least enough that I didn't want him to go to jail for two murders he didn't commit. Maybe even enough that I didn't really want him to go to jail for committing the robberies, even though I knew he was guilty. On that score, though, Detective Grimaldi had every right to lock him up and throw away the key, and she wouldn't get any argument from me if she chose to exercise her option. The funny thing was, I didn't think Rafe would argue the point, either. He'd do what he could to stay out of jail for as long as he could, but if he was caught, fair and square, he'd take it like a man.

"You know," Heather said, "someone else who worked in all three of the houses—Connie's and the two that were robbed—was that really hot house cleaner guy."

"Beau Riggins? The House Boy?"

"That's the guy. The one who cleans in his underwear."

"Wonderjocks," I said. Heather looked surprised, and I added, "He showed them to me. How do you know that he worked for all three of the houses?"

She counted on her fingers. "He was at the funeral the other day with Connie, and she told me she'd hired him. I saw him at the Caldwell family's house when I was staging it a couple of weeks ago, and Kieran's clients have his business card on their refrigerator. Behind a magnet of a guy whose clothes come off, like a paper doll's."

"I must have missed that," I said. "Not to be crude or anything, but why would he rape someone?" Looking like he did, Beau probably had all the female—or male—companionship he could want.

"He has to be a little weird to clean houses in his underwear," Heather said.

"Wonderjocks. And I don't think he does all that much cleaning. He probably just bends and stretches a lot. He said his clients like to watch while he works."

"I'm not surprised," Heather said.

Personally, I'm not someone who enjoys nudity, my own or anyone else's. I don't even wear a bikini on the beach, but prefer to cover up in a bathing suit when I go at all. Beau's easy sexuality had made me feel uncomfortable. But he hadn't seemed like the type who'd tie up, rape, and strangle someone. Rather, I thought he was an exhibitionist; someone who got off on being watched, not someone who'd do nasty deeds under cover of darkness. To Beau, his job was probably the equivalent of working as a stripper or being a porn star. Totally icky professions, both, but the total opposite of whoever had killed Lila and Connie. At least that was how it seemed to me, but I'd be the first to admit I have no personal knowledge and can't be expected to know what I'm talking about.

"It sounds like I'll have to give Beau a call," I said, and looked up as someone stopped next to our table. It was the waiter. I expected him to ask if everything was OK, the way waiters do, and maybe inquire if we needed a refill on our drinks, but instead he addressed Heather.

"Ms. Price? There is someone to see you in the lobby."

Heather looked surprised for a moment, and then her eyes lit up. I guessed maybe she'd left Julio a message about where she was going to be, and she thought he'd tracked her down after being released by the police. Personally, I wasn't so optimistic. There was no reason why Julio wouldn't just come over to the table. Unless he was wearing jeans and the maitre d' had refused to let him pass. However, I didn't let her see my doubt, but just smiled encouragingly. "Go ahead."

Heather didn't have to be asked twice, but jumped up and hurried toward the reception area, leaving her summer jacket hanging over the back of her chair and her handbag sitting on the floor beside it. The waiter smiled apologetically as he picked them up and followed.

She didn't come back, but the waiter did. Eventually. "Ms. Price was compelled to leave," he murmured as he placed the check on the table next to me.

"Did her boyfriend come for her?" I dug through my wallet, looking for the credit card I thought would be most likely to withstand the charge. I hadn't expected to have to pay for Heather's lunch as well as my own.

196 | Jenna Bennett

The waiter shook his head, dropping his voice another notch, to where I almost couldn't hear him over the clinking of silverware and muted conversations all around us. "The police escorted her out. A uniformed patrol officer in an official car." He shuddered.

"Dear me," I said, not at all surprised. "I hope nothing's wrong."

The waiter rolled his eyes and shrugged in an eloquent, Gallic way. "I shall return momentarily, Mademoiselle."

I nodded and sat back on my chair, hoping he wouldn't return momentarily to tell me my credit card has been rejected.

Gary Lee and Charlene Hodges arrived at the office promptly at 3:30, but before they got there, I had found the time for a few phone calls. The first was to Tamara Grimaldi, made just after I left Fidelio's and was walking to my car. I figured that by then she must have gotten tired of talking to Julio Melendez, but that Heather wouldn't have had time to get there yet, and I might catch her between interviews.

"Detective? Savannah Martin."

"Hello, Ms. Martin," the detective said resignedly.

"I just wanted to know if there was any news."

"You know, the general public isn't supposed to call the police for updates on ongoing investigations."

"Oh." I guessed that was probably true, although it hadn't actually occurred to me before she mentioned it. "Sorry."

"It's my fault. I've talked to you about too many things I shouldn't have mentioned."

"I did help you catch Walker Lamont," I reminded her. "And without me, you wouldn't have known that there was a connection between the open house robberies and Lila's murder."

"I assure you, Ms. Martin, that's a connection we would have found sooner or later."

I opened my mouth to protest, but she continued, "However, I guess I do owe you a little something. What do you want to know?"

For a second or two, too many possible questions swirled around in my head, making me dizzy. Then I grabbed one, the one that seemed the most important to me at the moment. "Did you just arrest Heather Price?"

"How do you know about that?"

"I was having lunch with her," I said, as I unlocked my car door and put my handbag inside. "The waiter said a uniformed officer in a squad car came and escorted her away."

Detective Grimaldi sounded resigned. "How do you manage to always be in the thick of things, Ms. Martin? It's not even because you try, is it?"

I didn't answer, and she added, her voice dry once more, "No, we haven't arrested Ms. Price. She is assisting the police in their inquiries."

"But that means you suspect her, doesn't it? In mystery novels, that's what it means."

I got into the car and fumbled the key into the ignition.

"We're trying to ascertain whether or not she was aware of her boyfriend's actions with regards to the robberies," Tamara Grimaldi said. "Clearly, it was her knowledge of the houses and their contents that spurred the idea for the robberies, but we're not sure whether she participated in their planning, or if Mr. Melendez used her for his own purposes."

"Oh, God, I hope not!" I said.

Detective Grimaldi's silence was eloquent, and I added, reluctantly, "She's obviously worried about him. She cares what happens to him. She'll be devastated if she finds out that he was using her all along."

"You hope she helped him plan the robberies instead?"

"Well..." I said. No, I guess I didn't really hope that, either. "I'm not sure what I hope. Whatever she did, though, I don't think she had anything to do with the murders. Did Julio say anything about them?"

I looked both ways before I eased the Volvo out into traffic on Murphy Road.

"He admitted to receiving stolen goods, and that he accepted the items from the robberies, but he denied killing anyone. He and Heather were together Wednesday after the funeral, until she went to Brentwood and found Connie Fortunato, so in other circumstances he'd have an alibi. But of course, with her possible involvement, I can't accept it on its own, without some corroboration. They stayed at home, so nobody else can vouch for either of them."

"What about the night Lila died? Does he have an alibi for that?"

"Yes and no." It was another alibi the detective couldn't take seriously. "He said he was playing pool with some men in a dive in South Nashville. A place called the Shortstop Sports Bar."

"Did he give you their names?" I asked, my heart starting to beat faster.

Grimaldi sounded disgusted. "He said he didn't know their names. However, when I threatened to charge him with murder unless he gave me something to work with, he managed to remember something. I've identified one of the men. His name is Ishmael Jackson, and he has a rap sheet as long as my arm. Among other things, he's served time for breaking and entering before."

"No kidding." My mouth was dry. If she had Ishmael Jackson's name, how long could it be before she had Rafe's?

"Every black-and-white in Nashville is looking for him, and I'm sure it's just a matter of time before I identify the others."

"Congratulations," I said.

"Thank you." The detective's voice was triumphant, so much so that she didn't notice how my voice was anything but. "And now I guess I'd better go. Lots to do before Spicer and Truman show up with Ms. Price."

"Let me know what happens, would you? If it's acceptable for me to ask, that is. Being a member of the general public, and all."

"When this is over, Ms. Martin," Detective Grimaldi said, "we'll go out to lunch again, and go over all the details, just like we did after Mr. Lamont confessed. In the meantime, I'll let you know what I think you need to know, and you can do the same. Deal?"

"I suppose," I said grudgingly, and hung up.

My second call was made when I got to the office, and it was to the beautiful Beau Riggins. But Beau must have been working—posing in the semi-nude with a feather duster in his hand in someone's house somewhere—because I got his voice mail. "You've reached the voice mail of Beau Riggins, house boy *extraordinaire*. Sorry I missed your call," he cooed, in a voice as rich as Elvis Presley's. "Please leave me a message, and I'll call you back just as soon as I can. Promise!" I could practically envision him winking as he said it.

"Hi, Beau," I said, and was pleased to notice that my voice didn't wobble at all. "This is Savannah Martin with Lamont, Briggs, and Associates. I had a question I wanted to ask you. When you have a minute to talk, would you mind giving me a call?" I left my number and hung up.

By the time Gary Lee and Charlene walked through the door, Beau still hadn't called back. I left my teeny-tiny office and ushered the two of them into the conference room, where the three of us could fit more comfortably. "Have a seat."

Gary Lee and Charlene exchanged a glance before they sat down beside each other on one side of the conference table. I seated myself on the other, folded my hands demurely on the glass table top, and smiled. "What can I do for you?"

They looked at each other again, and it was painfully obvious that neither of them wanted to speak. Eventually, Gary Lee cleared his throat. "We have something to tell you, Savannah."

"Great," I said.

More silence. Finally, Charlene took charge. "Listen, Savannah. When we first met you, at that open house over on Potsdam Street..."

"Yes?"

"We weren't really there looking to buy the house."

I nodded. No surprise there. Most people who come to open houses are gawkers; they're not serious about buying, they just want to see how other people live. That had been especially true for the open house at 101 Potsdam Street, where the majority of the visitors had come to stare at the place on the floor where Brenda Puckett had had her throat cut. One woman had even sat down and attempted to contact Brenda's disembodied spirit. Unsuccessfully, I'm happy to say. At least Rafe hadn't mentioned anything about an overweight woman haunting the place (apart from Marquita), and it was reasonable to assume that he would have, had he encountered her.

"But then you offered to show us other houses, and we figured it would be fun to... um..."

"See which bedroom had, like, the best vibe," Gary Lee finished.

"I see."

Charlene shook her head. "I don't think you do, Savannah. See, we rent this apartment in Germantown. It's on the top floor of an old Victorian house, and the walls are thin, and the floors sag, and there are gaps under all the doors, and whenever we want to... um..."

She glanced over at Gary Lee for help. He shrugged.

"Make love?" I suggested.

She nodded gratefully. "Whenever we want to make love, the old woman who owns the house complains about the noise. We'd probably be arrested for indecent exposure if we went outside, and you can only do it in elevators and fitting rooms and the back seat of the car so many times before that becomes old hat."

I've never made love in an elevator, a fitting room, or the back seat of a car—mine or anyone else's—and I couldn't imagine it becoming old hat, but I'd take her word for it. "So you thought telling me you were interested in buying a house and making me waste my time showing you houses you had no intention of buying was the way to go?

So that you could make love in other people's bedrooms? I'm sorry, but that's just creepy. Not to mention probably illegal. It's certainly enough to ruin my career. If word about this gets out, I'll be known as the Realtor for the sex-crazed."

Gary Lee and Charlene exchanged a look. "We're sorry, Savannah," Gary Lee said, but not without a betraying twitching of the lips. Charlene wasn't even trying to hide her smile.

I fumed in silence for another moment—it was a serious matter, darn it!—before I opened my mouth again. "Fine. You've told the truth. Now what?"

"Well..." They glanced at each other. "See, there's this house we want to see..."

I shook my head. "Oh, no! We're not going through that again."

"But this time we're serious, Savannah. We really think this might be the one. It's the perfect price, and the perfect size, and it's got mirrors on the ceiling above the bed, just like that house in Brentwood..."

"I'm not letting you into another house so you can have sex in the bedroom!" I yelled, and then subsided, with a guilty look at the closed door. Lord, what if somebody heard me?!

"Please, Savannah. Just one more. If we like this one, we'll buy it. I promise."

Charlene folded her hands and was giving me what my brother Dix refers to as his daughter Abby's 'frog-face', with bulging eyes and an out-thrust lower lip. My niece Abigail is so firmly convinced of its efficacy that none of us have the heart to disillusion her by refusing to give her whatever it is she's trying to obtain by the use of it.

"Well..." I said, weakening. (Yes, it was the possible commission that did it. Shallow and horribly immoral of me, no doubt, but I desperately needed the money.)

Charlene saw the opening and took it. "Oh, thank you, Savannah!" She jumped up and ran around the table and threw herself around my neck. I grimaced, but allowed the hug.

202 | Jenna Bennett

"You're welcome. But that's it. If I catch you doing something you shouldn't be I'm never showing you another house. And I'll tell every other Realtor in Nashville what you're doing, so they'll watch you every minute you're inside someone else's house."

It was an empty threat—I hoped to God no one else ever heard about what had been going on—but it worked. Gary Lee and Charlene exchanged another look. "OK, Savannah," Charlene said meekly. Gary Lee nodded.

We agreed to meet the next day at the usual time—I tried not to see any significance in that—and then I walked them out through the reception area and to the front door, just in case they had some idea of going at it like rabbits on the conference room table if I left them alone.

Eighteen

Beau didn't call back until after 5 pm, and then he told me he couldn't get together until the next day, if then. "I've got a date, sweetie," he said, "with the most gorgeous little Latin spitfire..!"

I winced, picturing Beau and some swarthy guy named Jorge doing the town. "Spare me the details, if you don't mind. We can just talk on the phone, if that works for you."

"Sorry, darling," Beau said, "but I've got a lot to do between now and 6:30. Cleaning can be so hard on the hands, and I wanna do a manicure and paraffin wrap, to be sure I'm ready for whatever might happen later. It's no good touching all that soft skin with work-roughened hands, you know."

"Fine," I said. "I'm doing floor-duty at the office tomorrow from 8 until noon, and then I've got an appointment to show a house at 3:30, but I'm free in-between, if that'll work for you."

"Unfortunately, I have to do floor-duty too. So to speak. I'm doing Caleb Horwitz tomorrow."

"Doing...?"

"His house, darling. I'm doing his house."

"Right," I said, flushing. "Sorry."

He waved it away. "Happens all the time. How about Sunday? It's the Lord's Day, and I don't figure He'd want me strutting my stuff, so I don't work."

"That's fine. What time?"

"How about I call you in the morning?" Beau suggested. "I like to sleep in, seeing as it's the only day of the week I don't have to be up early."

I agreed that that would be fine, and we hung up. No sooner had I put the phone down, than it rang again. "Savannah? Todd."

"Oh," I said.

Todd hesitated. "You don't sound very excited to hear from me."

I did my best to force some cheer into my voice. "Forgive me, Todd. Of course I'm excited to hear from you. It's just... it's been a long couple of days, and I'm tired and not really in the mood to argue."

"Why would we have to argue?" Todd wanted to know, with what sounded like genuine surprise.

I suppressed a sigh. "I assume you'll bring up the subject of Rafe Collier again, just like you always do, and if you do, then we'll argue."

"You make it sound as if we never talk about anything else," Todd said stiffly. When I didn't answer—because, frankly, I felt as if we never did talk about anything else, or not at any length—he added, "How about if I promise not to mention Collier's name at all? Would you have dinner with me tonight?"

"I'm not sure..." I hedged. Partially it was because mother always told me not to appear too available, but more so, it was because I really, really didn't want a repeat of Tuesday night's dinner. Plus, I really was tired. Ever since Todd had dropped his bomb on me, I felt as if it had been just one thing after another.

But Todd was persistent. "How about tomorrow night?"

"Well..."

"Fidelio's at 6:30? I'll pick you up at 6?"

"I guess..."

"Wonderful," Todd said. "I'll see you then."

He hung up before I could say anything else.

I spent the rest of the evening at home with a book, alternately hoping for and dreading the next phone call. It might be Rafe, calling to tell me he was in Arkansas or Florida, or Detective Grimaldi, telling me he was in jail. It could be a potential client, calling to ask me to show him or her a house, or it could be my mother, if Todd had gotten around to showing her those pictures of me. All in all, it was more a relief than a disappointment when the phone stayed silent for the rest of the night.

Ever since I got my real estate license, I had made a habit of doing floor duty in the office every Saturday morning. I'm not sure exactly why, because it wasn't as if the phone rang a lot there either. Mostly I guess it just made me feel as if I was doing something. Leaving no stone unturned in my quest to become a successful Realtor. Nobody else was there, so it was nice and quiet, and on the occasions when the phone did ring, unless the caller specifically asked for someone else by name, the call went to the agent on duty, i.e. me. That was how I'd ended up with Rafe Collier for a client a few weeks back. He had arranged to meet Brenda Puckett one Saturday morning, to see the house on Potsdam Street, and when she didn't show up—because she was dead—he'd called the office. Tim and Heidi and Clarice Webb, Walker's second victim, had kicked up a fuss about it later, because they thought Rafe should have been referred to one of them, but Walker had backed me up. I wasn't quite sure how I felt about it at this point. On the one hand, my life might have been a heck of a lot easier if someone else had gone to meet him, but on the other hand, I hadn't done too badly. I had gotten him his grandmother's house back, and had kept Mrs. Jenkins alive (despite overwhelming odds), and—in spite of what I was telling Todd and Dix and anyone else—I rather liked Rafe. Or maybe I just liked the way he made me feel. Being with him was relaxing, because he didn't put any pressure on me to pretend to be anything but what I was. I could ask him anything I wanted, without having to worry that I'd shock him, and he wouldn't judge me, or think less of me, or tell my mother.

Anyway, today I started out surfing the internet, because I was thinking about getting myself a real estate website, just in case I'd get some leads that way. I also familiarized myself with the houses that had come on the market in the past couple of days, while I'd been too busy worrying about Lila and Connie and Rafe to keep my mind on business. It's important to keep up with what's going on, even if I didn't actually have any clients looking to buy anything right then.

No, I didn't have great hopes for Gary Lee and Charlene. Mostly, I assumed they were trying to throw me a bone, to make up for having dragged me around to house after house to cool my heels while they were having sex inside. If it hadn't been for Connie's murder, and Gary Lee's DNA, and Detective Grimaldi's no doubt stern lecture, I doubted they would have told me anything about it at all. Nonetheless, I looked up the information on the house they wanted to see later, and printed out an information sheet. It looked like a nice house, apart from the mirrored ceiling. I could see why it would appeal to the artistic Gary Lee; the construction was modern, the paint colors were funky—deep teal, dark mustard, rich burgundy—and it was in the heart of a neighborhood that was rapidly becoming one of the choice areas for musicians and artists. In a moment of abandon and outrageous optimism, I fished a Purchase and Sale Agreement out of the file-drawer and put it in my briefcase. It never hurts to be prepared.

Once that was done, I sat back in my chair and waited for the phone to ring. And while I waited, I did my best to finish my book. But for once, Barbara Botticelli's beautiful, blonde heroine and dark and dangerous hero failed to hold my attention. Usually, I identified with the heroine and her token struggles against the hero's smoldering sex-appeal, even if I knew she'd surrender in the end, but today, like last time, I pictured Elspeth swooning in Rafe's arms, and the image just wasn't sitting right with me.

The phone rang just before I was ready to head out. My cell phone, not the office phone. The display number was unfamiliar, but the overly familiar voice on the other end wasn't. "Savannah? This is Perry."

"Oh," I said. "Hello, Mr. Fortunato."

Perry chuckled. "Don't let's be so formal. After all, you've made out in my house, haven't you?"

"I beg your pardon?"

"Well," said Perry in a reasonable voice, "you brought your boyfriend to the open house last weekend, and of course I couldn't help but notice that the bed had been used…"

"I'm sorry," I said icily; not sounding a bit like I meant it, but quite a lot like my mother, "but I have no idea what you're talking about. He's not my boyfriend, and even if he were, we'd certainly not be making love in your bed. Such a thing would be totally inappropriate, not to mention grossly unprofessional on my part. It would never cross my mind. And if someone else made use of your bed…" Gary Lee and Charlene, obviously, "then I apologize for it having happened on my watch, but I assure you, I had no part in it."

"I see," Perry said, and had the nerve to sound disappointed. I guess he liked the idea that I'd been having sex in his bed, even if it was with someone else. Hypothetically with someone else. "In that case, please accept my apologies. I guess I jumped to conclusions."

"That's OK," I said graciously.

"I was really calling to ask a favor. When you called me yesterday—thank you so much—you said for me to call if there was anything you could do…?"

"Yes?" I crossed my fingers, and for good measure my legs too, hoping he wouldn't ask for anything icky.

"...and I was hoping that maybe you'd be willing to host another open house here tomorrow. Now that my dear wife is gone..." His smooth voice wobbled, "...it's more important than ever to sell the house quickly. The memories..."

He trailed off.

"Of course," I said. Poor man! "I'd be happy to."

"Thank you," Perry choked out.

"It's no problem. Although I'd only just met her, I liked your wife. It's nice to know I'm able to do something to make things easier for her widower during this trying time."

Hopefully that little zinger would keep him in line and off my back while I was at his house tomorrow. "I'll be there a little before two, like last time."

"Thank you," Perry said again. I assured him, again, that it was no problem, and hung up.

I STILL HAD PLENTY OF TIME to kill before I had to go meet Charlene and Gary Lee at their latest house of choice, so I stopped off at home for some lunch—a dry crust of bread with some Brie and a pear, which was all the refrigerator yielded—and then I headed back out. Call me a Nervous Nellie, but with two women already dead, one of them in the very house I'd be going to tomorrow, I decided I'd feel better with some protection. So I dug the piece of paper with the address Detective Grimaldi had given me earlier in the week out of my bag, and set out for the store that sold the Mace and other police issued self-protective gear.

I guess I expected it to be dark and dingy and scary—maybe an industrial-looking building in a not-so-nice area of downtown—but as it turned out, the store was located in a sunny, renovated bungalow in the heart of the antique district on 8th Avenue South. Its big windows and high ceilings had nothing dark or dingy about them; in fact, the only scary thing about the place was the proprietor.

She looked to be in her late forties, and if she couldn't bench-press my weight without breaking a sweat, I'd be very surprised. Her upper arms bulged with muscle, nicely off-set by the sleeveless shirt she wore with her skin-tight jeans, and her hair was shaved on the sides and left in a mohawk on top. It was colored a virulent red, like a particularly brilliant sunset, and made her look like a rooster. "Hello, princess," she said, looking me up and down from her vantage point behind the counter.

"Hi," I answered, picking my delicate way through the displays of tasers, surveillance equipment, and spray-bottles full of various lethal and non-lethal substances. "My name is Savannah Martin." I gave her one of my business cards.

She glanced at it. "Realtor, huh? Guess you want some personal protection, dontcha, Miss Priss?"

"I do," I said, deciding not to take the name-calling personally. "Detective Tamara Grimaldi told me to come here."

"Oh, you know Tamara, do you? Well, tell me what you want, missy, and I'll see what I can do."

"I don't know what I want," I said.

"Well, how big a hole d'ya wanna put in the bad guy, missy? D'ya want him to get back up again, or stay down?"

"I'd prefer for him to stay down," I said, "but I don't want to kill anyone, if it's all the same to you. I'd prefer something debilitating, but not fatal."

"Faint heart never won fair lady, princess. Much safer to get him down and keep him there. But you're the customer. I guess what you're looking for would be a nice, safe defensive spray, then?"

"Something like that," I agreed, relieved. "I mean, I'm sure a gun would be more useful in certain situations, but I just don't know that I'd be able to use it, you know. And if I can't, I figure I'm better off not having one. I'd rather have something I feel comfortable with."

She sneered, but didn't argue. "I have just the thing. Look at this." She pulled out a tray from under the counter. It was full of what looked like lipsticks, their holsters shiny and glossy in three different colors, plus black and silver. They looked exactly like what I sold from behind the make-up counter at Dillard's back in my retail days, six months ago. Not to mention that they looked exactly like what I'd taken Walker down with two weeks ago. I wrinkled my brows.

"I don't get it."

"They're pepper sprays. Here." She grabbed one and pulled the cap off, just like a real lipstick. A tiny nozzle appeared. "Weighs just a half ounce, but contains 6-10 one second bursts, and can spray up to eight feet. Available in five classy colors. Just the thing for a pretty girl to carry in her purse. Indistinguishable from all the other lipsticks." She grinned.

"I guess I'll take one of those. I just point and shoot, right?"

"That's right. Now, how about a little something else to go with it?"

She selected another tube and twisted it apart. I took an involuntary step back as the harmless-looking cosmetic transformed itself into a miniscule knife, its blade glittering wickedly. She smiled fondly at it as she explained. "By twisting the applicator, you get a 1.25" serrated blade, and no one will know it isn't just another lipstick. The blade ain't long enough to reach the heart, lungs, or kidneys, so it won't kill anyone, unless you use it to cut a wrist or a throat."

"Great," I said, trying to keep myself from remembering what Brenda Puckett's throat had looked like after Walker cut it. "I'll take one of those, too. Matching colors, please."

"Of course." She selected two that matched—silver—and put them in a brown paper baggie. I handed her my credit card, with a silent prayer that the machine wouldn't emit strident jeers of derision when she tried to run the charge through.

Once the deal was done, I said my goodbyes, took my bag and headed for the door. Just as I got there, another customer walked up the steps outside, and held the door for me. I passed him with a murmur of thanks and a bright, impersonal smile, the way one does a stranger under the circumstances, and then I did a double take when I realized that I actually knew him. Or didn't know him exactly, but at least I'd met him before.

He recognized me, too. "Afternoon, Miz Martin."

"Good afternoon. Are you… um… looking for me?"

"Why'd I be lookin' for you?" Wendell wanted to know.

I shrugged, blushing. "I thought maybe you had a message for me, or something. Or maybe Rafe asked you to keep an eye on me while he's gone."

"He ain't gone," Wendell said.

"What do you mean, he isn't gone?" I had assumed, once he realized that Julio Melendez would probably give the police his name, he'd be leaving Nashville as quickly as he could.

"The job ain't done," Wendell said.

I hesitated. "When you say 'the job', I suppose you're talking about the robberies? The open house robberies?"

Wendell didn't answer, and his eyes were as flat and uncommunicative as brown pebbles.

I decided not to think too hard about what 'the job' might be, or which part of it wasn't finished. Instead, I returned to what was really, ultimately, the most important thing. In this exchange, anyway. "So Rafe hasn't left town?"

"Not as of last night," Wendell answered.

"He's not in jail, is he? Or in hiding?"

An almost-smile tugged at the corners of Wendell's mouth. "No, he ain't hiding. Just goin' about his business, as usual."

"I see," I said. And because I saw that I was asking too many questions about a man I professed to have little interest in, I added, with an attempt at off-handedness which didn't quite come off, "Well, if you see him, tell him I said hello."

"Sure thing, Miz Martin." Wendell inclined his head politely. I did the same. He brushed past me into the store, and I continued down the steps and across the parking lot to the Volvo.

GARY LEE AND CHARLENE WERE ready and waiting by the time I got to the latest in the long line of houses they wanted to see. It looked like it might be a nice one, too; not too big, not too small, new, but with enough character to blend in with the older homes surrounding it. I opened the door for them, and we all went inside, into the living room/dining room/kitchen combo, where we stopped and looked around at the fireplace, gleaming wood floors, and granite-topped breakfast bar. "Nice place," Gary Lee commented. Charlene nodded.

"The bedrooms are upstairs," I said, consulting the MLS-sheet I had brought with me. "There are three of them, although one is pretty small and might be a better music room or study."

Charlene and Gary Lee exchanged a glance. "Um, Savannah..." Charlene said. "Are you going to follow us around everywhere?"

"Do I have to follow you around everywhere?" I asked, looking from one to the other of them. They both shook their heads. "In that case, I guess not. Have a look around on your own. Don't do anything I wouldn't do, and if you do, make sure you clean up after yourselves. Perry Fortunato noticed the bed had been used last weekend."

"OK." They glanced at each other and started looking around. I watched them walk up the stairs to the second floor before I headed back out to the porch. Out of sight, out of mind, kind of. If they were going to do anything icky, I'd just as soon not know about it. If it hadn't been for Connie's murder and the MNPD's no doubt fine-tooth-combing of the Fortunatos' bedroom, no one would ever have known what Charlene and Gary Lee had been up to, and I was just fine with that.

They stayed gone for long enough to have managed a quickie, and when they came back out, Charlene's cheeks were flushed and her hair was messy. So was Gary Lee's, although it always was, so that wasn't indicative of anything except a disinclination to comb it.

"We really like it, Savannah!" Charlene burbled.

"Great," I said, and because I still felt put-upon by the whole thing, I turned to Gary Lee. "And was it good for you, too?"

Gary Lee had the grace to look embarrassed, but he nodded. "We think we might like to live in this house."

"Really?" If I sounded surprised, it was because I was. I had expected some run-around about waiting and thinking about it, and to be put off and put off until I forgot I'd ever known Gary Lee and Charlene, but maybe there was hope after all. "Are you sure?"

They looked at each other. "Um… pretty much…"

"Great!" I said. "I brought a purchase and sale agreement with me. All we have to do is fill it out. Then you give me an earnest money check, and I'll call the other Realtor."

"Oh. Um…" They exchanged another glance.

"Yes?"

"We didn't bring the checkbook."

"Oh," I said. And rallied. "OK. We can go to your place and write the contract there. That way you can get the checkbook."

"Oh. Um…"

"Yes?"

"How much does an earnest money check have to be for?"

"Enough to show you're serious about making the offer. That's why they call it earnest money."

"Oh. Um…"

"Yes?"

"We think we need to talk about this before we do anything."

"OK," I said, giving up. I should have known it was too good to be true. "Give me a call, then, when you've finished talking. Hopefully the house will still be on the market."

"Right." They didn't look at each other, or at me, when they said their goodbyes and headed for the car. I locked up and got into my own car, grumbling.

Nineteen

Todd rang the doorbell promptly at six, and handed me a big bunch of roses. They were interspersed with tiny sprigs of baby's breath, like a wedding bouquet. Had they been red, I would have been worried. As it was, they were yellow, so I decided I had no cause for concern. At least not tonight.

I had gotten dressed up for the occasion in one of my nicest cocktail-dresses, bright blue with little beads along the décolletage, and Todd was very complimentary. "You look absolutely stunning, Savannah," he said sincerely, looking deeply into my eyes across the table in Fidelio's Restaurant. I preened.

Both the maitre d' and the waiter had greeted me familiarly when we arrived. I'd been there so many times over the past couple of weeks, I guess I was becoming something of a regular. Maybe they were as heartily sick of seeing me as I was of being here.

We were seated at our usual table, in the darkly romantic section of the restaurant, screened by ferny plants and surrounded by tinkling fountains to drown out private conversation. Not that there was anything to drown out tonight; Todd had taken my warning to heart, and was careful not to mention Rafe by name or in any other way. Not even obliquely. It was wonderful not to have to watch my every word, nor to keep looking for hidden meanings in everything Todd said. It brought me back to my sophomore year in high school, when life had been simple and Todd and I had been an item. He and I, along with Dix and my best friend Charlotte, had gone everywhere together that year. Football games, swimming, ice skating, the prom...

"Have you seen Charlotte recently?" Todd wanted to know, as if he'd been reading my mind.

I shook my head. Charlotte had married a cosmetic surgeon after college, and had moved to—of all places—Charlotte, North Carolina. The last time I'd seen her was four years earlier, at my wedding to Bradley. "She calls me every so often, just to talk, but I haven't heard from her for a couple of months. I guess she's busy."

I took a dainty bite of chicken and rosemary stuffed ravioli and chewed.

"That's a shame," Todd said, picking at his veal piccata. "You two were such good friends in high school."

I shrugged. "It's what happens when people move away. You lose contact. And we're in different places in our lives. She's still married with a husband and children. I'm not."

"That could change, though," Todd said. I swallowed too quickly, and had to take a sip of wine to stop coughing, totally ruining my intention of changing the subject before he could say anything else about it. But then he didn't. Or not directly. "Did you hear about old Mr. Patton?"

I shook my head. I didn't even know who old Mr. Patton was, let alone what had happened to him. The name was vaguely familiar, but that was all.

"He owned that big farmhouse down by the river, near where we used to go swimming in the summer," Todd said. "You know the place. White house, a barn or two, flagpole..."

"Oh, yes." I remembered Mr. Patton. "What about him?"

"He passed away recently."

"Really?" Why did Todd think I might be interested in curmudgeonly old Mr. Patton's passing?

Todd forked up a piece of veal. "Dix is handling the estate. He says they'll probably end up selling the house once they've gotten through probate. The old man didn't have any children, and his sister's children and grandchildren don't want to move back to Sweetwater."

"I see," I said.

"I've always thought it would make a great place to live and raise a family."

It seemed to me he already had a great place to live—with his father in the house on the square—but I decided to let it lie. "Well, of course it would. Nice, old house, lots of land, beautiful view, and that private stretch of river…"

Todd grinned. "We had some fun, didn't we, Savannah?"

I smiled back. "Yes, we did."

"Do you remember that time I bet Dix he couldn't hoist Charlotte's pom-poms to the top of Mr. Patton's flagpole without the old man seeing him, and he did it?"

I nodded. Who could forget something like that?

The conversation lingered in the past all the way through dessert. It was nice and comfortable, like a familiar place after a long absence. And I'm not talking about the past so much as Todd's and my relationship. Until he came back to Sweetwater and started giving me a hard time about Rafe, I'd always felt very comfortable with him. He'd been my brother's best friend growing up, so I'd known him practically my whole life, and although our going steady in high school had been more about making my parents—and Dix—happy than because I was so much in love with Todd, we'd always been friendly. When he didn't hassle me, he was good company, very charming and considerate, with the old-fashioned manners of a true Southern gentleman. We had a lot in common. If he hadn't left Sweetwater to go to law school, and I hadn't gone to Nashville and met Bradley while he was gone, I might have ended up becoming Mrs. Todd Satterfield.

In its way, it was a seductive, comfortable fantasy. It was what I had signed on for when I married Bradley. But then fate—and Shelby—had intervened, and the perfect life I had envisioned—the perfect life I had been led to believe I'd have if I did everything correctly—had fallen apart. Instead of being the safe, cherished, protected wife of a successful attorney, with a townhouse in Green Hills and no worries, I was single, celibate, and hustling to try to make a success of myself in one of the most competitive businesses in the country, before the savings account ran dry and I started defaulting on my rent and my bills.

But that's neither here nor there. Todd and I talked about old times, and people we both knew, and his father, and my mother, and Dix and Sheila, and interests we shared, like theatre and art. Anything and everything except Rafe Collier, or any subject remotely related to him. No crimes—murders, rapes or robberies—marred the conversation, and by the time dinner was over and we were on our way back to my place, I was relaxed and mellow and feeling more kindly towards Todd than I had in a while. When he took me in his arms outside the door, I was pliant enough that the kiss developed into an embrace more passionate than I was comfortable with in the hallway outside my apartment.

All in all I have to say I was relieved when he let me go and stepped back. My voice sounded funny when I thanked him for dinner, and so did his when he answered. It was husky and low. "You're welcome. Any time. Good night, Savannah."

"Good night, Todd," I said, and I didn't look up until he had turned around and was walking away from me down the hallway toward the stairs.

GARY LEE AND CHARLENE DID not call me on Sunday morning, and neither did Beau Riggins. Beau I could forgive—he was probably sleeping in, after his no doubt exhausting night with his Latin spitfire—but I was seriously put out with the Hodgeses. Their behavior was totally inappropriate and disgusting, and I felt foolish for letting them con me again. They'd probably had themselves one last quickie under the mirrored ceiling while I was standing on the front porch waiting for them finish, and now I'd never see them again. Maybe everyone who'd warned me about getting into real estate had been right. Maybe I really wasn't cut out for it. Surely Tim would have caught on much sooner than I had—especially considering how sex-fixated he was—and I wouldn't be surprised if Rafe had had his suspicions last weekend, too, at the Fortunatos' house. There had been something in his voice and his eyes at the time, that I had taken for just the usual amusement, but in retrospect, I thought he had probably been having a good, if silent, laugh at my expense.

And where the hell was he, anyway? Wendell had assured me that he was still in town, so why didn't he get in touch? I could understand why he'd want to stay away from Detective Grimaldi, who'd probably lock him up if she saw him, but surely he could spare the time to give me a call? Especially after the conversation we'd had in the car on Thursday, and the way we'd been interrupted.

Or maybe that had all been an act, too. As gullible as I seemed to be, an accomplished liar like Rafe could probably play me like a violin. Which just went to show that I should just give up trying to make my own way in the world, and when Todd proposed again, which he was bound to do sooner or later, I could say yes and put all this aggravation behind me. I wouldn't have to worry about making ends meet, or converting prospects to clients, or making sales… I could just marry someone who'd take care of me, and be the perfect wife and, in a year or two, the mother that my mother taught me to be.

But first, there was Perry Fortunato's open house to get through. And I was still a Realtor and had an image to uphold, so I dressed in proper business attire—black skirt and pink blouse with high-heeled pumps and pearls in my ears—and set out for Brentwood.

The open house sign had been put in the yard—probably by Perry himself—and he was just leaving when I pulled up into the driveway. When he saw me, he got back out of his car and waited for me to stop mine before he grabbed the door handle and opened my door for me. "Good afternoon, Savannah."

Considering that his wife had only been dead for a couple of days, and wasn't even in the ground yet, his gaze was a mite too appreciative. He had dark rings under his eyes, however, and looked like he had lost weight since last week, so I decided to cut him a break. "Good afternoon, Mr. Fortunato. Thank you."

He smiled. "No problem. Let me get that for you." He leaned into the car, brushing up against me on the way, and grabbed my bag of paraphernalia—scented candles, sign-in sheets, pens, and so on—from the passenger seat.

"Thank you," I said again.

"No problem. Let me walk you in." He started up the stairs, and I had no choice but to follow, although I didn't really want the company. It's always recommended that an owner leave his or her open house to the agent, so as not to make any visitors feel uncomfortable, plus, I really didn't enjoy Perry's attentions. Bad enough that he'd been paying attention to me in the first place, being a good ten years too old for me and married to boot, but now, with his wife lying on a slab in the morgue...!

However, I needn't have worried. He opened the door and walked the bag into the kitchen, where he left it on the island and turned to me. "Anything else I can do for you before I go?"

I shook my head. "I've been here before, I know where everything is."

"I put the open house sign in the yard," Perry said, like a little boy fishing for praise.

"I noticed. Thank you."

"There are sodas and things in the fridge if you get hungry or thirsty, and of course there's the bar in the den…"

"I'm on duty," I said with a smile, "so I'm afraid drinking is out of the question, but thank you."

He looked around vaguely. "Connie had some magazines and such sitting around, in case you get bored. There's no ad in the paper today, so you may not get a whole lot of visitors."

"I'm sure it'll be fine," I said, wondering why he didn't just leave. "Thanks for your concern, but I brought a book, just in case."

Perry stuck his hand into the bag and pulled the book out. It was the same bodice ripper I'd tried to read for the past few days, without luck. I'd figured if I brought it here, where I had nothing else to do, maybe I'd actually get through it. However, when Perry looked at the cover and arched his brows and pursed his lips, I flushed in embarrassment. Like all of Barbara Botticelli's books, the cover showed a swooning blonde whose blouse was gaping open over her more-than-ample breasts, being leered at by a swarthy and bare-chested rogue. The rogue in this case was a pirate, as evidenced by the sea in the background and the skull-and-crossbones waving in the breeze. The girl was tied to the mast of the pirate ship, and the title, emblazoned in crimson letters across the top half of the book, proclaimed her as 'Pirate's Booty'. The double entendre was no doubt intentional.

I waited for Perry to comment, but he didn't, just dropped the book back into the bag, and asked, "Are you expecting company?"

I wrinkled my brows. That was the point, wasn't it? For people to show up?

"Your boyfriend," Perry clarified. "The one who was here last weekend. Are you expecting him again?"

Oh.

"He's not my boyfriend. And no, I'm not expecting him." Of course, I hadn't expected him last week, either, but at least then I'd told him beforehand that I was going to be here. Today, it would take almost supernatural powers to find me. That realization was a little uncomfortable; not because I suspected Perry of anything in particular, other than of trying to flirt with me under circumstances when he really shouldn't be, but because two women were dead and I didn't want to end up as third time unlucky.

For a second I thought about asking Perry to stay, but then common sense prevailed. I'd just use the phone to call someone as soon as he left. And if I kept the doors closed, and made sure I didn't let anyone in who looked the least bit suspicious, I ought to be all right.

"Why do you ask?" I added, belatedly.

Perry made an apologetic moue. "I don't mean to offend..."

"Don't worry." My voice was dry. "I know him too well to take offense at anything anyone has to say about him."

"Well..." Perry still looked apologetic. "If you'll forgive the impertinence, he didn't seem like the type of person I'd expect would interest a well-brought-up young woman like yourself. I was wondering if perhaps he was using you."

"Oh." I blushed. "No. He's not."

"Not necessarily in a sexual way," Perry said, with a penetrating look at me. "But perhaps... well, I wondered if he might have had something to do with what happened to my poor, dear Connie. That he was using you to gain entrance to the house."

I shook my head. "Absolutely not."

"How can you be sure?"

"I trust him," I said firmly. "I know he wouldn't kill anyone." Stealing the painting, yes; I could maybe see that. But not murder. And certainly not rape and murder. "He's not the type who has to resort to rape to get a woman. No offense."

Perry didn't answer, just looked at me. For long enough to make me squirm.

"If you say so," he said—finally!—and headed for the door.

I breathed a sigh of relief, which I did my best to hide with a breezy goodbye. And then I waited for him to disappear down the drive before I locked the door behind him and went back to the kitchen to find my phone.

I wish I could tell you that the open house was a smashing success and that several people showed up who seemed seriously interested in buying the place, but unfortunately, such was not the case. In actuality, nobody showed up at all, save for a couple who seemed to find the opulence of the house a little oppressive, and a few gawkers who mostly were interested in seeing the bedroom where the murder had taken place. I'd dealt with the same phenomenon after Brenda Puckett's death, when I hosted an open house at 101 Potsdam Street. The one where Walker tried to kill me. At least no one was trying to hurt me today, and no one was chanting and trying to contact Connie's wandering spirit, either. Thank God.

Just before 3:30 Beau Riggins finally called. "Good afternoon, gorgeous."

"Same to you," I said.

Beau giggled. "What are you doing with yourself?"

"Hosting an open house at the Fortunatos'. You?"

"Just rolling out of bed. Late night." As if to provide proof, he yawned and then apologized.

"No problem," I said. "Now that I've got hold of you, would you be willing to answer a couple of questions for me?"

"For you," Beau said expansively, "anything."

"Thank you. It's about the open house robberies and the murders. You know, Lila Vaughn's murder, and now Connie Fortunato's."

Beau shuddered. I could hear it through the phone. "Awful business. Just shocking. I don't know how I'll ever be able to go back to the Fortunatos' again."

After a moment he added prosaically, with most of the drama gone from his voice, "Of course, I may not have a job there anymore. With Connie gone, I doubt Perry'll keep me on."

"Perry doesn't swing that way?"

I meant it facetiously. Beau took me seriously. "Oh, no. Perry's got his problems, but that isn't one of them."

"What kind of problems does he have?"

I hadn't contacted Beau to find out about Perry Fortunato—I was more interested in Beau himself, and the coincidence that he'd worked for all three of the houses that had had items stolen—but I thought discussing Perry might open the door for further confidences. If I gave him the chance to tell me about Perry first, maybe he'd be more willing to talk about himself later.

"Money, mostly," Beau said with an audible shrug. "He likes to visit pay-per-click porn sites, from what I understand."

Eeeuw. "How can he afford to pay your salary if he's wasting all his money on the internet?"

"Oh, it isn't his money," Beau said. "Or I guess it is now. But Connie was the one with the money. Her father made a pile in the stock-market—one of those guys who started with nothing and ended up raking in money the way the rest of us rake leaves in the fall—and he left it all to his little girl when he died. Perry's been making inroads, but the money is Connie's. Or was."

"So it was Connie who was paying you." And presumably watching him swing his feather duster.

Beau knew what I was thinking. "She was a nice lady. I'm gonna miss her."

"And her money."

Beau giggled. "There are plenty of other people who'll gladly pay my salary, sweetie. I won't be hurting. But I liked her. She deserved better than that idiot she married."

"Somebody else said that, as well," I said. "That same someone also told me that you work for all three of the houses that have been robbed."

I had hoped for some kind of reaction, but I got none at all. "I work for a lot of people," Beau said.

"Mr. Givens," I said, "and his boyfriend. The Caldwells and the Fortunatos."

"So?"

"So don't you think it's a bit of a coincidence that three of your clients have been robbed in the past three weeks?"

"Maybe so," Beau said, "but that's all it is. A coincidence. I didn't rob anyone. Why would I? I make good money doing what I do."

"Not as good as you could on what went missing. Paul and Simon's art collection must have been worth a pretty penny, and I'm sure the Fortunatos' O'Keeffe was worth even more."

Beau mentioned a price that made my jaw drop and my eyes bug out of my skull. "How do you know?"

"Heard them talking about it," Beau said. "I was dusting that little room of Perry's behind the master bedroom, and I guess they didn't realize I was there."

"Perry has a room behind the master bedroom? I never noticed it." And as a result, never mentioned it to any potential buyers, either. Granted, in a house this size, one little room wouldn't make much of an impression, but still: a room is a room.

"You won't," Beau said, "unless you know it's there. It isn't a secret or anything; it isn't even much of a room. More of a big closet, really, behind the other closet. With racks to hang clothes and shelves to store things on. He keeps his dirty magazines in there, and his collection of porn videos."

"Yuck!"

"A lot of people have goody-drawers," Beau said tolerantly. "Perry's goody-closet is a little bigger than most, is all."

"Double-yuck! Oh, gack!"

Beau chuckled. "You should see Paul and Simon's goody-drawer. Perry's collection looks tame compared to theirs. And there's not much in the way of… um… tools. Anyway, I was there, dusting, and they started arguing in the bedroom. Perry asked for money, and Connie said no. He brought up the O'Keeffe, saying that she wasn't hurting for money with that thing hanging on the wall, and she could afford to give him some more. But Connie refused, and told him if he didn't stop wasting her daddy's money on online whores she'd divorce him, and they got into a filthy row, which ended with him banging out and slamming the door."

"Yikes," I said.

"Yep. And then Connie freaked out again when she realized I'd heard the whole thing. I had to do some stuff I'm not proud of to calm her down."

He was on the other end of the phone line—for all I knew on the other side of town—or I'm not sure I would have dared to challenge him. "I don't suppose you mean that you tied her to the bed and strangled her?"

"Of course not!" Beau said. "I told you, I liked her. I'd never do anything to hurt her. If you have to know, I slept with her."

"Oh," I said. "Sorry."

"No need to apologize. It wasn't that bad." He hesitated for a moment before adding, "I can't imagine why she put up with Perry's crap."

I couldn't, either. Bradley has been normal to the point of boring in bed, but if my husband had had a goody-closet full of dirty magazines and videos, I couldn't imagine letting him touch me.

"So was that all you wanted to know, darling?" Beau asked.

"Pretty much, I guess…"

"In that case I'm going back to bed. All this talk about goody-drawers has put me in mind of certain things. I'll talk to you later." He hung up before I had the chance to say goodbye, let alone to thank him for his help.

Of course the mention of Perry's secret closet had piqued my interest. Not because I wanted to look at his collection of dirty magazines and videos, let alone his sex-toys, but we have a secret room at the Martin plantation too. Rumor has it that a Martin lady from the time of the War Against Northern Aggression hid a Confederate spy there while the Union soldiers were mucking about outside. Which was a whole different ballgame than what I found in Perry's cubby.

As Beau had said, the 'secret' room wasn't all that secret once you knew where to look for it, and it also wasn't much of a room. More of a walk-in closet, really. The access was through a wall of shelves that swung out when I pulled on it. I stepped into the small space and looked around.

Beau hadn't been kidding. There must be hundreds of dirty magazines in there, in stacks on the shelves. Most of them looked well-used, as if someone had been thumbing through them a lot. And they weren't the soft, suggestive variety of which Dix had owned a couple back in his teens. (He'd hid them under the mattress in the old slave cabin so mother wouldn't find them.) These were the hard-core kind, with nothing suggestive about them at all. If Perry had been my husband, he would have ceased to be so as soon as I got a look at his collection. To call it disturbing didn't even begin to cover it.

The movies were of the same caliber, with titles that made me blush, although a few looked like home movies. They were dated, not labeled. Counting back on my fingers, I realized that the last one was dated for Friday a week ago, which just happened to be the day of Lila's murder. There was also a folder with photographs, some of which Perry must have downloaded off the internet, and some of Connie. One was of Connie with a man, one who looked a lot like Beau Riggins. I turned it face down, blushing. How totally icky of Perry, to photograph his wife having sex with someone else.

Entirely apart from the fact that the display was making me feel nauseous and creeped out, I didn't want to linger in the secret room too long. It was getting on for 4 PM and the end of the open house, and I had a duty to Perry—no matter how disgusting he was. I was just about to close the shelves behind me when I noticed a black gym bag over in the corner. It looked out of place; where everything else in Perry's personal space was obsessively neat and orderly, the bag seemed to have been negligently tossed there at some point. Curiosity got the better of me, and I tiptoed back into the little room and dragged it out from under the shelf. It had a zipper across the top, and when I pulled it, the bag opened. I stuck my hand in, grabbed the topmost thing—black and woolen—and pulled. And dropped it with an exclamation a moment later. It was a black ski mask.

Twenty

"Yoo-hoo!" a voice called. "Anybody home?"

I swung around on my heel with a terrified squeak. It wasn't 4 o'clock yet; Perry wasn't supposed to be back!

Yet he was. Clearly. It was his voice I heard. "Hello? Savannah?"

What happened next can only be put down to extreme stupidity on my part. Instead of stepping out of the closet and trying to spin what was going on in a way that might get me out of the house with my skin intact, I did the worst possible thing: I slammed the shelf shut, closing myself up inside Perry's special closet.

Of course I realized almost immediately how dumb I had been, but by then it was too late. I couldn't find a way out. There had to be one, but in the dark, with my hands shaking and with no clue where to look, I wasn't able to locate the latch or lock that kept the secret closet a secret. My handbag and open house paraphernalia were still on the kitchen island, so Perry would know I was around somewhere—unless he thought I'd been abducted—and sooner or later he'd find me. And what would happen to me then was too terrifying to contemplate. The ski mask I'd seen made him a prime suspect in Lila's murder, the videos and magazines were additional evidence of his liking for bondage and rough sex, and I could come up with several reasons why he might have killed Connie. She had the money in the family and he didn't. He wanted her to sell the O'Keeffe and she wouldn't. She had threatened to divorce him. Plus, she might have suspected him of killing Lila, and if what Heather had said was true, Connie wouldn't have stood for being publicly humiliated. Or she might have walked in on him taking the O'Keeffe, and he killed her over that. The open house robberies and Lila's murder had probably given him the idea, and if Perry had taken the painting, that would explain why there was no sign of forced entry. If he could pin both the robbery and the two murders on someone else—like Rafe and his associates—he'd be home free. At least until I'd stumbled into his closet and found his bag.

All of these thoughts went through my mind in flash, before I could jolt myself into action. Hands shaking, I pulled my cell phone out of my pocket, thanking God for my habit of keeping it in my pocket instead of in my bag, and used the lighted display to dial Detective Grimaldi's number. And got her voice mail. Cursing—silently, of course—I hung up and tried again. 911 this time. Only to be put on hold. Which really shouldn't happen when one's in mortal danger. I hung up again, feeling as if time was running short. I couldn't count on Dix to answer, or Todd, or Tim. The only other person whose number I knew by heart, and whose phone had always been answered by a live person—someone who might actually be of some use to me—was Rafe. Or more accurately, Wendell. I heard Perry come into the bedroom as I fumbled to punch the numbers into the phone. His voice was playful and joking, but not in a good way. "Come out, come out, wherever you are!"

I put the phone to my ear with a shaking hand, listening to it ring on the other end. *Pick up; come on, pick up!*

The closet shelves swung outward just as Wendell answered. "Grocery store."

"I need Rafe," I said, as quickly and succinctly as I could. "I need help. Perry Fortunato…"

And that was all I got out, before Perry reached down and snatched the phone out of my hand. I heard Wendell's stock answer float into thin air, "Nobody here by that name," before Perry snapped the phone shut and tossed it over his shoulder into the recesses of the closet. Looking at me and shaking his head sadly, he clicked his tongue. "Savannah, Savannah. What am I going to do with you?"

It wasn't a question I wanted to answer, and judging from the light in his eyes and the excitement distorting his features, I thought he had a pretty good idea anyway, without my input.

When he grabbed me by the arm and yanked me to my feet, I did my best to fight and get free, but all it got me was a clout on the side of the head which made me see stars. While I was blinking away tears and trying to pull myself together to try again, I heard Perry scrabbling in the dark, and then I heard a fizzing sound, and the next second, everything went black.

When I woke up, I was still in the Fortunatos' house. For that matter, I was still in the master bedroom. The sun outside the window was a little lower in the sky, so I estimated that an hour or so might have passed, but no more. My head hurt, and I was feeling nauseous. This time it wasn't just from fear and disgust, though; it was physical. From everything I had read and seen on TV, I rather thought Perry had hit me with a taser and knocked my cells for a loop.

While I was unconscious, he had moved me from the closet onto the bed, and tied my hands to the headboard with a piece of twine. He had also undressed me.

I wasn't totally naked, so I suppose it could have been worse. The idea of Perry stripping off my underwear while I was out cold, was beyond disgusting and terrifying; it was abhorrent.

On the other hand, the fact that he'd taken off my blouse and skirt was bad enough. I was still wearing the pink bra and panties I had put on that morning to match my pink blouse. Other than that, all I had on were earrings and black pumps with an ankle strap. My own. They looked a lot tartier without proper clothes to dress them up. And I had a perfect view of them, and of everything else, in the mirrored ceiling.

Perry was nowhere to be seen, which was the one positive aspect of the situation. The flipside was that although he wasn't here now, he was sure to be coming back, and there was nothing I could do but wait, since I couldn't free my hands without help. I tugged as hard as I could, and twisted my hands, but all I accomplished was to make the rope bite into my wrists. An image of Lila's hands, wrists abraded, in the photograph that Detective Grimaldi had shown me the day after Lila's death, flashed through my mind, and I closed my eyes to fight back the tears.

The door to hallway was closed, but after another few minutes, something seemed to happen downstairs. I heard what sounded like a thump, and then, unmistakably, footsteps on the stairs. Rapid, impatient steps. I pictured Perry bearing down on me, and renewed my thrashings. I knew it wouldn't do any good, but it was the only thing I could do, so I did it. A hand grabbed the doorknob and twisted, but the door didn't open. It strained, as if something heavy was pushing against it from the other side. For a breathless second, nothing happened, and then the door exploded inward with a splintering noise and an almighty bang as it slammed against the wall and bounced back. Rafe stood in the doorway, looking like the avenging hero in one of my favorite bodice rippers: muscles rippling, chest expanding, and eyes black as pitch.

"Thank God!" I breathed.

He didn't answer, just stood there for a second, staring at me, catching his breath. I didn't realize it until later, when I replayed the whole scene in my head, but he probably hadn't been sure what he'd find behind the door, and he needed a moment to process the fact that I was alive, awake, and seemingly unharmed. Oh, yes, and practically naked. Once he had, his face settled into smooth expressionlessness again, and his voice was bland and courteous. Or as courteous as Rafe ever is.

"Evening, darlin'." He came into the room, his feet making no noise on the fluffy shag rug.

"Hi," I said, a little unsure how I felt about the flash of heat in his eyes.

"Got yourself in a fix, ain't you?"

He stopped at the side of the bed and reached out to touch me. Gently, with just the tip of a finger, running it lightly up the inside of my arm from shoulder to wrist. I broke out in goosebumps, and if I didn't gasp, it was a near thing. Gritting my teeth, I fought to keep my voice steady.

"Please, Rafe, not now. Just untie me, OK? Before he comes back."

He didn't move. "Oh, he ain't gonna be back anytime soon. I left him downstairs."

Curiosity reared its head long enough for me to ask, "What did you do to him?"

"Knocked him out on my way past. We've got some time."

"I don't want any time," I said, squirming. "I just want to get untied."

"But surely you don't expect me not to take advantage of the situation, darlin'? Not when I've got you just where I want you?"

If he was feeling any urgency at all, I couldn't tell by looking at him.

"Tell you what," I said desperately, "if you untie me, I'll let you take advantage of me some other time instead."

"Yeah?"

"I promise. Just get me out of here in one piece and without letting Perry touch me, and I'll do whatever you want."

"Now, there's an offer that's hard to refuse. *Anything* I want?"

I hesitated. This was Rafe; he might want something I wasn't prepared to give. "Within reason."

He smiled. "That ain't what you said a second ago."

"Fine. Anything you want. Anything at all. Just please untie me!"

"You gonna give that to me in writing, darlin'?"

"I'm sorry," I said, my patience as well as my fear quotient stretched very thin, "I'm a little tied up here."

"How about we seal it with a kiss, then?" He winked.

"As long as it's *after* you've untied me."

"Sure thing, darlin'." He moved to the head of the bed to go to work on the knotted ropes, but before he got that far, Perry burst through the door. I'd been so focused on Rafe that I hadn't even heard Perry come thundering up the stairs. And I must say he looked a little the worse for wear. He had a puffy lip, a swollen eye, and a burgeoning bruise on the side of his jaw. He also had murder in his eyes. Up until this moment, I had thought that to be a figure of speech. Now I realized I'd been wrong.

"You!" He pointed a shaking finger at Rafe.

"I thought you said you knocked him out!" I squeaked.

Rafe shrugged. "Thought I did. Guess I was in a hurry. I'll do better next time."

"There won't be a next time!" Perry snarled, pulling a gun out of his pocket.

The world stopped for a moment, while I processed the fact that this was the second time in a month I'd come face to face with a killer waving a gun.

Unlike last time, this gun wasn't aimed at me. Perry had it pointed straight at Rafe's stomach, with a hand that didn't shake at all anymore. I suppose the fact that he wasn't threatening to shoot me ought to have made me feel better, but there was nothing to keep him from turning the gun on me once he'd shot Rafe, and if it came down to it, I didn't particularly want to watch Rafe die, either. And at least when Walker had pointed his gun at me, I'd had the option of running away. Not so this time. I was stuck here, like a tethered goat. My demise seemed inevitable.

Of course, I'd probably rather take a quick bullet to the head than have the life slowly squeezed out of me like Lila and Connie, but when the rubber met the road, I'd prefer not to die at all.

Rafe probably didn't want to die either, but he didn't show it.

"Shit," he said, his voice even and unemotional, and his face expressionless. One would think he'd looked down the barrels of so many guns that they'd become old hat. It wasn't an entirely comfortable thought, and I didn't think I'd ever want to get to that point myself. Then again, if I ever did, at least I'd still be alive, and that was something.

"What are you going to do to us?" I asked. And unlike Rafe's voice, mine shook nervously. Perry turned to me, and it was a toss-up whether my semi-nudity or my fear excited him more. Either way, he was clearly flying high. His eyes shone and his nostrils flared.

"First," he said gaily, gesturing with the gun, "I figure I'll shoot your boyfriend. It'll be easier that way; I won't have to worry about him butting in. Or maybe I should make him watch. That might prove interesting…"

He eyed Rafe speculatively. Rafe stared back, his face a hard mask.

"He's not my boyfriend," I said. Perry nodded, but solicitously, like he didn't really believe me. "No," I insisted, "he's really not. My mother would disown me if I had anything to do with him."

Rafe looked at me, but didn't speak.

"Is that so?" Perry assessed him for a moment before turning back to me. "Why?"

"Why, what?"

"Why would your mother disown you if you had anything to do with him?"

I lowered my voice apologetically, as if I could somehow prevent Rafe from hearing me. "Well… he's not a gentleman."

"Not a gentleman?" Perry repeated blankly. One would think he had never heard the term before.

I shook my head. "He's really not. I mean, he grew up in a trailer. On the wrong side of town. With a single mother. One who got herself in the family way at fourteen. By a colored boy. He went to jail before he could vote. On top of that, he drives a motorcycle. And most importantly, he's not a lawyer."

"A lawyer?" Perry said, blinking under the onslaught of mostly irrelevant information. I nodded, determined to distract him for as long as possible. Maybe if I could keep him talking, Rafe could come up with a way to overpower him. Unless I was seriously annoying Rafe, of course, and he decided not to bother trying to save me.

"Everyone in my family is a lawyer. My father was a lawyer. My grandfather was a lawyer. My brother's a lawyer. My brother-in-law is a lawyer. My ex-husband's a lawyer. Even my ex-boyfriend…"

"I get the point," Perry said.

"Well, I'm supposed to marry a lawyer. Or if not a lawyer, at least someone who'll be an asset to the family. Not a common criminal. And of course it has to be someone my mother will approve of. He has to be successful, from a good family, and have a nice house and a nice car and enough money to provide for me. And the proper background and the right manners."

"Of course," Perry said.

"So you can see why I couldn't possibly have anything to do with…" I lowered my voice apologetically and shot a glance in Rafe's direction, "…*him*."

Perry contemplated him in silence for a moment before he nodded. The gun was still fixed on Rafe's stomach, but Perry was clearly distracted. Rafe looked angry. There was heightened color in his cheeks, and the look he sent me could have pinned me to the wall, had I not already been pinned to the bed. I won't repeat the words he used to describe what he'd like to do to me and my social attitudes, but they were blunt, coarse, and very rude. I blushed. Perry giggled, and Rafe turned to him. His eyes were dark and dangerous.

"How about I make you a deal? With the mirrors and cameras and all…"

Cameras? There were cameras?

I twisted around frantically, trying to discover where they were, while Rafe continued smoothly, "…I figure you probably enjoy watching. If you're gonna shoot her anyway, how about you let me take a turn with her first?"

"How do I know you won't do anything stupid?" Perry asked reasonably.

Rafe shrugged. "You can always do her yourself, after. She ain't a virgin, so it ain't like I'm cheating you out of anything."

Perry hesitated. I could tell he was torn. On the one hand, he probably wanted first dibs on me, and was loath to give them up to someone else. On the other, I couldn't blame him for preferring to work *with* Rafe rather than against him. Rafe looked like a formidable foe, and his explanation for why he wanted to 'do' me sounded reasonable. And Perry was just disgusting enough to find the prospect of watching Rafe rape me exciting.

"Please," I blurted, "don't let him touch me!"

Both men looked at me. "You afraid of me, darlin'?" Rafe asked. His voice was low and husky, and along with the anger, there was heat simmering in his eyes. He both looked and sounded frighteningly convincing.

I nodded. Hell, yes. For the most part I had managed to get over my fear of him, but it wasn't buried so deep that something like this couldn't bring it back to the surface. At the moment, I found it only too easy to be afraid.

Perry giggled. "You know what they say, Savannah. If it's unavoidable, just lie back and enjoy it."

"Is that what you said to Lila?" I asked, as Rafe's lips curved in what looked like appreciation. "Before you raped and strangled her?"

Perry's face darkened. "Lila Vaughn was a tramp," he said. "Always coming on to men. Always making eyes and showing her body. And then always saying no."

"Sounds like you, darlin'," Rafe commented. I stared at him, shocked. "Always making promises and never delivering."

"I've never…!" I began, indignantly.

His voice changed, and his mimicry of my tone and inflection was devastatingly accurate. "*Please, Rafe. I'll do anything you want. Just please help me.*"

It was only a couple of minutes since I'd used those words. Perry said, "Why don't you take her up on that promise now?"

"My pleasure." Rafe turned to me. One of his hands—the one closest to Perry—went to the zipper in his jeans. I gulped. Out of the corner of my eye, I saw him slip the other hand into his pocket, but I didn't pay a whole lot of attention to it. All of my senses were focused on his face, on the smile that pulled the corners of his mouth up, and the desire licking at his pupils.

"No," I breathed, shaking my head and trying to scoot away. Perry giggled, and moved closer for a better view.

The next thing that happened, happened so quickly that I didn't see it. I saw the movement and the result, but not the act itself. Rafe's hand whipped out of his jeans pocket in a flashing arc, and the next second, Perry's gun went off. The bullet hit the bed a few inches from my thigh, and I screamed and twisted away. And then I screamed again when I saw Perry drop the gun and clutch at his stomach with both hands. Blood trickled between his fingers, and he looked down and up at Rafe again with shock on his face. Then his knees buckled, and he folded up on the shaggy carpet.

Rafe didn't move. He just stood there for a moment, making sure that Perry wouldn't get up again, and then he kicked the gun under the bed, where Perry couldn't reach it. When he turned to me, I caught my breath quickly at the sight of the knife in his hand. He must have had it in his pocket this whole time, and just waited for his chance when Perry's concentration faltered.

"You OK, darlin'?"

Whatever huskiness and heat had been in his eyes and voice were gone. His eyes were flat and his voice even. I, on the other hand, was a basket-case. Trembling with fear and pain and exhaustion, I had tears running down my cheeks. "I think so," I managed, through chattering teeth. "Is he dead?"

Rafe glanced negligently at the huddled mess on the floor. Perry was curled into himself, clutching his stomach and breathing in short, shallow gasps. "Not yet."

"Shouldn't we call an ambulance or something?"

"Considering that he's looking at two counts of murder and two more of attempted murder, not to mention the rapes and the theft, it'd be kinder just to let him bleed out. But it's up to you."

He lifted the knife. A drop of blood—Perry's blood—fell on my arm, and I shuddered in revulsion. Rafe wiped it off with his hand, unemotionally, and then dried the blade of the knife on the black satin sheet, where the wet blood disappeared against the fabric. My hands were shaking so much it was a miracle he didn't cut an artery as he released me, but I guess it was because his own hands were rock steady. As I sat up, wincing at the pins and needles in my arms, I worried for a moment that I'd lost control of my bladder in the heat of the moment. But then I realized that the bullet had penetrated the cover of the waterbed, which had sprung a slow leak, and I was sitting in a widening puddle of water.

"Let's get you out of here," Rafe said, and without any more ado, he scooped me up and stood. For once, the fact that I was practically naked in the arms of a man who wasn't my husband, failed to worry me. I threw my arms around his neck and held on for dear life while he moved past Perry, out the door and down the stairs, into the living room. However, it wasn't until he put me down on the edge of the sofa and straightened up, and I reluctantly let go, that I noticed the glistening crimson stain on his T-shirt.

"Oh, my God!" I choked out, staring, "is that *your* blood?"

"What?" He followed the direction of my eyes. "Oh, this? The bullet nicked me on the way past. No big deal."

"You're bleeding!"

"It's just a scratch." He sounded like the larger-than-life hero of the bodice ripper currently nestled in my bag, but I couldn't summon enough air to say so. He must have seen my eyes turn glassy, because he added, quickly, "Look, I'll show you. It's nothing. No worse than a skinned knee. I've been hurt much worse than this before. See?"

While he continued to talk soothingly, apparently intent on keeping me from fainting, he peeled the white T-shirt up and over his head. I'll never know if the ploy might have worked had the circumstances been different, but overwrought and over-stimulated as I was, the sight of him—silky smooth skin, hard muscles, bloody furrow and all—stole the remaining breath out of my lungs, and I slid to the floor in a dead faint.

WHEN I WOKE UP, I was on the sofa, and Rafe was slapping my face with a wet washcloth. He had taken the time to put a couple of Band-Aids over his injury, but not to put his shirt back on, and all of that masculinity leaning over me made me feel faint all over again. I pushed his hand away weakly and sat up, folding my arms across my breasts. "Sorry."

"For what?" He straightened up, too.

I shrugged, making sure I didn't look below his chin. "Everything. Almost getting you killed. Acting like a girl. Fainting."

"You're entitled. Some scary stuff happened to you."

"Have you called the police yet?"

"Figured I'd leave that to you." He got up and snagged the cordless phone from the table. "Here."

He headed into the bathroom with the wash-rag. I dialed Tamara Grimaldi's number and this time caught her. "Detective? Savannah Martin."

"What are you doing, calling from the Fortunatos' house?"

No flies on the detective. Of course, it wasn't omniscience, just caller ID.

"I was hosting another open house," I explained. "Perry called and asked me to. While I was here, I stumbled over his collection of pornography, and also over a black ski mask and coveralls. He found me going through his stuff and tried to kill me."

"Holy Mother of God!" the detective said. "Are you all right? What happened?"

"How about you come down here, and I'll tell you?"

"Are you hurt? Do you need an ambulance?"

"I don't, but Perry might. He's in pretty bad shape. Or he might be dead by now."

"Good," the detective said callously. "Stay where you are. I'm sending an ambulance, and I'll be there in 30 minutes myself. Don't go anywhere, and don't open the door to anyone else."

I promised I wouldn't, and hung up. "They're on their way."

"Seems a shame to cover you up," Rafe remarked, with another glance at my scantily clad charms, "but you should prob'ly get dressed."

"I would if I could find my clothes," I said, "but I didn't see them upstairs. And my cell phone is somewhere in the closet. Perry snatched it out of my hand and threw it." My voice began shaking again.

"At least you managed to call first," Rafe answered.

I nodded. "Good thing Perry didn't know that Wendell always says you're not there. If he had realized I'd actually gotten through, he might have killed me right away."

"Today I really wasn't there," Rafe said. "But Wendell called me as soon as your phone went dead, and told me to get the hell over here."

"Thank you."

He shrugged. "I'll go upstairs and see if I can find your clothes. If I can't, I'll find something of Mrs. Fortunato's. You two were about the same size."

Connie had been as thin as a rake and at least an inch shorter than me, but I didn't point it out. "Maybe Perry has a shirt that'll fit you. You should get dressed again, too."

Rafe didn't answer, but he turned to grin at me before he headed up the stairs, as if he knew that the main reason I wanted him to cover up, was so that I wouldn't be tempted to sneak peeks at him.

He came back a few minutes later, wearing a dark green T-shirt and carrying my cell phone and a pair of Connie's jeans and a stretchy top. "I couldn't find yours, but I figure these'll do."

I had my doubts, but I took them anyway, and started putting them on. "How's Perry?"

Rafe was watching me, but I don't think it was because he was enjoying the show. Or not solely because he was enjoying the show. Probably, it was just as much to gauge my reactions. "Dead."

"Oh, my God!" I could feel the blood drain out of my face as I pulled the white top over my head and yanked it down. It failed to meet the top of the—skintight—jeans by several inches, leaving a strip of my stomach bare. Rafe's lips curved in momentary appreciation, but he didn't comment.

"He's better off," he said instead. "I've been where he was headed, and believe me, I know what I'd choose."

I didn't answer. He'd been there, yes, so maybe he did know, but all the same, it was difficult for me to admit that Perry was better off dead than alive.

"I gotta go," Rafe added when I didn't say anything.

I stared up at him, mouth open. "What do you mean, you have to go? You can't leave me here alone!"

"I can't take you with me," Rafe said. And added, with a toss of his head up the stairs, "*He* ain't gonna bother you. Just stay down here and wait for the cops."

242 | Jenna Bennett

"Why can't *you* stay here and wait for the cops?"

His voice was patient, as if this was something I ought to have reasoned out for myself. "Cause they'll arrest me. And now ain't a good time for me to be in jail."

"Oh." I bit my lip. I'd forgotten about the tiny matter of the robberies in the flush of having found Lila's and Connie's killer.

Rafe's voice gentled. "Don't worry, you'll be fine. Just keep the front door locked, and don't go upstairs."

I shook my head. No danger of that. "But what do I tell them?"

He spread his hands. "Anything you want."

"But..." *But I don't want you to go!*

He looked at me for a moment, as if he could read my mind, before he said, "I'll call you."

"Isn't that what every man says? And never does?"

He looked at me for another second, and then he came back. And grabbed me by the shoulders, lifted me off the sofa, and planted a kiss on my lips. It was quick and hard and surprisingly thorough, and when he let me go, I sat down again with a thump.

"I'll call you," he said again, with emphasis. I didn't bother arguing. I wouldn't have bothered to argue even if I could have gotten my vocal chords to cooperate. There is no sense in arguing with something like that.

Twenty-One

By the time Detective Grimaldi arrived, Rafe was gone. I was outside, sitting on the front steps in my borrowed jeans and top, still feeling chilled in spite of the September heat, and the paramedics were upstairs deciding that there was nothing they could do for Perry.

They hadn't come down the stairs to tell me that, of course, but dead is dead, and I wasn't fool enough to believe that Rafe might have been mistaken about Perry's state.

Grimaldi stopped in front of me for a moment and waited until I looked up. "Are you OK?" Her dark eyes were concerned.

"As good as I can expect to be," I said.

"I'm going to go inside for a minute, and talk to the paramedics. Then I'll come back out and talk to you. Don't go anywhere."

I shook my head.

True to her word, she came back a few minutes later and sat down next to me. In her hand was a plastic baggie containing the bloody knife that had killed Perry, and another holding the gun. "Tell me what happened," she said.

I avoided looking at the bags as I went over the progression of events again, in a little more detail this time. Perry's phone call to me, and my agreement to host another open house for him. Beau Riggins's phone call, spurring my nosiness. What I'd found in Perry's secret cubby, and Perry coming home and finding me there.

"And then?"

"He knocked me out. Elbow to the head, I think—it felt that way—and taser. When I woke up, I was tied to the bed."

Tamara Grimaldi nodded. "We saw the ropes. How did you cut yourself loose?"

I hesitated. Cutting myself loose while my hands were tied would have been an impossible task. "I didn't. I talked Perry into doing it."

She arched her brows. "How did you manage that?"

"I… um… made him think I wanted to participate." I blushed.

"I see. That was very resourceful of you. So this knife…" she lifted the baggie, "…belonged to Mr. Fortunato?"

"Um…" I hesitated for another moment while my brain scrambled to consider all the pros and cons of all my possible answers. Lying to the police is such a hassle. "Actually, no. It's mine. Or rather, it's Rafe's. He gave it to me."

Better to own up to that part of it. The police would probably check the knife for fingerprints and find his.

"You don't say?" Detective Grimaldi eyed it speculatively. "When was this?"

"Um… a few days ago?"

"On Thursday, perhaps? When Spicer and Truman caught you two making out in the parking lot across from Julio Melendez's place?"

"We weren't making out," I said, but without heat. I didn't have any energy to spare to set the record straight; I was too busy trying to muddy the waters. "But it might have been then. I'm almost sure it was."

"Right," Grimaldi said. "You're a terrible liar, Ms. Martin."

I stared at her, wide-eyed, and she added, "I'm not saying it isn't Mr. Collier's knife. I'm sure it is. As a matter of fact, I think I've seen it before. We tested it for traces of blood after Mrs. Puckett's murder, I believe. But I don't think he gave it to you several days ago. If he had, you wouldn't have had to visit Sally's shop yesterday, to buy your own knife."

Darn. I'd forgotten about that.

"So why don't you tell me what really happened? Not that I can't venture a pretty good guess."

"Fine," I said, resignedly. "When I discovered Perry's stash of porn and goodies, I tried to call you. You didn't answer, and I didn't have time to leave a message, because I could hear him outside. I needed someone who always picks up the phone, so I called Rafe instead. Then Perry found me and knocked me out. By the time I woke up, Rafe had gotten here. He'd knocked Perry out; that's why the... um... corpse looks like it's been in a fight. But before he could untie me, Perry came upstairs and pulled out a gun. Rafe was the one who made him believe he wanted to participate, not me."

Although my not entirely fake fear had helped to make the deception possible.

"I see," Detective Grimaldi said. "So when we look at the tapes from the hidden cameras, that's what we'll see?"

The cameras! I'd forgotten all about them.

"Pretty much, yes. Perry believed him, and let his guard down. Rafe pulled the knife out of his pocket and stabbed Perry in the stomach. I was still tied up then. He didn't cut me loose until afterward."

"I see," Grimaldi said again. "And where is he now?"

I made a face. "He left."

"He *left*?!"

"He said this wasn't a good time for him to be in jail."

"Great," Detective Grimaldi said, breathing through her aquiline nose. "He stabs a man to death—in a particularly efficient, brutal way, I might add—and you let him walk off."

"What was I supposed to do? Knock him down and sit on him?"

"Oh, he would have loved that!" Grimaldi said, through her teeth.

I shrugged. "I'm not a cop, Detective. I don't have the authority to tell a man not to leave. Although I tried."

"Uh-huh," the detective said, grumpily. "I'm going to need that telephone number, if you please."

"Sure." I rattled it off. "He doesn't deserve to be arrested for killing Perry, though. It was self defense. Perry had a gun, and he had threatened to use it. When Rafe stabbed him, Perry tried to shoot. The bullet grazed Rafe and ended up in the waterbed. Either of us could have been hit, and if Rafe hadn't stopped Perry, I would certainly be dead by now."

Detective Grimaldi didn't answer. "Will you be OK driving home on your own, Ms. Martin? I'm going to have my hands full here for a while."

I blinked. "That's it? You're just going to let me leave?"

"I'd appreciate it if you'd stop by downtown tomorrow, to go over things again. Late morning, perhaps? I'll have some lunch delivered and we can talk things over in private. For right now, I need to look at the evidence and the video tapes. But if everything turns out to be as straight-forward as it seems, yes, this is it."

"Wow!" I said, getting to my feet. "Sure. I'll be fine driving home by myself. My hands have mostly stopped shaking. If you have any more questions, you know my number. And... um... if you come across a black skirt and a pink blouse in there, they're mine. Rafe couldn't find them, so he borrowed some of Connie's instead."

"The shortest and tightest he could find, no doubt." Detective Grimaldi looked me over.

I smiled apologetically. "I'll have them cleaned and bring them to you tomorrow. If you find mine, you can just throw them away, unless you need them for evidence. I don't think I'll be comfortable wearing them again, knowing that Perry took them off me while I was unconscious."

The detective nodded. "I'll see you tomorrow, then. Elevenish?"

I agreed to be at Police Plaza by eleven the following day, and Tamara Grimaldi went back into the house while I headed in the opposite direction, for my car and the safety of home.

WHEN I SHOWED UP AT eleven the next morning, she had ordered lunch from Monell's Restaurant and spread it out in an unused interview room on the top floor, with a view of the Cumberland River and the barges floating slowly by outside. "Have a seat."

"Thanks," I said, "I think."

"What's the matter?"

"Nothing. I guess I'm just worried about all this niceness. Like, you're going to wait until my mouth is full and then spring something on me."

Tamara Grimaldi shook her head. "There's nothing to spring. The evidence bears out everything you told me. The knife has Mr. Collier's fingerprints all over it, and some of Mr. Fortunato's blood. We also found a tiny fiber from the rope lodged between the blade and the handle, and traces of blood on the rope. Obviously, the knife was used to stab Mr. Fortunato and then wiped on the sheets and used to cut the ropes that tied you to the bed. The bullet was right where you said it would be, and the gun had Mr. Fortunato's fingerprints on it, and no one else's. We discovered a white T-shirt with Mr. Collier's blood in the downstairs trash can. I hope he wasn't badly hurt?"

"It was just a scratch. Or so he said."

"That's good to know. We also found your clothes tossed in a corner of the closet. For now, I'm going to hold on to them, but if there comes a time when I don't need them anymore, I'll get rid of them for you."

"Thanks," I said.

"No problem. I've looked at the video from the camera behind the air vent, and that bears out your story, as well. Both you and

Mr. Collier performed well, I might add. I'm not surprised that Mr. Fortunato believed him."

"For a minute or two, I believed him myself," I admitted.

Detective Grimaldi allowed herself a faint smile. "I'd still like to talk to him about this, but I don't suppose there's any chance you'll tell me where to find him?"

"I already gave you his phone number, and you know where he lives."

"I called the number and asked for Mr. Collier, and I was told there was nobody there by that name. When I tried again, there was no answer. What's so funny?"

"Wendell always says there's nobody there by that name," I explained, not bothering to try to hide my smile. "And he always answers the phone differently. I don't know what kind of place it is, but so far he's called it a car lot, a pawn shop, a storage place, and a grocery store. You're the police, can't you trace the number?"

"Prepaid cell phone," Grimaldi said, "so no. I sent Spicer and Truman over to Potsdam Street to look for Mr. Collier, but he wasn't there, and the nurse said she hadn't seen him for days."

"Sorry. If the number doesn't work, and he's not in the house on Potsdam, I don't know where to tell you to look. All I can do is wait for him to get in touch with me."

"Figures," Detective Grimaldi growled. "Well, when he does, tell him I want to talk to him, will you?"

I promised I would, for all the good I thought it would do. "So can you prove that Perry killed Lila? And his wife?"

She nodded. "Oh, yes. No doubt about it. One of Lila's hairs was on the ski mask. If he'd survived his encounter with you and Mr. Collier, we would have charged him with murder."

"What about Connie?" I asked, feeling nauseous. "Surely he didn't tape himself strangling her, too?"

Detective Grimaldi shook her head. "There were tapes of Connie

Fortunato having sex with a very good-looking young man, however. In her own bed. Dated just a week or so before her murder."

"Early twenties, with brown hair and dark blue eyes and a very nice body? Wearing underwear that said *Property of Australia*? Sounds like Beau Riggins, the house boy. He told me he'd had sex with Connie after he overheard her and Perry arguing about the O'Keeffe. Perry wanted Connie to sell it, but she refused."

"I see," Tamara Grimaldi said. "I haven't spoken to Mr. Riggins, but it sounds like I should."

I smiled. "You'll enjoy Beau. He's so over the top I'm not sure whether he's for real or just playing a part, but he's a lot of fun. He's the one who told me about Perry's secret closet."

"That's what you said. I have a line on the O'Keeffe, by the way. In Perry's cell phone records, we found the number of a shady art dealer in Atlanta, who might know something about it. The police down there are looking into it for us."

"Sounds like you're covering all the bases."

The detective shrugged modestly. "I wish I knew a little more about his motivations, but with him being dead, I don't know that we'll ever know exactly why he did what he did."

"I can venture a guess," I said, "if you don't mind listening to wild speculation."

"Sure." She gave me the floor with a gesture of her hand, and devoted herself to eating her chicken and dumplings instead.

"He told us—me and Rafe—that Lila was always coming on to men and then saying no. But after the open house robbery, Lila was telling everyone who'd listen about this guy who'd tied her to the chair and what she'd said to him. Connie probably told Perry, and he decided to pay Lila a visit. I don't know if he really thought he could fool her into believing he was... I mean, I don't know how he thought he could avoid having her recognize him, but he must have dressed up in the ski mask and coveralls I found in the closet, and tried to fool her for long enough to get her to open the door for him. But when she recognized him, and probably threatened to tell his wife, he killed her."

Detective Grimaldi nodded. "I'm with you so far. Go on."

"I think Connie was considering divorcing him. Beau said she threatened to. I don't know if she knew about Lila or whether she was just tired of him spending all her money, but if she did file for divorce, he'd lose everything. All the money was hers, from her father. So maybe he figured he'd take advantage of the open house robberies to stage a botched robbery at his own house, with the O'Keeffe as the target, and that way he'd get rid of his wife as well as make twice the money off the painting. Once by selling it, and once by getting the insurance money for it."

"That makes sense," Detective Grimaldi said.

"He probably figured that the police were working on a connection between the robberies and Lila's murder—as in, someone involved in the robberies killed Lila—and this would reinforce that idea. Excuse me." My cell phone rang and I reached for it. The number was unfamiliar, but I decided to answer it anyway, just in case it was a potential client. "This is Savannah."

"Hi, darlin'," a voice said.

"Oh, God!" I blurted, followed by a guilty glance at the detective. "Sorry. Hi, Mom. How are you?"

The other end of the line was silent for a moment. "Let me guess. You're talking to Tammy?"

"That's right," I said brightly. "Now's not really a good time. Can I call you back?"

"I'd rather you didn't. How about dinner tonight?"

"I have to go to the planning meeting for the Eye Ball," I said. "They've lost two, maybe three of their volunteers…" if Heather Price wasn't coming back, "…and I can't duck out as well."

"When is it over?"

"Um… eight?"

"I'll meet you at Fidelio's at 8:30. That'll give you time to slip into something comfortable."

He hung up before I could respond. Detective Grimaldi was watching me narrowly and I dredged up a weak smile. "My mother can be a little overprotective. I guess word got out that I was almost killed again. Or maybe she heard that I was practically naked in someone else's house. And on video. That'd do it, too."

"I see," Tamara Grimaldi said.

I tucked the phone away. "About those tapes…"

"They're evidence. But since the murderer and rapist is dead, and the case won't ever go to trial, nobody needs to see them."

"Can you keep all the male cops from having a look? If word gets around that there are sex tapes in the evidence room…"

I wasn't sure I could face Spicer and Truman again, if I thought they'd watched that tape.

"I'll make sure of it," Detective Grimaldi promised.

"What happened to Heather Price and Julio Melendez? Have you arrested them both? Are you charging them with anything?"

"We're holding Melendez on trafficking in stolen goods and masterminding the robberies. As for Ms. Price, there isn't a whole lot I can do. She swears he used her information without her knowledge, and he's not saying differently. So I can't charge her with anything."

"But you think she was in on it?"

Detective Grimaldi hesitated. "If she didn't take part in the actual planning, I think she knew what he was doing. If not beforehand, then after the first, and certainly after the second, robbery. But I think Lila's murder scared her sufficiently that she'll never admit it. And without a confession, I can't convict. There's no other solid evidence implicating her."

"So you've let her go?"

Tamara Grimaldi shrugged. "You win some, you lose some," she said philosophically.

I nodded. You sure do.

NATURALLY, TIMOTHY BRIGGS WASN'T THRILLED about what had happened. Three weeks ago, I had single-handedly put Walker Lamont in jail, and now I had killed one of Tim's clients. Or if I couldn't claim that honor myself, it was my fault that he was dead. At least it seemed so to Tim. Although it wasn't actually the arrest and the death that bothered him as much as the fact that the Fortunatos' house had to be taken off the market pending probate, and Tim would miss out on the commission.

"Couldn't you just have left well enough alone, Savannah?" he grumbled. "I mean, did you have to get mixed up in another crime spree? This isn't going to reflect well on Lamont, Briggs and Associates, you know!"

"I suppose you wanted me to just ignore the fact that he'd murdered two women? Or was this a situation where I should have taken one for the team and, as Perry put it, laid back and enjoyed it?"

Tim didn't answer. Not surprisingly, as there wasn't really a good answer to my question. I added, "You know, I wasn't actually the one who killed him. Rafe did."

Tim's eyes lit up at the mention of Rafe, and suddenly he seemed to take Perry's death in stride, just the way I had hoped he would. It was probably mean of me to capitalize on Tim's fascination with Rafe, but it sure came in handy sometimes. "And how is the scrumptious Mr. Collier today?" he wondered archly.

"I'm sure he's fine," I said, "although I won't actually see him until tonight."

"Ooooh!" Tim tittered. "Fidelio's again? Or somewhere less... restrained?"

I made a face. "Fidelio's, unfortunately. I'll have to let him know that I really don't like it there, and maybe he won't suggest it again."

"But that's where you'll be tonight? You won't mind if I just stop by to say hello, will you, darling? I promise I won't be a pest."

"Knock yourself out," I said. "It's a free country."

And then I added, prudently, "But don't expect us to ask you to join us. No offense."

"None taken." Tim rubbed his well-manicured hands together gleefully. "Oh, goody-goody! I can't wait. When will you be there?"

"*I'll* be there at 8:30. He may be there earlier, or later, or not at all, if Detective Grimaldi finds him and arrests him before tonight."

I got up from the chair I'd been sitting in, across the desk from Tim, and headed for the door. "I guess I'll see you there."

"Count on it," Tim said, with a display of blindingly white teeth.

Twenty-Two

I started agonizing over what to wear a little after 4 o'clock, with two hours to go before I had to leave. Whatever I wore had to be subdued enough for a business meeting, which was what the gala planning meeting was. On the other hand, I wanted to look good for my date with Rafe. (And yes, it was a date. I'd spent enough time trying to rationalize and explain away the obvious.) He'd asked me out, so he deserved a modicum of effort on my part—I did my best to look pretty when Todd asked me out, after all—and after what he did for me last night, Rafe deserved a whole lot more than that. If he hadn't killed Perry, I would be lying on a steel table in the medical examiner's office right now.

All right, so let me modify the statement I made earlier. I didn't want to look merely good; I wanted to look amazing. Stunning. Gorgeous. Or at least good enough to wipe out the image he must be carrying in his head of my far from perfect body clad in nothing but a bra and matching pink panties.

His last statement to me on the phone earlier was also playing havoc with my head. I hadn't had time to worry about it at the time, while I was trying to make sure that Tamara Grimaldi didn't realize who was calling, but now I allowed my insecurities full reign. What exactly had he meant by 'something comfortable'…?

In fiction, the phrase usually has a very specific meaning. The sultry heroine disappears into the bedroom to 'slip into something more comfortable,' leaving the hero to cool his heels on the living room sofa, and when she comes back, she's wearing a negligee. But surely Rafe didn't expect me to show up at Fidelio's dressed in my bathrobe…?

Well, if he did, he could just forget it. There are limits. However, I owed him something more than just my usual business attire. He'd always made a big deal out of the slinky cocktail-dresses I wore to have dinner with Todd—mainly because I didn't wear them when I went anywhere with him—so maybe I should wear one of those. They didn't fit the description of comfortable, though. And what if by 'comfortable', he'd really meant 'easy to get off'…?

That thought threw my emotions onto a whole new plane, one where I was walking a tightrope between abject terror and breathless, if unwilling, anticipation. Either seemed treacherous; it was a long fall regardless, and no soft landing to be expected on either side.

But he probably hadn't meant 'easy to get off'. And if he had, he wasn't going to get it. Again, there are limits. Although I supposed it couldn't hurt to compromise just a little, in case it *was* what he had meant...

I owned this little, black wrap-around dress, which I didn't wear very often because… well, frankly, because it was so easy to get off. All someone had to do was untie the bow, and he could spread the dress out like a picnic. Which made me worry that I'd accidentally snag my string on something, like a door knob, and before I knew it, I'd be standing there showing the world my underwear. Not an experience I sought. But tonight might be the perfect occasion for just such a dress.

Not that I *wanted* Rafe to take it off me, of course; I didn't mean that. But if that was what he'd planned, I couldn't very well refuse. Not after telling him just yesterday that if he got me out of Perry's clutches unharmed, I'd let him take advantage of me, no holds barred. He'd kept his end of the bargain, and I couldn't really back out now.

So I put on the black wrap-around dress, and black stockings, and black shoes—yes, the ones with the ankle straps—and black underwear (just in case), and then I fussed with my hair until it fell over my shoulders in—if I do say so myself—fetching disarray. I spent a good twenty minutes slathering on eye make-up, to make my eyes appear bigger and brighter and more luminous, and then I painted my lips the perfect heathery mauvy color, to look soft and inviting and kissable. Not because I wanted him to kiss me, of course, but... oh, what the hell; yes I did. I'd totally missed the first kiss he gave me, because I'd passed out from sheer terror, but I wouldn't miss this one. If he gave me one. Which he'd damned well better, because if he didn't, I'd have something to say about it.

When I walked into the small salon at Cheekwood at a few minutes before 6:30, people turned and stared, and a few of the men even whistled. Which was exactly the effect I was going for, so I blushed and smiled and felt pretty good about myself.

The meeting got underway shortly, minus Lila—of course—and Connie, and even Heather Price. Detective Grimaldi had assured me she wasn't in jail, so I guess maybe the embarrassment of the situation had made her decide to make herself scarce. Laura Burgess, the event coordinator, held another one-minute silence for Connie, like she had done for Lila last week, but beyond that, she didn't discuss the matter. Nobody seemed to realize that I'd been in the middle of it all, and I saw no reason to enlighten them.

An hour and half later it was over, and I got in the car and headed for Fidelio's, making sure to check my make-up in the rearview mirror before I got out of the car, and to fluff my hair and ensure that my dress draped properly as I minced across the parking lot to the front door.

The maitre d' recognized me, of course, and sent me what I can only describe as a disappointed look along with his usual polite bow. "Good evening, signorina."

"Good evening," I answered, inclining my head and wondering what I'd done now.

"Signorina's young man is waiting." He was far too dignified to comment directly on my choice of dinner partner, but he managed to convey his opinion quite well nonetheless, with the flaring of his nostrils and the inflection in his voice. "Would signorina like me to escort her to the table?"

"No, thank you," I said, "Signorina can make it on her own."

"Very well." He looked at me down the length of his Roman nose. "The... gentleman is waiting at table 4." The slight pause before the word 'gentleman' indicated the opposite. "Table 4 is located behind the pygmy date palm." He indicated a small, green tree with fluffy leaves, beyond which I could see Rafe's unmistakable shoulders.

"Oh," I said, relieved. "Thank you."

He inclined his dignified head, but didn't tell me to enjoy my meal. I guess maybe he thought there was no way I would.

The men at Fidelio's were just as gratifyingly attentive as those at Cheekwood had been. I got more than a few looks as I walked through the restaurant to the table behind the pygmy date palm, and I admit I soaked it all up. There's nothing quite like admiration from the opposite sex to make a woman feel her best. And I needed all the encouragement I could get. My knees were shaking as I made my way across the room.

Last time we'd been here together, I'd arrived to find Rafe flirting with all three of the women at a neighboring table. Not so today; he was alone, and his attention was on me. Fully. The whole way across the floor. By the time I arrived at the table, I had a hard time looking up to meet his eyes.

"Evening, darlin'." He gave me a cool peck on the cheek, and held the chair for me before he walked back around the table and sat down himself. And grinned. "That dress ain't much like what you wore last time we were here. I'm surprised Satterfield let you out the door in it."

Last time, I had followed Todd's directive not to wear anything suggestive and/or revealing in front of Rafe. I had dressed in my most prim and proper business-blouse and calf-length, black skirt, with my hair slicked back in a tight chignon and practically no make-up. The very opposite of today, in fact.

"You told me to wear something comfortable," I said defensively.

He was much too quick on the uptake, and the way he could read my mind was downright disconcerting. "And you figured I wanted you to wear something it'd be easy for me to take off of you later?"

"The thought crossed my mind," I admitted, blushing.

He laughed. "I appreciate the effort, darlin', but the only reason I told you that, was to yank your chain. I didn't think you'd actually do it. Not that I'm complaining."

"No, I can see that. I suppose it would probably boost your ego to know that that remark made me worry all day long?"

He grinned. "At least you were thinking of me, right?"

I shrugged. I supposed I couldn't very well deny that I had been. "So I'm not actually going to have to fight you off tonight?"

"Course not." He turned away from me just as the waiter approached. "I'll have a beer. In the bottle, no glass. And the lady'll have white wine."

As the waiter moved off, nose in the air, Rafe turned back to me and continued smoothly, "I mean, we had a deal, right? I said I'd get you out of Perry's house in one piece and without letting him touch you. As I recall, what you said you'd do in return didn't include fighting me off."

I didn't answer. I couldn't. Although I could feel my face turn pale. Rafe looked at me for a moment, savoring my expression, before he started laughing. "Maybe you oughta put your head between your knees if you're gonna pass out, darlin'. Good Lord, it's just sex, not marriage. What are you afraid I'm gonna do to you?"

"I'm not sure," I admitted. "I just know that the idea scares me out of my mind."

"No kidding. Well, you can relax. I don't plan on taking advantage of the fact that you'd have promised me anything yesterday. You probably didn't expect to live long enough to have to deliver."

"So I'm not going to have to sleep with you?"

He smiled. "Sure you are. Just not tonight. No time for sex tonight."

"What are we doing?" I lifted the glass of Sauvignon Blanc the waiter put in front of me and took a healthy swallow. After a moment, I could feel some color creep back into my cheeks. "I'll have the Chicken Marsala, please."

"Same." Rafe waited until the waiter had moved off, and then he added, "*We* ain't doing anything. I, on the other hand…"

I put my glass down. "Uh-oh. What's wrong now?"

"Nothing's wrong. I just wanted to let you know I'm gonna be going away for a while."

My eyes widened. "You're not going to jail, are you? Are Spicer and Truman waiting outside to drag you off as soon as we've finished eating, or something?" I looked around wildly.

"You've seen too many bad movies," Rafe answered. "It's only in old westerns that the outlaw gets to say a proper goodbye before they haul him off to be hanged. No, I'm between a rock and hard place here, with Tammy wanting to talk to me about Perry, and Julio's boss wanting to talk to me about why Julio's in jail, and by tomorrow, one or the other'll be ready to move on me. So I'm getting out while the gettin's good."

"If you knew that when you called me this morning, why didn't you just leave then?"

"Wanted to say a proper goodbye," Rafe answered, with a grin. I flushed, and tried to hide it by lowering my eyes to the table. It didn't work, and he chuckled. "Bedding you properly would take too long, but I'm sure I can find time for a proper kiss."

Goodness, I thought, distracted, how long did he expect a proper bedding to take? Gary Lee and Charlene had certainly managed their encounters in record time, and when Bradley and I had had sex, it had been over practically before it started. At least for me. But Rafe made it sound like he'd need twelve solid hours of uninterrupted time to do the job right, and the idea of it made my head spin and my toes curl.

"Savannah," Rafe said, and I resurfaced, blinking to dispel the slideshow currently running on a loop in my head. He so rarely used my name, seeming to prefer that Southern catch-all phrase, *darlin'*, that it sounded foreign to me. It also sounded serious.

"Yes?" I said apprehensively.

"I want you to do something for me."

"OK."

"While I'm gone, will you check in on my grandma once in a while? Just to make sure she's all right? Marquita's over there, but she's getting paid to care, and it ain't the same."

"Sure," I said. "I'd be happy to. I like your grandmother. When do you expect to be back?"

He avoided my eyes. "No idea. Depends on how long it takes for this to blow over."

"Can you give me some idea? A couple of days? A month? A year? Ever?!"

He shrugged. "I'd like to avoid that, but yeah, that's a possibility. If the wrong people find out where I'm at."

"Julio's boss?"

"Among others. Over the past couple years I've pissed off some pretty bad people, and some of 'em may try to settle the score."

"Todd told me what you've been doing since you got out of prison," I said tentatively. It was his turn to arch a brow.

"How does Satterfield know? That ain't something that shoulda shown up on that background check he did last month. If it did, I'm in even deeper shit than I thought."

"Actually, he's gone a little beyond that." I made an apologetic face as I dug in my purse. "Last week he told me he was having you followed. The private investigator took this. Along with a lot of other photographs." I handed him the picture of the two of us at the Shortstop Sports Bar, the one I had taken from Todd. Rafe looked at it in silence for a moment.

"Nice shot of you," he said eventually.

"Thank you. Todd thought so, too."

"Gave you a hard time, did he?" One corner of his mouth turned up.

"He thought I looked like I was enjoying myself a little too much, yes. He accused me of flirting with you."

Rafe grinned. "I should be so lucky. Course, if someone had shown me a picture of you looking like this, across the table from some other guy, I mighta felt a little jealous, too."

I snorted. "I'm sure."

He smiled. "So Satterfield's figured out how I've spent the past ten years. What do you think?"

"I wish you'd stop. It's dangerous."

"So's life, darlin'. Besides, somebody's gotta do it."

"I don't see why," I said, "but never mind. You sound like Beau Riggins."

"Yeah? Who's Beau Riggins? Somebody else I gotta worry about you marrying while I'm gone?"

I giggled. "Hardly. Although if you wanted to resign from your life of crime, you could make a killing in Beau's profession. No pun intended."

He leaned back on his chair and folded his arms across his chest. I could see the outline of the snake tattoo curled around his left bicep through the thin sleeve of the white shirt. "What's his profession? Assassin?"

"House boy," I said.

"Come again?"

"He cleans houses." I went on to explain exactly what Beau did and how he did it, and had the pleasure of hearing an unguarded, totally spontaneous laugh from Rafe. Not an everyday occurrence, and one that made me feel good on those rare occasions when I witnessed it.

"In his underwear?" he repeated, his voice uneven.

I nodded, blushing. "He pulled down his zipper and showed them to me."

Todd would have been shocked and appalled, first at Beau for exposing himself—or his underwear—to me, and then at me for looking at it. Rafe clicked his tongue in mock disapproval. "Shame on you."

I shrugged. "Like you said once, there's no harm in looking."

"Depends what you're looking at, don't it, darlin'? To be fair, maybe I oughta pull down my zipper too, so you can compare."

"No thanks," I said. "That wouldn't be fair at all. Beau wears Wonderjocks."

"He wears what?"

I was in the process of explaining to Rafe what a Wonderjock was, and how it worked, when the food arrived, and hard on the heels of the waiter, Timothy Briggs. Who did a theatrical double-take when he saw us. If that was the best he could do, I wasn't surprised that Broadway hadn't worked out.

"Oh, Savannah! I didn't realize you'd be here!"

"Of course not," I said dryly, "how could you?"

Tim didn't answer. He had already switched his attention from me to Rafe. "Hello, handsome." His voice was a sultry purr, and his posture—shoulders cocked and hands on his hips—was pure teenage vixen. I had to turn away to hide my smile.

"Hi, Tim." Rafe's voice wasn't sultry at all, but his wicked grin and flash of dark eyes more than made up for it. Tim sighed appreciatively.

I rolled my eyes. "What are you doing here, Tim?"

"Oh, I'm just having dinner with some friends," Tim said airily, waving a languid hand. "What about you kids?" His eyes returned to Rafe.

"We're actually having dinner, too," I said. "Quite a coincidence, isn't it? Especially since this is a restaurant."

Tim didn't answer, and I'm not even sure he heard me. He seemed to be too busy watching Rafe breathe to pay attention to anything else. "What a wonderful surprise to see you again, Rafael." The way he pronounced Rafe's name was positively caressing.

"The pleasure's all mine," Rafe answered, and although his tone didn't match Tim's for plummy suggestiveness, it was as close to audible sex-appeal as it's possible to come. If I could have bottled and sold it, I could have made a fortune. Tim turned to me, lowering his voice confidingly. "Such a pity he's straight, darling."

"Isn't it?" I admitted demurely.

Tim tittered. "So what were you two sitting here talking about? It must have been something exciting, to make you blush so prettily!" He sent me an arch look.

Rafe grinned. "Underwear, actually. I got a look at Savannah's yesterday, so I figured I'd offer to show her mine. Tit for tat." He winked. Annoyingly, I blushed again.

"Oooooh!" Tim fluted. "Can I be included in that offer, too? Pretty please! I'd love to see your tat."

"Unfortunately," Rafe said smoothly, "for both of us, Savannah said no."

"Shame on you." Tim pouted, sending me a wounded glance for ruining his fun. Then he lowered his voice and leaned a little closer to Rafe. "Forgive me, Rafael, but would you mind settling a question for us? Savannah and I talked about this the other day. Is that..." He glanced down into Rafe's lap, pausing delicately, "the Wonderjock?"

From the way he pronounced the brand name, he might almost have been talking about a priceless work of art. Like Connie Fortunato's Georgia O'Keeffe.

Rafe arched his brows in my direction. "You were talking about this the other day?"

Tim nodded innocently. I blushed, bit my lip, and shrugged. Rafe grinned. "Sorry to disappoint you, but this is all me."

"Good Lord!" Tim said, fanning himself with a limp hand.

"Well, you know what they say." Rafe looked at me and winked. I couldn't keep another blush from staining my cheeks crimson.

Tim must have been so overcome by this news that he didn't demur when I pushed him on his way, still glassy-eyed and breathing fast. He joined a threesome of other good-looking, obviously gay men on the other side of the restaurant, and they stuck their heads together, with frequent glances in our direction. They weren't looking at me, and it didn't seem to bother Rafe, so I decided not to draw attention to it.

"So you and Tim were talking about my underwear the other day?" Rafe said, picking up his knife and fork and going to work on his chicken. "You musta forgotten to mention that."

I lifted my own fork and picked at my food. "We were talking about you and about the Wonderjock, but not necessarily at the same time. I mean, I wasn't telling Tim that you wore one. I mean…"

"I should hope not," Rafe said with a grin. "I guess if you're discussing my equipment with other people, there's hope that I'll get you to use it sometime, right?"

I shrugged. "Anything's possible, if you wait long enough. Why don't you just make sure you come back to Nashville in one piece, and we'll see?"

"Now, there's a thought that's guaranteed to distract a man from his duty. I'll do my best." He popped a bit of chicken in his mouth and started chewing. I picked on my food some more.

"You know," I said tentatively, after a minute or two, with a glance at him from under my lashes, "yesterday, at the Fortunatos' house, when I said those things about you …"

He glanced up, eyes wary. "Yeah?"

"I didn't mean… I mean, I didn't intend… I was just trying to make Perry think…"

He didn't answer, just let me run out of words on my own. When I finally did, he opened his mouth, and all the laughter was gone from both his eyes and his voice. "I am what I am, darlin'. If you or your mama have a problem with me because of it, that's too bad, but it ain't something I can change."

"I don't have a problem with it," I said firmly.

He smiled. "Sure you do. Everything you told Perry was true. That's why he believed you. You'll forgive me for saying this, darlin', but you're a terrible liar."

I bit my lip. "Sorry." And not for being a terrible liar.

"No problem. It got us outta there alive; I ain't about to complain. If it saves my life, you can call me anything you want."

He went back to eating. I watched him for another minute, while I pushed my own food around on the plate. "Since we're talking about Perry…"

"Yeah?"

"There was a minute or two yesterday when you scared me."

He cocked a brow. "Just a minute or two?"

"When you were talking to Perry about what you wanted to do to me…"

"Unlike you, I'm an excellent liar." His voice was easy.

"So it wasn't true? None of it?"

"Well… not the way I made it sound."

"I see," I said. Whispered, really.

He looked at me for a moment without speaking, and then he put his knife and fork down and faced me across the table. "I'm sorry I scared you, Savannah. But because I did—because you were scared and you weren't just pretending to be—Perry believed us. We walked outta there. You did good." He lifted his beer bottle and toasted me.

"Yes," I said, "but…"

It was weak of me, no doubt, but I wanted more reassurance. I wanted him to tell me that that all-consuming heat in his eyes, that darkness I'd glimpsed, was just play-acting and wouldn't come back to swallow me if I ever got that close to him again. If I ever made good on that promise I'd made.

He watched me wring my hands for a moment, and then he spoke. Lightly. "I'm a man, darlin'. A mostly naked woman tied to a bed is gonna tempt me. Especially when she looks like you. I ain't gonna apologize for it."

I nodded, shakily. He added, "But you were scared out of your mind, and there ain't nothing attractive about that."

"Thank you," I whispered.

He shrugged. "One of these days I figure you'll believe me, as long as I keep saying it. I ain't gonna hurt you."

Twenty-Three

We spent the rest of dinner talking about mostly inconsequential things. I told him about Gary Lee and Charlene and what they had been doing every time I showed them a house, and Rafe told me he'd suspected as much, but he'd figured it was better not to tell me. I asked him if he knew anything about what had happened to the other men who had been involved in the open house robberies, and he said as far as he knew, the police had arrested all three of them, along with Julio Melendez. In the process, he confirmed that the other three robbers had indeed been the three men I'd seen him with at the Shortstop bar last week.

"Though if I'd known they were gonna be there, I wouldn't have suggested going. Ishmael likes women, but it don't seem to occur to him that they don't always like him."

"Ishmael was the one who kept staring at me? No, I didn't like him all that much. As a matter of fact, I wondered if it might have been him who killed Lila. He was almost as tall as you, and had those pretty, dark eyes."

Rafe shook his head. "He already had a girl that night. And he ain't that bad. Just ended up on the wrong side of the law when he was young, and stayed there."

"Kind of like you," I said dryly.

He grinned. "Nothing like me. Women always adore me, or hadn't you noticed?"

I rolled my eyes. "If you say so."

We left Fidelio's around ten o'clock. Tim and his friends were still eating and drinking, and shooting us glances out of the corners of their eyes. As he passed by, Rafe paused for a second to put a hand on Tim's shoulder and flash a smile that ought to have melted the ice cubes in every glass on the table. His voice was equally melting, and would probably be responsible for quite a few wet-dreams later. "Nice to see you again, Tim. Have a good night."

I glanced over my shoulder when he walked away, and saw that all four of the men had reached for their water glasses at the same time.

"That was mean," I said when we reached the street.

Rafe grinned. "But fun. They'd been staring at me for the past hour, so I figured I might as well give'em something to think about."

He looked around and added, "Can you give me a ride? I had Wendell leave my bike outside your place earlier."

"Sure," I said. "Here. You can drive."

"Don't mind if I do." He took the keys I handed him in one hand and my elbow in the other, and steered me toward the car.

We spent most of the drive in silence. I was full of food, just a little drowsy from the wine, and I had a lot on my mind. Rafe must have been in similar straits, because he didn't seem to have much to say, either. He pulled the car up to the curb outside the building—I could see his Harley-Davidson parked a little further down the street—and we got out and stood on the sidewalk in front of the gate, a little awkwardly.

"Um…" I glanced over my shoulder. "Do you want to come upstairs for a cup of coffee or something?"

He smiled. "I guess you feel safe asking me that, seeing as you know I'm in a hurry, don't you?"

I shrugged, and he added, "I don't think that'd be a good idea, darlin'. Don't wanna start something I don't have time to finish, and if I start something anyway, I'll likely end up in jail."

I nodded. A part of me had counted on his saying no. I don't think I would have suggested it, had I not been absolutely certain he'd say no. However, there was another part that wished, secretly, that he'd accepted. Although that part was probably just tipsy and a little sentimental, and certainly too self-absorbed to think about what would be best for him. "I guess this is it, then."

"Guess so."

We looked at each other for a moment. "Take care of yourself," I said.

"You, too. And don't marry nobody while I'm gone. If Satterfield proposes, put him off for a while. I've got plans for when I get back, and if you're married to somebody else, that's gonna cramp my style." He winked.

"Sure," I said sarcastically, fighting back a blush. "If Todd proposes, I'll just tell him that Rafe wanted me to wait, so he could sleep with me before I got engaged. I'm sure Todd will understand."

He laughed. "Oh, he'll understand, all right. He won't like it, but he'll understand."

We stood and looked at each other for another few seconds. "I'll miss you," I said impulsively, surprised to realize it was true. In just a few weeks, he'd become a part of my life. Not a huge or permanent part, more like a part that came and went, but one that was usually there when I needed it.

He grinned. "I'll miss you, too. At least when some other gorgeous blonde isn't throwing herself at me."

"Thanks." Here I was, trying to be sincere and serious, and all he could do was make bad jokes. "Your sentimentality is heart-warming."

He flashed another grin. "I do my best." And then the grin faded and he reached out and touched my cheek with his knuckles. It was a surprisingly tender gesture, and one that, for all its gentleness, felt more like a quick jab in the stomach. "I gotta go, darlin'."

I nodded. "Is this where you kiss me goodbye and ride off into the sunset?"

He glanced over his shoulder at the Harley-Davidson. "More like I drive hell for leather down the interstate with the law on my tail, but yeah. I guess."

"OK," I said softly.

He arched a brow. "You ain't gonna fight me over it?"

I shook my head.

"Well, hot damn," Rafe said. "I need to go away more often. Come here, darlin'."

He put both hands on my waist and pulled me closer, close enough to feel the heat from his body through my dress. If I took a deep breath, my chest would probably touch his. Good thing I couldn't seem to get that much air into my lungs.

Looking up into his eyes was uncomfortable, so I focused on his lips instead. They were beautiful lips: nicely shaped and just full enough without being too full; made for kissing.

As I stared, those nice lips moved, and I concentrated to hear what they were saying. Rafe's voice was rough, and the buzzing in my ears didn't help, but I could just make out the words. "Christ, Savannah! I oughta be halfway to Memphis by now, and if you look at me like that, I'll never even make it down the street."

The shock cleared my head, and I stared up at him, eyes wide and lips parted in shock. The next second he had yanked me up against him; chest to chest, hips to hips, and mouth to mouth. My body stiffened, and then melted against his. As his tongue slipped into my mouth, my eyes rolled back in my head and my knees turned to water. If he hadn't been holding me up, I would have melted into a puddle at his feet.

This state of affairs went on for a while. I'm not sure how long, since I was mostly unconscious. But eventually an insistent noise intruded on the moment, and after listening to it for a while, my body got the message that it needed to respond. It took incredible effort, but I managed to get both hands against Rafe's chest and push.

Once I was away from the heat and pull of his body, the noise distilled itself into words. "Break it up, you two! This is a public place; you can't do that here!"

I looked around, blinking, my lips swollen and my hair straggling, only to be confronted with a black-and-white squad car and the smirking face of patrol officer George Truman. Spicer was leaning across the passenger seat, grinning. "Shoulda figured it'd be you two again," he said. "No better'n a couple of kids. Take it upstairs or we're gonna have to run you in for indecent behavior."

"Sorry," I managed. Rafe didn't say a word, but I could feel his body strum with tension. Difficult to say whether it was because of what we'd just been doing or the fact that Spicer and Truman might be here to haul him off to jail. "We'll move."

Spicer put the squad car in gear. "See that you do. Or you'll be spending the night downtown. And not together, either."

He pulled away from the curb. We watched the car drive away, and then I turned to Rafe. It took effort to make my voice steady, but I managed. "You should go."

I couldn't bring myself to look up and meet his eyes, so I kept mine on the top button of his shirt instead. He nodded, but didn't move. I added, "Before they realize they made a mistake and come back for you."

Grimaldi had said that next time, she's make sure Spicer and Truman knew not to let him leave.

"Right. I'll see you around, darlin'." He hesitated for a second before he leaned down and kissed me again. This time on the cheek. His lips were cool against my skin, and he smelled faintly of something clean and spicy, that I hadn't noticed in the sensory overload earlier.

"Be careful," I said. Darn it, we were back where we started, standing awkwardly on the sidewalk with nothing to say!

He grinned at me. "Sure thing. You too."

"I'll try," I said.

"I'll be in touch."

And with another quick grin he turned on his heel and walked away. I stood where I was and watched him get on the bike, start it up, and pull into traffic. He lifted his hand once, and then he was gone. I watched the taillight of the bike until I lost it among the others, merging onto the interstate down at the corner of 5th and Main. And then I went upstairs to my—I admit it—lonely apartment and went to bed. Alone. And if I felt just a touch of regret, that's nobody's business but my own.

About the Author

Jenna Bennett writes the USA Today bestselling Savannah Martin mystery series for her own gratification, as well as the New York Times bestselling Do-It-Yourself home renovation mysteries from Berkley Prime Crime under the pseudonym Jennie Bentley. For a change of pace, she writes a variety of romance, from contemporary to futuristic, and from paranormal to suspense.

FOR MORE INFORMATION, PLEASE VISIT HER WEBSITE:
WWW.JENNABENNETT.COM

Made in the USA
Middletown, DE
28 February 2018